THREE DAYS IN APRIL

THREE DAYS IN APRIL

EDWARD ASHTON

An Imprint of HarperCollinsPublishers

This is a work of fiction. Names, characters, places, and incidents are products of the author's imagination or are used fictitiously and are not to be construed as real. Any resemblance to actual events, locales, organizations, or persons, living or dead, is entirely coincidental.

EPub Edition SEPTEMBER 2015 ISBN: 9780062439284

Print Edition ISBN: 9780062439291

HB 05.26.2023

For Bonnie. I wish you were here to see this.

1. ANDERS

I'm turning away from the bar, drink in hand, when I feel a glass bump against my chest. I look down to see a girl with her mouth hanging open, a bright blue stain spreading down her white silk shirt. She's barely five feet tall, with curly red hair, shoulders like a line-backer, and biceps that look like short, angry pythons under ghost-pale skin. She looks up at me, and yeah, there's the brow ridge. This is not going to go well.

"Shit!" she says. "Shit! This was a brand-new shirt, you asshole!"

She puts a hand to my chest and pushes me back. I hit the bar at kidney level, hard enough to leave a bruise. Beer sloshes over my hand and runs down my arm. By the time I look back, she's already swinging. I slip to the side, and watch her fist sail by. The bar-tender is reaching for something under the bar, and the bouncer is starting our way. My hands are up, palms open. If I have to hit her, it'll be a slap. I have no problem with punching a girl in principle, but Neanderthals have heads like bricks. She looks me in the eye. I can see the wheels turning. That wasn't as fast as I can move, but it was fast enough to make an impression. She straightens up, and drops her fists.

"I'm Terry," she says. "Buy me a drink and call it even?"

"So let me guess," I say. "Dad wanted a football star?"

Terry leans her elbows on the table and takes a surprisingly dainty sip from her drink. She called it a parrot, but it looks and smells like blue Drano.

"Something like that, yeah. Didn't have the money for a real engineer, though. They even botched the gender, obviously. I was supposed to just get the muscles and the extra bone strength, but . . . well, you can see what I got. What about you? Manufactured for the NBA?"

"What makes you think that?" I ask, and finish my beer in one long pull. I'm not actually much of a drinker, but I'm still winding down from our scuffle by the bar, and I feel like I need to take the edge off.

"Come on," she says. "What are you, seven feet tall?"

I laugh.

"Not quite," I say. "I'm six-seven, and it's one-hundred-percent natural. I come from a long line of giant, gangly Swedes."

"Maybe." She takes another sip and leans back in her chair, tilts it up on two legs and balances for a moment, then drops the front legs back to the floor with a bang. "But you'd be surprised how many times I've taken a swing at someone in a bar, and I don't usually miss that badly."

I laugh again, a little harder this time. Alcohol-wise, I might actually be moving past taking the edge off at this point.

"Nah," I say. "I wouldn't be surprised. If the original Neanderthals were as douchey as you guys are, it's no wonder we wiped them out."

Her eyes narrow. I'd guess she's thinking about taking another poke at me, but instead she leans back in her chair and smiles.

"You're avoiding, my gigantic friend. I hang out with a lot of Engineered, and I've never seen anyone move that fast. Even the military exoskeletons are more strength than speed. I don't know if you're mechanical or biological, but you're definitely something. What did they give you?"

I raise one eyebrow.

"That's a pretty direct question."

"I'm a Neanderthal. We're douchey but direct."

She grins and takes another sip of her parrot. She has a wide, toothy smile, and I catch myself thinking that she's really kind of cute when she's not trying to punch me.

"My mods are biological," I say finally. "I'm a genetic chimera, technically. They cut me with mouse genes. I've got something like eight percent type C muscle fibers."

That earns me a flat, blank stare. Apparently, I need to elaborate.

"Ever try to catch a mouse?" I ask. "They've got tiny little legs. They ought to be easy to get hold of, right?"

"Sure," she says. "But they're quick."

I nod.

"Right. Big mammals have fast-twitch and slow-twitch muscles. Little ones have a third type. Think of it as fast twitch plus. It's what keeps them a step ahead of the cat. That's what I got."

Her smile turns into an almost-smirk.

"But you don't have an entourage, and I've never seen you on the vids. So, I'm guessing there's a catch."

I run a hand back through my hair and sigh.

"Yeah, there's a catch. It turns out there's a reason that only tiny animals have type C fibers. I can jump through the roof—but only once every six weeks or so, because pretty much every time I try, I pull a muscle or break a bone. I played ball in high school and for a year in college. I was one of the first Engineered to play at that level, and for a while there was actually some fuss about whether it was fair for me to compete with the unmodified kids. I gave it up after my freshman year, though. I got tired of getting crap from the other players, I got tired of having to be careful all the time, and I got tired of hanging out with the trainers."

She leans back, and laces her fingers behind her head.

"Did you ever ask them what they were thinking?"

"What who were thinking?"

"Your parents. You look like you're about the same age as I am—north of twenty-five, south of thirty, right?"

I nod. I'm thirty-six, but she's close enough.

"So," she says, "germ-line mods weren't even legal in most places when they cut us. And even where they were, nobody knew what they were doing." She looks down at herself and scowls. "I mean, obviously, right? So, what were they thinking? You wouldn't buy the first model year of a new car, would you? But they took a flyer on the first model year of a new species."

I shrug. She's right, of course. And the fact is, I did once ask my dad why he did it. I was nineteen then, in the hospital with a shattered femur, the morning after my last basketball game. I was bitter and sulking, blaming Dad for the fact that I was hurt, that I hadn't been able to keep a lid on it, that I hadn't been able to stay under control.

He probably should have just smacked me in the back of the head and walked out of the room, but he didn't. Instead, he said, "I knew we were taking chances, Anders, and I'm sorry that things didn't entirely work out. But even back then, I could see what was coming. Twenty years from now, unmodified kids won't be able to make a high school basketball team, let alone play in college. Twenty years after that, unmodified kids won't be able to get a job. That's where we're going, son, and I thought it would be better for you to be one of the first ones of the new breed than one of the last ones of the old."

And you know, I get that. I really do. Dad was afraid of being left behind when the species moved on. He was probably right, honestly. He was just twenty years too early.

At least he had plenty of money, so I didn't have some dipshit grad student cutting DNA on me like my new friend here apparently did. Even with that, though—the best-laid plans.

Of mice and men. Get it?

Terry pushes back from the table and heads over to the bar. I take the opportunity to check messages. Nothing. I was actually supposed to meet someone here tonight, but as far as I can tell, she never showed. Or maybe she did, and when she saw me mixing it up at the bar, she bolted. Doesn't matter. I only knew her through the nets anyway, and my track record with transitioning virtual relationships to real ones is pretty poor for some reason. I pocket my phone. Terry sits down again, and sets another beer in front of me.

"So," she says. "Are we on a date now?"

I wake up. The sun is red through my eyelids, and I can't feel my right arm. I open my eyes. The reason I can't feel my arm is that it's pinned underneath a red-headed bowling ball. I lift my head and look around. This is not my bedroom. I'm in a twin canopy bed with lacy pink curtains. The sun is pouring through the half-open window and boring a hole through my brain. I close my eyes and let my head fall back again.

Terry coughs. A spray of hot spittle hits my chest. She groans and rolls away from me. I take the opportunity to pull my arm back. It flops across my stomach like a dead fish. I lift the covers and take a quick glance down. I'm naked. Terry's wearing a pink tee shirt and panties. There are ugly purple bruises on both of my thighs.

I close my eyes again. My head is throbbing, but I don't know where Terry keeps her painkillers and I don't have the energy to try to find out. As I drift off, I half-dream a sound like a bird scratching at the windowpane. I try to open my eyes to see what it is, but at this point even that's too much effort.

I wake up again. The sun is higher now, making a bright rectangle on the floor instead of on the inside of my skull. My head is pounding, and my mouth feels like someone put little fuzzy socks on each of my teeth. I'm alone in the bed. I sit up slowly. The room spins once or twice around before settling back into place.

The door swings open and Terry comes in, wearing a sweatshirt and jeans now, looking freshly scrubbed. Her hair is pulled back in a ponytail. She tosses me a water bottle. It bounces off of my forehead and drops to my lap.

"Thanks," I say. Or try to, anyway. What comes out is more like a croak. I open the bottle and drink half of it down without stopping to breathe.

"You're a late riser," she says. "I wonder if maybe you had too much to drink last night."

"Maybe." I rub my face with both hands, then use my knuckles to dig the crust out of the corners of my eyes. Terry clears her throat.

"So," she says. "You got big plans this morning?"

"Uh . . ."

"Don't misunderstand—I'm not asking you to stay. I'm asking you to leave."

"Oh."

I take another long drink. She watches me expectantly.

"So," I say finally. "We hit it last night, huh?"

She rolls her eyes.

"Yeah. Pretty disappointing. Apparently, you're super fast at that, too."

Ouch.

"Really?"

She smiles. My head is still aching, but for some reason I smile back.

"No, not really. You passed out before I could get your pants off."

I take another quick glance under the sheet.

"Oh. So why am I naked?"

Her smile widens until it's almost a leer.

"I didn't say I didn't get your pants off. I just said you passed out first."

I finish the water bottle. My mouth still tastes like ass.

"Any idea how my legs got bruised?"

"You fell over my coffee table."

"Ah." I rub my face again. "What time is it?"

She glances down at her phone.

"Almost eleven."

I groan and swing my feet off the bed and onto the floor.

"I actually do have somewhere to be," I say. "Think you could hand me my pants?"

It's a perfect spring morning, cool and crisp, with a deep blue sky and just a hint of a breeze. Terry's apartment is on Thirty-third, not too far from JHU. I need to get to a diner on North Charles, up closer to Loyola. I give a few seconds of thought to pinging for a cab, but I'm not supposed to meet Doug until noon, and I'm thinking maybe the walk will do me some good.

Baltimore's always been a pretty town. The sun dances on the glassphalt on West University—something I'd appreciate a lot more right now if every glitter didn't feel like an ice pick in my brain. I cut through the Hopkins campus and turn up Linkwood, past the student housing and into the professors' neighborhood. The trees here are old and thick limbed, leaning out over the sidewalk, and the houses are neat and clean and well maintained. I'm basically a squatter in a run-down townhouse on Twenty-eighth. I'd love to move up here, have a little bit of yard and a deck, but I'm not a professor. I'm a part-time instructor at three different schools, which is not the sort of career that supports the good life.

My mother calls me every week or so. Almost every time, she asks me when I'm going to get a real job, when I'm going to start my life. It's a valid question, and I haven't come up with a valid answer. Honestly, I'm not sure what a real job is at this point. I don't know anyone who does anything that she would recognize as work. I have a friend who makes a bit as a product promoter, and one who does temporary art installations for parties and weddings. I know a couple of guys who live on government credits, and one who works for his dad, but never actually seems to do any work.

And then, there's Doug. I have no idea what Doug does.

I walk into the diner at 12:04. I don't bother wondering if Doug is here yet. I know that he walked through the door at precisely 12:00. I glance around, and there he is, just being seated by the hostess at a table near the back. I'd prefer a booth, but his exoskeleton doesn't fit into the bench seats very well, and when he kicks your shin under the table, it really, really hurts. I walk over. The hostess has my place set up across from him, but I pull the chair around to the side of the table.

"Hey," he says. "You look like crap."

I drop into my seat and rub my temples with both hands.

"No doubt. How're things on the far side of the singularity?"

"Good," he says. "I just ordered waffles."

"Awesome. With your brain thingie, you mean?"

He scowls.

"Don't be a dick, Anders. It's a wireless neural interface. You know this."

I shrug.

"Did you order anything for me?"

"Depends. Are you going to call it a brain thingie again?"

"Probably."

"Then no."

I wave a waitress over. She's a Pretty—flawless skin, white-blonde hair, eyes, nose and ears symmetrical to the micrometer. She looks me up and down, then rolls her eyes at Doug.

"I can take your order," she says, "but you know you gotta tip for him, too, right?"

I nod. I've had brunch with Doug before.

"Fine. So what can I getcha, hon?"

I don't bother to look at the menu. I always get the same thing here.

"Pancakes, two eggs scrambled, bacon, white toast?"

"Juice and coffee?"

"Hot tea."

"Got it."

She swishes away. Doug's left eye is twitching. Apparently he's downloading something fun.

"Let me guess," I say. "Monkey porn? Donkey porn? Monkey on donkey porn?"

His eyes focus, and he squints at me.

"No," he says. "Science stuff. You wouldn't understand."

My jaw sags open.

"I wouldn't understand? I'm the one with the doctorate in engineering, Doug. Do you even have a high-school diploma?"

He scowls, which through the metal mesh that covers half his face is actually kind of terrifying.

"Formal education is meaningless after the singularity," he says.

"Right," I say. "It was porn, wasn't it?"

"Yeah. But no monkeys or donkeys. Just the regular kind."

I've known Doug for fifteen years now. When I first met him, he just had an ocular implant that he could use to access the nets, but every few months he's added something new—visual overlays, exoskeleton, medical nanobots, blah blah blah. The brain thingie is his newest toy. It's not clear to me exactly what the brain thingie does for him that the ocular didn't, but apparently it's something that was worth drilling a hole in his skull. It's like he's an addict. I imagine he'll eventually look like a walking garbage can, with laser eyes and a giant robotic dong.

I've never actually looked into what these kind of mods cost, but it's got to be a fortune, which is weird considering that I've never seen any indication that Doug does anything that anyone would pay money for.

"So," I say. "What's up with your arm?"

Doug's left arm has been clamped to his side since I sat down. He's not ordinarily a fidgeter, but he hasn't even wiggled a finger today.

"Servos are locked up. Haven't been able to move it since last night."

"Huh. Planning on doing something about that?"

He half shrugs.

"Yeah, I'll get it looked at. Can't do it until Monday morning."

"So why don't you take it off?"

He looks at me blankly.

"Take what off?"

I wave a hand at him.

"The exoskeleton, Doug. Why don't you take it off until you can get it fixed?"

The scowl comes back. Definitely terrifying.

"I dunno, Anders. Why don't you take off your endoskeleton every time somebody startles you, and you bang your head on the ceiling and break your own leg?"

Well. That was unnecessary.

"Oh, don't look at me like that," he says. "It's exactly the same thing. This isn't a suit I'm wearing. It's just as much a part of me as my organics."

I lean forward.

"Except that you actually could take it off, right? You can't do that with your balls, for example."

"In fact," he says, "right now it would be easier to take off my balls than this rig. The left arm is frozen. I may not have mentioned that."

The waitress comes by with our food. She smiles at me, and asks if I need anything else. I shake my head. She gives Doug a sideways glance, glowers, and walks away. I pick up a slice of bacon. It's perfectly crispy brown, and still hot. I take a bite and chew slowly, letting the salt clear the taste of rat anus that's still lingering in my mouth. Doug is trying to cut his waffles into precise squares one-handed. It's not going well.

"You know," he says. "That bacon is nothing but fat and sodium."

I shrug.

"And you know that waitress wiped her perfectly proportioned ass with your waffles, right? Explain again why you don't feel the need to tip?"

Doug sighs. We've been through this before.

"Tipping allows the management to continue to employ low-cost human labor, where an automaton would clearly be more efficient. If nobody tips, the servers will eventually demand better pay, which will prompt management to replace them."

"But it's not everybody who's not tipping, Doug. It's just you—which means that the servers are not replaced by hyperefficient mechanical men, but I do have to sit here catching backsplash from the stink-eye they're constantly throwing you, and watching you eat waffles that spent the best time of their lives down the back of someone's shorts."

He stabs a forkful of waffle and shovels it into his mouth.

"Tastes okay to me."

We settle into eating. The waitress stops by to refill my tea. She really is a piece of work, and I find myself wondering if I could talk her into meeting up with me later. Hard to figure out how to start that conversation without coming off like a possibly dangerous weirdo, though, so I table the idea for the moment. I finish my last bite of eggs and give the pancakes a poke, but my stomach lets out a warning rumble. Doug finishes his waffle, drains his water glass, and leans back in his chair.

"So," he says. "I suppose you're wondering why I asked you here today."

I actually was not wondering that at all. I look at him expectantly.

"The answer," he says finally, "is that I have a proposition for you."

I raise one eyebrow.

"Not the naked, sweaty kind of proposition," he continues. "The business kind."

I lean back and fold my arms across my chest.

"I have some documents," he says. "I need you to review them for me. They're . . . outside my expertise."

"You mean not related to donkey porn?"

"No," he says. "Not related to donkey porn, or monkey porn, or monkey-on-donkey porn. Technical documents. I think they're close to your area of expertise, but I'm not sure. If they're not, just delete them, and I'll find somebody else."

"You're not sure because you don't know what's in the documents? Or because you swap to kitten cage-fighting videos every time I try to talk to you about my work?"

"Can't it be both?"

I sigh.

"I'm sure it is, Doug. Fine. What file sizes are we talking about?"

He shrugs.

"A couple of terabytes, I'm guessing mixed media. Shouldn't take more than a day or two to go through it, but unless you're a lot better informed than you've led me to believe, you'll probably need to do a fair amount of background digging as well."

I pull out my phone, and make a show of checking my calendar. Truth is, I have absolutely nothing going on.

"Great," I say. "I've got finals coming up, but I can probably get to it after that. What's the rate?"

"The what?"

"The consulting rate. What are you going to pay me for this?"

He looks genuinely startled.

"Pay? Come on, Anders. I thought we were friends."

I roll my eyes and wait for the laugh, but it's not coming.

"I understand that you're the cheapest cyborg on Earth," I say finally, "but did you or did you not just say that this was a business proposition?"

"Yeah," he says. "But I didn't mean the paying kind of business."

I close my eyes, and massage my temples again. The headache had been receding, but it's coming back now with a vengeance.

"Just to clarify," I say. "Is someone paying you to decipher these files?"

He manages to look offended.

"That's kind of personal, isn't it?"

"But you expect me to spend several days doing the actual work for you, for free."

He looks up at the ceiling and sighs.

"Well sure, it sounds bad if you put it that way."

"So let me put it this way instead: I bill out at six hundred an hour."

He shrugs.

"Fair enough. When can you get back to me with some answers?"

Considering that Doug didn't blink at my pulled-from-my-ass consulting rate, I'm feeling like I can spring for a cab to get back home. The car drops me off a little after two. I climb the six steps up to the stoop, and dig in my pockets for my keys. In addition to living next to a drug lab, I live in the only house left in Baltimore that doesn't have electronic entry. I'm about to let myself in when the door jerks open, and Gary pulls me into a full-body hug.

"Where were you last night?" he wails, and crushes his face against my chest. "I waited and waited, but you never came home."

I push my way inside, pull the door closed behind me and pat him on the head.

"Sorry, honey." I say. "I meant to call, but I was busy having sex with a prostitute. I hope you don't mind."

He laughs and lets me go.

"I figured as much. You smell like a Dumpster. Also, rent transfers tomorrow. Can you cover, or do I need to add it to your tab?"

"No," I say. "I'm good. I'll push it tonight."

I start upstairs. I want a shower and a nap before I start thinking about not taking a look at Doug's files.

"Hey," Gary says. "Somebody named Dimitri stopped by looking for you this morning. Do we know a Dimitri?"

I keep climbing.

"So many Dimitris," I say. "Russian hit man Dimitri? Ballet dancer Dimitri? Dancing bear Dimitri? What did he look like?"

I turn the corner at the landing. Gary's still talking, but I'm no longer listening. I peel off my shirt and drop it in the hallway, step into the bathroom and turn on the shower. As I turn to close the door, I'm surprised to see Gary standing at the top of the stairs.

"Seriously," he says. "This guy was definitely not a dancer and probably not a bear, and he seemed kind of torqued when I told him you weren't here."

I kick off my shoes and drop my pants.

"I don't know anybody named Dimitri. What did he look like?"

"Six feet, kinda stocky. Black hair. Brushy little beard. Pretty serious accent. Ukrainian maybe?"

This is not ringing any bells.

"Look," I say. "I've got nothing. I'll think about it, and if I come up with anything I'll ping you. Good enough?"

I close the door without waiting for an answer.

I spend ten minutes washing, then another fifteen letting the hot water steam the rest of the alcohol out of my system. I shut off the water, and by the time I'm finished toweling off, I feel like I could curl up and sleep on the bathroom floor. I collect my clothes and chuck them into the wicker hamper. As I do, my phone drops out of my pants and bounces off the tile. It pings when it sees that it has my attention. I've got a voice-only. I pick up the phone and acknowledge. It's from Terry.

"Hey," she says. "I heard you might have had a visitor this morning. Sorry."

"I did," I reply. "Can you elaborate?"

"Sorry, no. I'm a limited-interactive. Terry has authorized you for direct access, however. Would you like me to attempt connection?"

Just as well, I guess. I hate talking to fully interactive avatars. I get that they're just simulations, that they don't really have thoughts and hopes and dreams and whatnot, but the good ones have been able to pass the Turing test for a while now, and deleting them has always felt weirdly murder-ish to me. No such problem with the LIs, though. They're just annoying.

"No," I say. "Don't ping Terry now. I'll get back to her later. Delete."

Whatever this Dimitri thing is, I don't feel much like dealing with it at the moment. I open the door. Steam pours out into the hallway. My room is to the left, Gary's is to the right. He's sitting on his bed staring into space, either stroked out or watching something on his ocular. One eye focuses on me.

"Hey," he says. "Towel, maybe?"

I turn into my room and shut the door behind me, drop the phone on my nightstand and fall into bed.

I have a recurring dream where I'm downtown, wandering around the mess just north of the harbor in the middle of the night. I have a car, which I do not in real life, but I can't remember where I parked it, and the streets keep changing names and directions until I don't recognize anything. I usually wind up getting chased around by somebody. This time, it's a bear in a tutu who keeps yelling at me to stay away from his girlfriend. He corners me in a blind alley. I'm standing on top of a Dumpster, scrabbling at the brick wall of the building behind it, waiting for his bear teeth to sink into my ass, when I snap awake. The late afternoon sun is slanting through the window, and I'm soaked with sweat.

I'll later learn that while I was napping, the good citizens of Hagerstown, Maryland, more or less simultaneously crapped their pants and died.

2. TERRY

I'm just back from a run, dripping sweat and still panting, when my phone pings. I've got a full-interactive from Dimitri.

"Hey," it says. "Pick up. I saw you come in."

Shit. I keep meaning to deny incomings access to the house.

"Fine," I say. "Connect."

I walk into the kitchen, turn on the sink and splash cold water on my face. The avatar manifests as a talking bear. I don't have an ocular, so it shows up in the wallscreen instead of standing in front of me. Still, annoying.

"So," it says, in a cartoonish parody of Dimitri's accent. "Dimitri found your new boyfriend. He lives in a crack house. You should stay away from him."

"Really? That's what you're here for? Del—"

"Wait! Wait! I have other things to say!"

I can feel my face twisting into a scowl. The bear raises one eyebrow hopefully.

"Fine," I say finally. "Two minutes, and then I'm in the shower and you're in the recycle bin. What?"

"Your new boyfriend has contact with unsavory characters," it says. "Very bad people, with bad motives. Dimitri is concerned for you. He would not want you to get caught up when new boyfriend comes to bad end."

I roll my eyes as I turn off the water in the sink.

"Could you please drop the accent?" I say. "It's not cute. And could you also lose the bear suit?"

The bear smiles, which on a bear face is more creepy than reassuring.

"Is this better?"

The accent is gone, but now I'm looking at a fat guy in a leather thong. When did Dimitri's avatars turn into smart-asses?

"Look," I say. "I've been pretty clear that Dimitri and I are not a thing, haven't I? We are not lovers, sex pals, soul mates, or significant others. We have been friends, but honestly I'm starting to question that now. Who I choose to bring home with me and what I choose to do with them is none of his business. Understood?"

The avatar raises its hands in surrender.

"Really, Terry, this is not a jealousy thing. Your new friend is probably not a bad guy, but there's a good chance that he's going to be in some trouble soon. Dimitri would very much prefer that you stay out of it."

It seems sincere. But of course, that's the beauty of a full-interactive avatar. It honestly believes whatever information Dimitri fed it. That's why full-interactives are a favorite tool for people who are completely full of shit.

"I'll tell you what," I say finally. "I'll take it under advisement. Does that work for you?"

It shrugs.

"I suppose it will have to do. Please contact Dimitri directly at your earliest convenience."

"Yeah, I'll get right on that. Delete."

It gives me an ironic salute, and then disappears.

I'm not sure exactly what, if anything, Dimitri might have done to Anders, but whatever it was, I feel at least partly responsible. I don't know where Anders lives, but I did skim his number while he was passed out in my bedroom. I give him a ping, then drop him a quick voice-only by way of apology when he doesn't connect. I don't know if I'll see him again, but if I do, I don't want the first topic of conversation to be the nutjob I led to his doorstop.

Not that Dimitri's a nutjob, really. This jealousy thing, if that's what it is, is totally out of character. I've known Dimitri for three years now, and despite the fact that we met at a support group for people who'd recently lost loved ones, he's never really gotten into my personal life before. Also, the bear was pretty insistent that Dimitri's interest in Anders is professional.

Hard to see how Dimitri could have a professional interest in Anders, though. I don't know exactly what

Dimitri does, but I know he works for NatSec in some capacity. I asked him about it once, early on, when we were still trying to feel out what our relationship was going to be. I tried hinting around for a while, then asked him flat-out what he did for a living. He just smiled and shook his head.

"What?" I said. "If you told me you'd have to kill me?"

"No," he said. Dimitri's not exactly a laugh riot under the best of circumstances, but this was as serious as I've ever seen him. "I would not have to kill you, Terry. There is an excellent chance, however, that if I told you how I spend my workdays, someone would have to kill me."

Thinking about that conversation leads me to wonder for the first time if maybe Dimitri might have some actual justification for an interest in Anders. Anders didn't seem much like a terrorist last night—but then, I've never spent much personal time with a terrorist before, so what do I know? I try to picture his big, goofy, drunk-on-four-beers ass putting bombs together in his basement, or cooking up a super virus in a secret lab somewhere, but the image just makes me giggle. Dimitri developing a sudden, uncontrollable, possessive love for me seems a lot more plausible.

I strip out of my running gear and step into the bathroom. This room is the only thing I truly hate about my apartment. It's got an open shower stall on one side, facing a floor-to-ceiling wallscreen on the other. I do not like looking at myself naked, and I really don't like other people looking at me naked. I like to think I'm in pretty good shape, but between the big shoulders and the tiny breasts, and the brow ridge, I'm not ever gonna be a lingerie model. I actually asked the landlord to put in a closed stall when I first moved in. I do interior design for a living. Rich old ladies pay me obscene amounts of money to give them this kind of advice, and I offered it to him for free. He was pretty clear that he thinks this bathroom is a selling point for most tenants, though, and he was not interested in changing it.

I turn on the water, let it go from cold to lukewarm, and step under the spray. I did a pretty thorough scrub-down this morning, so this is really just a sweat rinse. I'm starting on my hair when the screen pings. I wipe my eyes clear and squint through the spray. It's my sister.

"Connect," I sigh. "Audio only."

The wallscreen stays blank, but I can hear the grin in her voice.

"Hi, Terry. No view?"

I close my eyes again, tilt my head back and let the water plaster my hair to the back of my neck.

"I'm in the shower, Elise. What do you need?"

"Just wanted to talk pretty dresses and appetizers," she says. "Nothing important. Want me to try back later?"

Ugh. I let my head fall forward until my chin almost touches my chest.

"If you don't mind?"

"No problem. Maybe an hour?"

"Sounds good, Elise. Disconnect."

There's something to look forward to. Elise is getting married in a month. I'm supposed to be the maid of honor. Her best friend, Grace, is a Pretty, and Elise might as well be—tall, thin, and blonde, with gravity-defying boobs and a face that looks like it's been digitally enhanced. The thought of standing up in front of everyone we know in between those two is enough to make me want to crawl into a deep, deep hole and pull the dirt in on top of me.

Not surprising considering that we're basically different species, but finding a dress style that Elise and I can agree on is proving to be a challenge. Her taste runs to wispy pastels that barely cover her privates, while I tend to prefer either sportswear, or dresses with enough fabric to cover up the fact that my shoulders are twice as wide as my hips.

Grace actually suggested that we do the entire ceremony nude. Elise wasn't going for that, but obviously I'm getting no help from her end.

The only quarter I'm getting any support from, in fact, is the boy—which is ironic, because in every other way, he's kind of an asshat. His name is Tariq. He's a performance artist. He claims to be one-hundred-percent natural—he's even turned Elise into a vegan, for God's sake—but I've seen him do some crazy stuff, and I've always assumed he actually has some pretty serious mods. Most times his whole "Mysterious Messenger from the Spirit World" bullshit makes me want to put my fist through his sunken chest, but he's pushing for the wedding to look like something out of the eighteenth century, with everyone wearing corsets and wrapped up in fifty yards of crinoline. So, in this case I'm counting him as an ally.

I give myself a last turn, run my hands back through my hair, and then shut off the water. I step out of the shower, take one of the towels from the rack on the door and wrap it around my hair, and rub myself down with the other.

"House," I say as I walk into the bedroom. "Look up Anders Jensen."

My house avatar pops up on the bedroom screen. She's made herself over to look like me today. Creepy.

"Location?"

"Baltimore."

"Four matches."

I'm out of underwear. I'm out of bras. I pull on a pair of bike shorts and a compression shirt. Close enough.

"Limit age range, twenty-five to thirty."

"No matches."

Bastard.

"Limit age range thirty to thirty-five."

"No matches."

Okay. That's disturbing.

"Limit age range thirty-five to forty."

"One match."

"Visuals?"

A half dozen stills pop up on the screen. Looks like most of them are from security cameras. It's definitely him. He's at least thirty-six years old. That makes him the oldest Engineered I've ever met, and probably one of the oldest in North America. Looking at him, I honestly wouldn't have thought he was over 25. He's not a Pretty, exactly, but I'm guessing now that his cutter probably gave him more than a little mouse juice.

"Residence?"

That gets me a visual of a beat-up townhouse, labeled 317 West Twenty-eighth. Apparently Anders hasn't been using his genetic superiority for financial gain. That's only a half mile or so from here, but the neighborhood deteriorates pretty quickly in between, and I'm guessing the upgrades in my bathroom are worth more than his house.

So, what is Dimitri's issue with this guy? The more I think about it, the less I believe that he's jealous. Dimitri and I have never been physical, and he's never given me any reason to think that he wants to change that. I don't bring a ton of guys home, but there have been a few over that last couple of years, and Dimitri has never raised a peep about any of them.

"House. Direct contact, Dimitri."

It patches straight to the bear.

"Hello, Terry," it says. "Dimitri would love to speak with you, but unfortunately he is occupied. Can I help?"

"Disconnect."

I need to go for a walk.

It's gotten steadily hotter and muggier as the day has worn on, and by the time I get to Anders' house, I'm wondering why I bothered with a shower. Honestly, it's probably only about eighty, but I don't do well with heat. I can feel the sweat trickling out from my hairline, beading over my eyes, and dripping down my cheeks like tears.

The visuals on my wallscreen didn't do this place justice. There are cracks in the concrete steps, cracks in the foundation, shutters on some of the windows and not on others. The paint has come off the siding in patches, and the power strips on the roof look like they're starting to peel up. I'd fault Anders, but the rest of the block actually looks worse, and I'm guessing that if he put any effort to fixing this place up, he'd just make himself a target for a home invasion.

I bump the door with my phone. Nothing happens. I try again. After the third time, it dawns on me that this door isn't reading my phone because it has no electronics. It's seriously just a big piece of wood on hinges. I give it a couple of whacks with the palm of my hand, wait five seconds, and give it a couple more. I'm about to try again when the door opens a crack, and I see a sliver of face and one eye peering out around a chain lock.

"We have a bell, you know. Are you with Dimitri?"

"No," I say. "I am not with Dimitri. You're not Anders. Is he in there?"

The door closes, and I hear the rattle of the chain lock being unlatched. The door swings halfway open, and not-Anders pokes his head out and looks around. He's a weedy-looking guy, skinny and pale, with a patchy little beard and blond dreads. He relaxes when he sees that I'm alone, steps back, and opens the door the rest of the way.

"Anders is sleeping," he says. "Apparently, he was up all night having sex with a prostitute. Wanna come in and wait for him to wake up?"

"Sure," I say, and extend my hand. "I'm Terry. You know—the prostitute."

He takes my hand, mock bows, and brushes my knuckles with his lips.

"Charmed," he says. "Please do come in."

I step past him, and he closes the door behind me. The interior is dim and cool, and much nicer than the street view would suggest. The foyer opens into a good-sized living room, with a short hallway to the kitchen. They've got a decent, unpatched leatherette sofa, and a couple of gaming recliners facing what looks like a recent vintage wallscreen. I drop into one of the recliners, pop the footrest and lean back.

"Make yourself comfortable," he says. "I'm Gary, by the way. Are you really the prostitute?"

I shrug.

"Apparently so."

He grins.

"Neat. That must've looked like a Great Dane humping a Chihuahua. Can I get you anything?"

"Some cold water? It's hot as a monkey's ass out there."

He gives me a quizzical look.

"Are monkey's asses really hot? Is that a thing?"

"It's an expression."

"No," he says. "I'm pretty sure it's not."

I scowl. Despite its many shortcomings, the brow ridge is excellent for scowling.

"It is now," I say. "Water?"

"Right," he says. "Coming up."

He backs out of the room, and shortly I hear running water, and the rattle of ice in a glass.

"House," I say. "Vids. Sports. Lacrosse."

"Sorry," it says, in Gary's voice. "You are not authorized."

I scowl again, but it apparently doesn't have the same effect on Gary's avatar.

"Not authorized?" I ask. "To turn on vids?"

"You're not authorized for jack in this house, sister."

A sassy avatar. Great. Gary comes back with a glass in each hand.

"So," I say. "You lock out your entertainment?"

"I use the system for work." He hands me my drink and flops onto the sofa. "I keep everything locked."

"Kinda paranoid?"

"Not really." He takes a long drink, and I can actually see his pupils dilate. I'm pretty sure his is not water. "You'd be surprised how easy it is to hack from one function to another once you get basic access to a house system. One minute you're watching lacrosse, and the next you're emptying my bank account, and replacing my avatars with goats or naked old ladies or something."

"Huh." I drain my water in one pull, hold up the glass and rattle the cubes. Gary stares at me blankly. I rattle them again. He raises one eyebrow. I smile. He rolls his eyes, climbs back to his feet, takes my glass and heads back into the kitchen.

"You know," I say. "If you were less paranoid and more sociable, poor Anders might not have to resort to banging prostitutes."

"Not true," he says as he comes back with my water. "Anders is ugly. He will always have to resort to banging prostitutes."

He sits back down and takes another long drink.

"You're not really a prostitute, are you?"

I smile.

"You're gonna feel pretty bad if I am, aren't you?"

"Yes," he says. "I am."

"I'm not."

"And Anders didn't really bang you, did he?"

"No," I say. "He did not."

He grins again.

"Good. If I found out that Anders was getting laid for free, I'd have to rethink my entire worldview."

I take a drink, and wipe the cold glass across my forehead. I'm cooling down now, sweat drying on my face and arms. I'm not entirely sure what to make of Gary. I'd like to know what kind of work he does that requires the level of security he's apparently put in place here, but given that he won't even let me watch lacrosse on his wallscreen, I'm guessing he's not going to tell me.

I wonder what Dimitri would think of this setup.

"So," Gary says after a long, awkward silence. "Who are you really?"

I finish my water and wipe the last of the sweat from my face with my sleeve.

"I'm really the girl Anders spent the night with," I say. "We met at the Green Goose last night. I'm pretty sure he tried to drink me under the table. It didn't work out for him."

Gary nods.

"Got it. As big as he is, you'd think he'd be able to hold his liquor."

I smile.

"But you'd be wrong."

"Right," he says. "So, what happened? You carried him home slung over your shoulder?"

"No," I say. "He was still walking when we got back to my apartment. I actually thought I might get lucky, until he fell over my coffee table and couldn't get back up."

He shakes his head.

"I don't think you're using the word 'lucky' correctly."

I laugh.

"I think you're wrong. Have you seen him naked?"

He finishes his drink.

"This conversation is making me uncomfortable. Can we talk about something else?"

"Sure," I say. "Let's talk about why two apparently well-educated and possibly employable young men are living next door to a crack house."

"No," Gary says. "That also makes me uncomfortable. Let's talk about why you're here. Did Anders steal your wallet or something? Because he does that, you know. You should probably stay away from him."

"Huh," I say. "You're the second person who's told me that today."

He looks genuinely surprised.

"Really? Who was the first?"

"My friend Dimitri. He said Anders was going to be in trouble soon, and that I should stay out of it."

Gary leans back. His eyes narrow, and he folds his arms across his chest.

"Oh, I got it now. Dimitri's your boyfriend? Is that what he was so wound up about this morning?"

"No," I say. "Dimitri is not my boyfriend. He's just someone I know."

"And he told you Anders is big, big trouble."

"He did."

Gary raises one eyebrow.

"Anders, the broke former Eagle Scout who has never had so much as a parking ticket. Mostly because he's never owned a car, but still."

"Broke, huh?"

"Totally. Seeming like less of a catch now?"

"Lots of nice stuff here."

"I didn't say *I* was broke."

I take another look around. His gear is actually better than I'd thought. The recliners are real leather, and on closer inspection, so is the sofa. The floor looks to be some kind of hardwood under the raggedy throw rugs, and the climate control is first rate.

"So what did you say you do for a living?"

He shrugs.

"You know. Stuff. Data entry and whatnot."

"Right. And you let Anders live here because . . ."

"He pays rent. Most of the time, anyway. And sometimes he helps out with . . . stuff."

"Data entry and whatnot."

"Right."

Another long silence follows. Finally, Gary says "House. Vids. General. *SpaceLab*."

The wallscreen comes alive. I've never heard of *SpaceLab*, but apparently it's an animation that takes place on an orbital platform. The characters all seem to be either drunk or mentally defective, which right from the jump doesn't make a ton of sense. I've met a few actual orbital jocks, and you really couldn't imagine a more sober and un-defective bunch.

Gary starts snickering about thirty seconds in, so I guess it's supposed to be a comedy, but I'm having a hard time figuring out the joke. On top of that, the animation is terrible. The characters' faces have a rubbery look to them that's just off enough to make you realize they're not real people, which in a weird way is more disturbing than if they were completely stylized. I tolerate about five minutes, then close my eyes and say "Is this really the best we can do?"

"Pause," he says. He looks profoundly hurt. "Don't tell me you're not a fan of *SpaceLab*?"

I turn to look at him.

"I've never seen this before, but based on the last five minutes, yeah, I think I can say with some confidence that I am not a fan of *SpaceLab*."

"How can you not appreciate *SpaceLab*?" He leans

forward and chops the air with one hand. "*SpaceLab* is classic social satire. It reflects modern society back to us through a funhouse mirror, and forces us to confront the absurdities in our everyday lives."

I shake my head.

"First, I'm pretty sure you just repeated back something that you read on somebody's vid-critic feed. Second, I just watched the science officer of a space station get into a feces-flinging fight with his captain, whose brain had apparently been switched with a chimpanzee's. Which parts of my everyday life is this reflecting back at me?"

"Well . . . it's not meant to be taken literally. It's a metaphor."

"A metaphor?"

"Or a simile. Maybe it's a simile? Which one has 'like' in it?"

"That's a simile."

"Then it's definitely a metaphor."

"You don't look like an idiot," I say after a long pause, "but you are one, aren't you?"

He slumps, and his voice drops an octave.

"Yes."

I sigh and run my fingers back through my hair.

"Fine. Satirize the crap out of me. Play."

"Gary?" says the House.

He perks up immediately.

"Yeah, play."

So I sit through the last seven minutes of the episode. It does not get noticeably better. We learn that the captain switched bodies with the chimp in order to negotiate with a band of space-faring monkeys who were threatening to destroy the station. He eventually returns from his mission and restores order by swapping back into his own body and placing the chimp under arrest for mutiny and insurrection. The chimp elects to act as his own lawyer. He is convicted and condemned to be ejected into the icy vacuum of space. The sentence is carried out in a slightly amusing sendup of *Billy Budd*. Seeing their fellow primate being chucked out of the airlock, the space monkeys blow up the station. Fade to theme music.

I sit in silence for a moment, while Gary looks at me expectantly.

"Well?" he says finally. "Pretty great, right?"

I'm not sure what to say to that.

"Was that the last episode?"

He looks at me like I've just grown an extra head.

"What? No. No, why would you think that? *SpaceLab* has been running since I was in high school. This is actually one of the older episodes."

"Didn't they just blow up the space station? That's a tough one to recover from, isn't it?"

He smiles.

"Oh, that? No, they do that every episode."

I stare at him. He just keeps smiling.

"Space monkeys blow up the station every episode?"

"Well, no," he says. "It's not always space monkeys. Sometimes it's terrorists or aliens or God. Usually it's one of the crew, though."

"Uh-huh. Tell me again what that was satirizing?"

"Well, this episode was a parody of a nineteenth-century novel called *Billy Budd*."

I roll my eyes.

"Only the last ninety seconds of that mess we just watched have any relationship whatsoever to *Billy Budd*."

The arms are crossed again, and now he's the one scowling. It's a lot less impressive on his flat little face, but still. Time to backtrack.

"Look," I say. "Maybe *SpaceLab* is an acquired taste. You said yourself that you've been watching this since you were in school. This was my first time. I might appreciate it better after I have a little more exposure."

That perks him up again.

"So you want to watch another clip?"

"Baby steps, Gary. Baby steps."

"Right," he says. "Sorry."

There's another long pause. Gary starts fidgeting, and I realize that if I don't say something soon, I'm liable to wind up watching something even more asinine than *SpaceLab*.

"So," I say. "How long have you known Anders?"

He shrugs.

"I dunno. Five years? I sat in on a class he was teaching at Hopkins. I needed a lot of help getting through the course, and he needed a lot of help with not being a starving hobo. So, here we are."

"What was the class?"

He drains the last of his drink.

"Intro to nanotech. That's why I had so much trouble. Not really my thing. I'm more of a virtual systems guy. Having to deal with actual physical laws is a gigantic pain in the ass."

"Nano, huh? Is that what Anders does?"

Gary laughs.

"Well," he says. "*does* is a very strong word. He showed me his thesis once, and 'nano' was definitely in the title, so I guess he knows something about it. But if he actually *did* nanotech, I'd be getting rent out of him a little more regularly. What he does is *talk* about nanotech to classes full of bored rich kids. Not the same thing, and very much less rewarding."

"Yeah," I say. "He told me he's a professor."

Gary laughs again, harder.

"A professor? Oh honey, no. No, no, no. Anders wishes he was a professor. Anders has gooey wet dreams about becoming a professor, but Anders is definitely not a professor. Anders is an instructor. A part-time instructor. Professor is to instructor as burger crew chief is to nugget fryer, and instructor is to part-time instructor as nugget fryer is to the guy the nugget fryer gets to cover for him while he goes out and takes a hit behind the Dumpster. That's Anders—the substitute nugget fryer of the academic world."

Apparently Gary has just amused the shit out of himself, because it takes him a solid two minutes to get his giggling under control. Definitely not water in his drink, and probably not alcohol, either. I wonder if maybe I should ask for one of whatever he's having, and then try watching another episode of *SpaceLab*.

"So look," I say finally. "This has been fun, but I actually did come here for a reason. Any chance you could go check in on Anders? Maybe see if he's ready to come down and say hello?"

He shakes his head.

"Sorry, Terry. No can do. Waking Anders up is a dicey prospect on a good day, and after he's been drinking, it's worse. If you really need to talk to him, you're gonna have to wait."

I get to my feet.

"So let me go get him. I don't really care if he gets pissy with me."

He shakes his head.

"No, you misunderstand. If you wake him up from a sound sleep, Anders has a tendency to startle."

"And?"

"Did he not mention the mouse thing?"

Oh. Right.

"Don't worry," he continues. "He never hurts anybody else. It's not like you were in mortal danger while you were not-banging him last night. He's put himself in the hospital a couple of times, though. Anyway, it's pretty much standard procedure around here to let him wake up on his own."

"Ah," I say. "Got it. So how long do his siestas usually last? I really would like to talk to him, but I can't wait around here all afternoon."

Which reminds me that I was supposed to be talking shrimp puffs and white lace bustiers a couple of hours ago. I pull out my phone. There's a voice-only from Elise. I must have missed the notification when it came through.

"Hi, Terry," she says. "I don't think I'm going to be able to talk about the wedding today. Bad things are happening here."

3. ELISE

I drop my phone back into my bag, take a deep breath, and gag so hard that I throw up a little into my mouth. The man in the next booth has finally stopped screaming. I can see his foot jutting out into the walkway between tables, twitching. Twitch. Twitch. Then still. My waitress is still facedown where she fell, two tables away. There's a bloody-looking puddle by her mouth, and something is starting to seep out from under her skirt. The smell is unbearable. I try mouth breathing. I can actually taste the stink. I need to get out of here, but I haven't gotten a check yet.

I half stand, and look around the restaurant. Other than a woman slumped over a table across the way whose hand is still shaking, nobody else seems to be moving. I ordered an artisanal field green salad, chamomile tea, and a slice of lemon tart. I never got the tart, though, and it doesn't look like I'm going to, so I'm pretty sure I don't need to pay for that. The salad was twenty-two dollars and the tea was seven. Tax is ten percent and the tip . . . ugh. I pull out two twenties and leave them on the table. I think I might be shorting the waitress. I glance over at her again. She's definitely not moving. It's probably okay.

Getting out of the restaurant is like walking through the world's grossest minefield. When people started screaming, a lot of the customers tried to either get to the bathroom or get out the door. Doesn't look like any of them made it, and they're everywhere—and not just them, but the goo that came out of them, which I definitely do not want on my shoes.

My shoes. Keep looking at my shoes. Two steps forward. One to the left. Step over a hand. Don't look at what it's attached to.

Up by the hostesses' stand, there's a kind of a logjam, with four people sprawled across the entrance and completely blocking the way. Two of them are a couple, lying side by side with their arms around each other. The one who's doing most of the blocking is a five-hundred-pounder, lying facedown with his arms at his sides.

He's not a person. He's a beached, incontinent whale. I know the hostess, though. Her name is Kelly, or maybe Kiley. She graduated from my high school a year ahead of me. She was a cheerleader. She's lying half in and half out of the door, propping it open. At least she's letting some fresh air in.

I pull off my shoes and tuck them into my bag.

They're strappy Roman sandals with four inch heels—perfect for either a day at the office or a night on the town, but not so much for walking across a dead whale and a former cheerleader. I'd really rather not step on anything that's oozing, so I hop up onto the whale's back with both feet. He shifts underneath me and lets out a long, low moan. I wave my arms for balance. It's like trying to stand on a beach ball. I jump forward onto the back of his neck, then onto Kelly's back, lean into the door and vault out onto the sidewalk, stagger forward two steps and sprawl across the hood of a car parked at the curb. There's a girl slumped over in the passenger seat. Her chin and chest are covered with blood. I slide down to the sidewalk, curl up into a ball, and scream. And scream. And scream.

I'm not sure how long it is before I think to try to call Tariq. Maybe a half hour? He's in Baltimore today, playing for the tourists in the harbor. I need to tell him not to come home this afternoon.

I need to tell him not to come home, ever.

I'm up and moving again by then, and mostly back from Crazytown. My phone won't link to any of the networks, though. It just sits there and beeps at me. At least I'm wearing shoes again. I've seen a couple of other still-alive people—one guy on a motorcycle flying up National Pike towards 68, and a woman looking out of a third-story window on Locust. Neither of them seemed to want to talk. I've also seen a whole lot of not-alive people—people in their cars, people on the sidewalks, people in stores, all of them with something awful seeping from their mouths and noses, none of them moving.

I've been trying not to think about the restaurant, but I'm starting to feel like I need to understand what's happening, and right now, I definitely don't understand what's happening. The only person I actually saw go down was my waitress. She'd just come by to refill my water glass. She took two steps away from my booth, then dropped the pitcher she was carrying, took one more staggering step, and fell. I was staring at her, wondering if she'd had a heart attack or something, wondering if I should be calling an ambulance, when . . .

Okay, don't think about that anymore. Keep moving forward.

I don't understand what's happened, but it looks like whatever it was happened really quickly, and at the same time everywhere. I don't see any more police cars around than usual, and no ambulances or fire trucks, either, so I'm guessing nobody even had time to call EMS. Like the waitress, like Kiley and the whale, it looks like everyone just dropped where they stood.

I'm not an expert on crazy doomsday stuff, but I don't know of anything that could just kill everyone in an entire city at once like that. I've read about black pox and dirty bombs and poison gas, the kinds of things that NatSec is always arresting and deporting and disappearing people for making, or trying to make, or thinking about making. But I'm pretty sure none of those things could do anything like this. Poison gas would be the closest, I guess, but if that's what this is, then what about me?

As I turn the corner onto North, I almost trip over a woman sitting on the sidewalk. She's leaning against a lamppost, hugging her knees and crying—pretty much doing what I was doing a little while ago. I stop, kneel down, touch her shoulder.

"Hey," I say. "Are you okay?"

She stops crying, and her eyes focus on mine.

"Am I okay?" she asks. "Are you a fucking idiot? No, I am not okay. Have you looked around? Fuck!"

I rock back on my heels. She seems pretty worked up.

"Seriously," she says. "Don't you know what's happened?"

I shake my head.

"It's the Rapture!" She's screaming now. "It's the Rapture, and I'm still here!"

I stand up and back away. She presses her head against her knees and wails.

"I don't think this is the Rapture," I say. I didn't pay a lot of attention in church when I was a kid, but I'm pretty sure there was nothing in there about everybody bleeding out through their anuses. She looks up at me. Her eyes are bloodshot and staring.

"So," she says. "What is it, then? What happened to everyone?"

I look around.

"They're dead," I say. "Everyone is dead."

She looks away again. At least she's being quiet now.

"Why aren't you dead?" she finally whispers. "Why aren't I?"

I turn away and keep walking.

I live in a two-bedroom bungalow that backs onto Reed Park. Walking down my street, I could almost convince myself that nothing bad is happening. The neighbor's dog charges across their front yard and stands barking at me from the driveway, and the sprinklers are on in front of the house across the street. There aren't any people out, but that's not too unusual, even on a sunny afternoon like this one. I can see a sliver of the soccer field in the park between the houses.

Sunday afternoons are a big time for league games.

I'm not going to look out there.

I let myself in the front door and close it behind me. "House," I say. "Are you there?"

"Yes, Elise."

Thank God. I was afraid my house avatar might be as dead as my phone.

"Direct contact, please. Terry."

There's a long pause. That isn't good.

"I'm sorry, Elise," House says finally. "Direct contact is not possible. Would you like to prime an avatar? I can queue it for transmission as soon as communications are restored."

"Yes," I say. "Voice only. Zero interactive. Terry, contact me. Now."

"Is that all?"

"Yes."

"Queued for transmit."

"House. Are incoming feeds active?"

"Yes, Elise. Reception is normal. Transmission is blocked."

"Blocked by who?"

"Blocked by whom?"

"What?"

"Correct phrasing is, 'Blocked by whom?' "

Terry set my house avatar to correct my grammar. I don't know how to unset it. This is not the time.

"Fine, jackass. Blocked by whom?"

"Unknown."

"Can I get vids?"

"Yes. Topic?"

"News. National. Live. Centrist. Kitchen wallscreen."

I hear the caster talking as I walk through the foyer and into the kitchen. He's saying something about rising bond rates in the European markets, and how that's good for some investors and bad for other investors. I've never understood why they bother with stories like this. As far as I can tell, every single thing that ever happens in the world is good for some investors and bad for other investors, and knowing which investors any particular thing is good for is only helpful if you know it before that thing happens.

Anyway, he's not talking about the apocalypse, which, if that were what was happening, you would think would be the lead story.

I run cold water in the sink, splash some on my face, and spend a solid thirty seconds scrubbing at my hands. When I look up again, the crawl across the bottom of the screen is saying something about a labor dispute in Uzbekistan that's threatening to undercut production of beryllium. The announcer has moved on to a story about the orbital power platform they're building over Nebraska, and how the locals are very, very upset with the location of the rectenna.

"House," I say. "Vids. Search topic: apocalypse."

"That search returns one-point-seven million results. How would you like to prioritize?"

"Eliminate all entertainment."

"Search now returns two hundred fifty thousand results."

"Limit to news, limit to North America, limit to segments produced today."

"Search now returns twelve results."

"Start with the most recent."

The wallscreen flips to two men in suits, sitting on a sofa. House includes an overlay that says "Local interest, Charleston, WV. Released today, 12:32:00."

"Welcome to *Good News Sunday*," the man on the right says. "Today we're joined by the Reverend Donald Blakesly, who believes that we are living through the final stages of the End Times. Welcome, Reverend Blakesly."

"Thank you, Jerome," says Reverend Blakesly. "It's a pleasure to be here."

I need to have a talk with House about what I mean

when I say 'news'—but actually, what's going on outside does seem kind of biblical, so I decide to let it run.

"Reverend Blakesly," Jerome says, "we've heard many times before that the prophecies laid out in the Book of Revelations are being fulfilled, and that the End of Days is nigh. Why do you believe that this time is different?"

"Well, Jerome," says Reverend Blakesly, "I know that others have claimed to have interpreted the signs before, and I also bear in mind our Lord and Savior's admonishment that he will come like a thief in the night, and that none will know the hour of his coming."

Jerome leans forward, one eyebrow raised.

"But Reverend Blakesly, you have said repeatedly in your public and private casts that you believe that the End of Days is nearly upon us. How can that be, if our Lord Himself has said that none can know the time?"

The reverend leans back in his seat and steeples his fingers.

"I have never claimed to have divined the day and time of our Lord's return, Jerome. However, I do think that if you look closely at the sixth chapter of the Book of Revelations, it becomes increasingly clear that the Seals are being opened, one by one.

"The first Rider, who comes upon a white horse, and the second, whose mount is red, are harbingers of warfare and slaughter. And are those not present in this world wherever one looks? In the south, the godless Brazilians run roughshod over their pious neighbors. In the east, the Chinese have subdued half of

Asia. In the north, Christian Russia kneels before the terrible Swedes. And in the west, California seems on the verge of passing Proposition 117."

"Proposition 117? The one allowing temporary contract marriages?"

"The very same."

This is too much.

"Search forward," I say. "Keyword 'apocalypse.' "

House skips the cast ahead. Jerome is leaning back in his seat now, and I'm guessing from the expression on his face that he's finally realized that he's booked a lunatic.

"So tell me," he says. "What form do you expect the final apocalypse to take?"

"Well, Jerome, this brings us to Chapter Fifteen, and the Seven Last Plagues. The first of these is shown by painful sores, which appear on those with the Mark of the Beast. Are you aware of how widespread antibiotic-resistant gonorrhea has become? The second plague involves the poisoning of the sea. The ever-accelerating acidification of our oceans certainly fills this bill. The third plague refers to the poisoning of groundwater, which I think we can take as a given, and the fourth refers to the increasing heat of the sun. The fifth plague is a plague of darkness. That I believe has not yet come. Nor have the sixth and seventh plagues, which are the drying of the Euphrates and a great earthquake and rain of fire. I believe that these will be fulfilled through a great asteroid strike, most likely somewhere in the Middle East."

Jerome leans forward again, moving in for the kill.

"Of course," he says, "our government has had a very thorough catalogue of all near-Earth asteroids for many years now, and we would know—"

"Pause," I say. I thought maybe we were making progress with the seven plagues, but none of the ones the good reverend talked about involved massive anal bleeding.

"House. Return to live newsfeed."

There's a new caster now, a very serious-looking blonde woman, and the crawl across the bottom reads "HORROR IN HAGERSTOWN" over and over.

" . . . repeat, nothing is yet known about the nature of the outbreak in Hagerstown. Government spokespersons have stated unequivocally that no disease research centers are located in Hagerstown, and that they have no knowledge of any terrorist threats that may have been made against the region. We now go live to the White House, where Press Secretary Darryl Browning is scheduled to make a statement."

Okay, now we're getting somewhere. The scene cuts to a podium in front of a plain blue background. A tall man with a gray crew cut steps into frame and looks directly into the camera.

"Ladies and gentlemen of the press," he says. "At approximately sixteen thirty, there was a massive outbreak of an unknown, highly contagious, and highly lethal disease in Hagerstown, Maryland. We know nothing at this point regarding the exact nature of the disease, but video from surveillance cameras and drones in the area indicates that it is most likely hemorrhagic in nature. Containment checkpoints have been set up on all access points to central Hagerstown, but no survivors have yet been observed. Likewise, surveillance indicates no movement whatsoever within the Hagerstown city limits. Our belief at this time is that the fatality rate within the affected area is one hundred percent."

That gets a few gasps from the audience, and I can hear some muttering in the background.

"I can now take questions, but please understand that we are still working with severely limited information."

I can't see the reporters in the audience, but from the long silence I assume they're all sitting with their jaws hanging open, possibly wetting themselves. Finally, Darryl Browning says, "Yes, Ms. Barringer."

The viewpoint pans to the gallery, where the bloggers and press hags look pretty much exactly the way I pictured them. An older woman is standing in the center of the front row.

"So . . ." she says. "What . . . what do we do now?"

Darryl Browning looks down at the podium for a long moment, then back up at the camera.

"Well," he says finally. "Considering the existential threat that this outbreak poses to our nation, it seems clear that our only option is the most thorough possible sterilization of the entire Hagerstown area."

He goes on, but I've stopped listening. Sterilization. I'm not sure what exactly he means by that, but

I'm pretty sure it can't be good. How do you sterilize things? Boiling water? Iodine? Fire?

Fire.

I need to get to one of those checkpoints.

Before I go, I swap my skirt for shorts, and my sandals for sneakers. I pull my road bike down from the rack on the entryway wall, drag it out the front door and into the street. There's a boy out on the sidewalk a few houses down. He's looking up, waving his hands in the air and yelling. He's maybe ten years old, barefoot and dirty, with a too-big Orioles cap turned backward over a mop of brown hair. Based on what I've seen so far today, I'm guessing his parents are dead. I catch myself wondering if I can adopt him when this is over.

"Hey," I yell as I climb into the saddle. "What are you doing?"

He pauses, turns and focuses on me.

"Oh, hey," he says. "That guy on the news vid says they don't think anybody's alive here. We need to get somebody out there to figure out that it's not true. I'm thinking maybe I can trigger the motion seeker on one of the news drones, get them to home in on me and push the feed out to one of the big outlets."

I start pedaling toward him.

"He also said they've got checkpoints around town," I say. "I'm gonna try to find one. You should come with me."

He looks down at his feet. I pull up to the curb beside him.

"Nah," he says. "I'd better stay here. Mom left me here when she went into work this morning. This is where she'll come looking for me."

I almost start to tell him that his mom's not coming back, but no, this is not the time for dropping truth bombs.

"You really should come with me," I say instead. "It sounds like they're planning on doing bad things here, and I don't know if your mom's going to be able to get back home before they do."

"Bad things, huh?" He looks up at me. "Do you know what an FAE is?"

I shake my head.

"I do," he says. "It's a fuel-air explosive, dumbass. It's the bad thing they're gonna do here. And if they decide to do it, there's no way your stupid bike is gonna get you out from under it."

I stare at him. He's much less adorable up close.

"I kinda doubt you're gonna find friendly doctors at your checkpoint, either," he says. "Probably army killbots. The guy on the vid said they think this is a hot zone. They're not gonna want anybody walking out of it."

"But . . ."

"The only way we don't get cooked is if we trigger a civilian drone. They won't let NatSec pull the trigger if they have vids of cute kids and pretty ladies still alive here. Or even you, I guess. So find a nice open spot, and start waving your arms."

I make a conscious effort to close my mouth. He

turns his back on me, and starts jumping up and down again. I shake my head and pedal away.

"Or, you could ride up the pike and get your boobs shot off," he yells after me. "That's good too."

There are definitely more people out and around now than there were when I walked home. Most of them are little kids, with just a few adults mixed in. None of this makes sense. Nobody's sick. They're either totally fine or totally dead. And anyway, aren't children supposed to have crappy immune systems? How could you make a virus or a poison or whatever that kills more adults than kids? Maybe Reverend Blakesly was onto something. Maybe the kids are still alive because they haven't had time to commit enough sins yet.

Of course, that doesn't explain why I'm still here.

I ride east along Jefferson. I pass a woman running, and a few minutes later a man in a car speeds past and almost runs me off the road. On and off, I hear a dull banging in the distance. The kids I see are mostly just wandering around and crying. I think about trying to help some of them, but I can't stop thinking about what that little shit said about the killbots.

The banging stops for a bit after I cross Eastern, and I hear what sounds like a voice coming through a loudspeaker. Then I see a sharp flash of light up ahead, and a second later there's a boom and a wash of heat that startles me into slamming on my brakes. I swerve back and forth twice, lose my balance, and go down in a heap. My head hits the pavement and I see another bright white flash, this time behind my eyelids.

I sit up. My hands are both scraped raw, and my mouth tastes like blood. I untangle myself from the bike. The handlebars are turned sideways. The front wheel is bent. I stand. My eyes unfocus, and I feel like I'm about to be sick. I double over, and have a moment of panic wondering if this is how the plague starts. But then my stomach settles, and I decide that maybe I'm just a little concussed. I straighten up again. I can still hear the loudspeaker voice, but I can't make out what it's saying. The sun is almost touching the horizon, and my shadow stretches out to infinity in front of me. I start walking.

After a hundred yards, I can see what made me crash. It's the car that passed me earlier. It's torn almost in half, rolled over on its roof in the middle of the road and burning. A little ways beyond it, just short of where Little Antietam splits off, something wide and squatty and green is blocking the road. Apparently it sees me, because it rises up on four splayed legs, and the turret on top turns to face me. There are a half dozen bodies in the road between the bot and the burning car.

"This area is under quarantine," it says. "You cannot pass this checkpoint. Return to your home, please, and await instructions."

It's the loudspeaker voice I heard earlier.

"I'm not sick!" I yell. I keep walking forward, slowly. "I'm not infected! I wasn't in town!"

"I'm sorry, miss," it says. "I can't let you pass. You need to turn around now, and go back home."

I stop just short of the car. I'm assuming that's its no-go radius.

"Are you a person?" I ask. "Can you talk to me?"

"I am a fully interactive avatar," it says. "I can talk to you, but I do not have discretion to let you past this checkpoint."

There's a thick stand of trees on the right side of the road. I take a tentative step in that direction. A bullet zings off the pavement in front of me.

"Sorry," the bot says. "I can't let you go that way either. If you don't head directly back the way you came, I'm going to have to shoot you."

Son of a bitch. That little bastard knew exactly what was going on. Why didn't I?

"Look," I say. "There are lots of people still alive here. They're mostly little kids. You can't just kill a bunch of little kids, can you?"

"I don't have any discretion in the matter," it says. It sounds genuinely apologetic. Off to the right, I can see another like it moving along the edge of the woods. As I watch, it fires twice. A high-pitched scream follows, then a third shot, then silence. I turn back to the bot blocking the road.

"They're going to burn us, aren't they?"

It hesitates, and shuffles its feet uncomfortably.

"I don't know."

I can feel tears welling up. I squeeze my eyes shut, and will them back down. I'm not going to die bawling in front of a killbot.

"Can you let me talk to a person?" I ask. "I mean an actual human?"

Its carapace shimmies in what might almost be a shrug. "I'm sorry, miss. I can't."

I look back over my shoulder. The sun is a fat red ball on the horizon, with pink and purple streamers stretching out as far as I can see to the north and south. It's kind of stunning, and I catch myself thinking that if this is my last sunset, at least it's a good one.

Tariq must have seen the feeds. He must think I'm already dead. I wonder if he's watching this sunset too.

After what feels like a long time, I turn back to the bot. "Which will hurt more?" I ask.

It had settled back down onto its belly, but it perks up again now.

"Please rephrase the question."

I take a deep breath in, then let it out.

"Will it hurt more to let you shoot me, or to wait for the bomb?"

It hesitates.

"I don't know, miss. I would shoot you in the head with a .50 caliber armor-piercing round. I doubt you would feel much. On the other hand, a fuel-air explosive is extremely powerful. Your subjective experience would likely be the same."

I turn my back on the bot. The sunset is like an oil painting. This would be a perfect evening if it weren't for the bot and the bombs and the stench of shit coming from the bodies in the road.

"If it makes you feel better," it says, "when the bomb comes, I'll be destroyed as well."

That really doesn't make me feel better at all.

"I don't understand," I say. "Why is that supposed to help?"

"Well," it says. "At least we're not dying alone."

I turn back to look at it. The anti-tank weapon on the turret is locked in on me.

"Does your offer still stand?" I ask.

"Yes," it says, "but I think you should decide soon."

Far off to the west, I hear a low, droning buzz. I shade my eyes and squint into the sunset. A black dot rises in front of the bloated red sun. Closer, a helmeted man on a three-wheeled cycle comes crashing out of the trees not far from the second bot. For some reason, it ignores him. He skids onto the road and speeds toward us. Behind me, the first bot comes two clanking steps closer, but it doesn't address him, doesn't even seem to notice that he's there. I imagine I can feel the warm spot of its targeting laser on the back of my neck. The man on the cycle is close now. He flips up his visor and screams, "Down! Elise, get down!"

Tariq?

The bot shuffles another step forward.

4. GARY

Terry drops her phone and says, "Get me a newsfeed."

I don't like the news. I've been drinking a mix of BrainBump and rum for the last two hours. The nanos are tickling my implants nicely, and I'm really kinda jonesing for a little more stupid.

"Hey," I say. "What about some more *SpaceLab*? There's an episode from last summer—"

She wings her empty glass at me. I flinch, and it whizzes past my head and explodes against the wall.

"Get me a newsfeed, you weedy little fuck! I don't have time for your burnout bullshit!"

I guess we're not bantering anymore.

"House," I say. "News. Local. Live. Liberal."

The screen cuts to what looks like a puff piece on Senator Nguyen. She's wearing a flannel shirt and jeans, and walking with a smiling younger woman through a soybean field.

"These are my roots," says the senator. "When Washington gets to be too much, when I need to ground myself, this is where I come. My family has been working this land for fifty years, and God willing we'll be here for a hundred and fifty more."

"Not this," says Terry. "Get me a local feed from Hagerstown."

"Gary?" says House.

"Authorized," I say. "She can watch whatever she wants, as long as she quits throwing my stuff at me."

The screen goes blank.

"No feeds available from Hagerstown at this time," says House.

"Frederick," Terry says. "Get me a feed from Frederick."

That gets us a pretty young caster wearing a gold tech shirt and shorts, standing beside a line of stopped cars on a highway on-ramp.

" . . . apparently stopping all traffic westbound on 70, which as you can see is creating a pretty nasty backup. There's been a steady stream of military copters passing overhead, heading northwest toward Hagerstown. Mickey Liu in Martinsburg tells me he's seeing the same thing on 81 North. I've tried pinging several colleagues in Hagerstown, but have gotten no replies. I have also tried to contact both local and national government agencies, so far without success."

The feed cuts to an older man in a suit. He's sitting on a porch in a glider chair.

"Strange goings-on in Hagerstown," he says. "I've

tried to patch to a number of civilian drones that should be in the area, but they all appear to have been taken offline between one and two hours ago. So have the local ground-based cameras and security systems. Whatever is happening there, someone with a very long reach does not want us to know—"

He pauses, and his left eye starts twitching. He's downloading something through an ocular. After a dozen seconds, his eyes refocus. "We're going to patch through to a national feed. Those with weak stomachs may want to drop off now."

The screen cuts to a static view of the interior of a McDonald's. There are probably fifteen people in the frame—in booths, on the floor, slumped over tables. None of them are moving, and most of them look like they've been puking up blood.

"Scenes like this are repeated throughout Hagerstown at this hour," says the voice-over. The POV jumps to a traffic cam at a downtown intersection showing a four-car pileup. The driver of one of the cars is hanging halfway out of his open door, a puddle of something vile on the pavement under his open mouth. It jumps again to what looks like an office, and again to a park, where eighteen or twenty guys apparently dropped dead in the middle of a soccer game.

"Authorities continue to review all available data sources," says the voice-over, "but as of this time, no evidence of survivors has been found."

"Oh, Jesus," Terry whispers.

"Have you got people there?" I ask.

"My sister," she says. She's crying now. I need to get Anders.

By the time I get to the top of the stairs, I've got feeds coming into my ocular—from my peeps, not the sheeple on the wallscreen downstairs. I get a twenty-second loop from what looks like low earth orbit that shows cars on a city street moving normally, then swerving out of control and smashing into each other. Nobody gets out to exchange insurance cards. That switches to a view from an air breather of the soccer field I saw in the living room, except that the players are still alive. Then one slows to a stop, clutches his belly, and drops to his knees. It's not more than five seconds before they're all down. A few are still thrashing when the POV spins crazily and cuts out.

"Gary?" Anders is standing in front of me. He snaps his fingers in my face. "You there, man? For shit's sake, it's Sunday afternoon. What are you on?"

I cut the feed and shake my head.

"Nothing. Well, not much. I had a couple of Bump-n-Dumps, but I'm fine. You need to come downstairs."

"That's where I was headed. What's going on?"

"You've got a visitor. Also, it looks like Hagerstown just got whacked. Also, your visitor's sister lives in Hagerstown, so she's not too happy. Also, something weird is going on with my feeds . . ."

"Stop." He holds up one hand. "What do you mean, 'Hagerstown just got whacked'? You mean bombed? Like a terrorist thing? What kind of a dipshit terrorist would go after freaking Hagerstown?"

"No," I say. "Not bombed. Just whacked. Killed. Looks like everybody in town just keeled over dead."

He blinks, slowly.

"You mean, all at once?"

I shrug.

"Yeah, pretty much."

"How do you do that?"

"Fuck if I know. I was just starting to get some feeds from my boys when you got all snappy with me."

He rubs his face with both hands.

"Okay. You said I had a visitor?"

"Yeah. It's your friend from last night. She's pretty upset."

"And she's got a sister there?"

"That's what she said."

"Shit. Okay."

He starts down the stairs. I tap back into my feeds. They're pretty much the same thing over and over again, from different vantages: people alive and doing people things, then people thrashing around and spewing shit and blood and puke out of every orifice, then people dead. They all cut out about ten or fifteen seconds after things start going crazy. The ends of the drone feeds all look like they lost flight control right before the cutout. The satellite and fixed-camera feeds just end. I pull up a chat frame next to the vid.

Sir Munchalot: <Hey. What's with the cut-outs?>

Drew P. Wiener: <Unknown. We've only got

these clips because one of my bots flagged them as unusual, and archived them off in realtime. They're all gone from the public nets.>

Sir Munchalot: <Sauron's Eye?>

Drew P. Wiener: <Must be. Don't know who else would have the resources/authority to wipe out every feed coming out of an area that big.>

The fact that Drew was able to pull the clips before Sauron's Eye redacted them means the NatSec bots are about ten seconds slower than Drew's. That's good to know. The fact that the feeds got redacted at all, on the other hand, means that NatSec has invoked terror-response protocols. This is also good to know, because it means that possession of these clips could probably get all of us tossed down the memory hole.

Hayley 9000: <Got some preliminary guesses on what could cause the biological effects seen here. Fenrir says there are a couple of dozen aerosols or gases that could rip out someone's alimentary canal like that. High oral doses of an alpha emitter might produce those kinds of symptoms as well.>

Argyle Dragon: <Fenrir is an idiot. Those clips were temporally synched. Everybody dropped at once. An aerosol or gas would have a temporal distribution pattern.

A radiological would have even worse distribution problems, and would have pinged every rad sensor for a hundred miles before anybody died.>

Fenrir: <Bite me, Argyle. What about biologicals? I've seen some tailored variants on hemorrhagic fever that kinda looked like that.>

Argyle Dragon: <Same problem. Temporal distribution. Try again.>

Fenrir: <What about a timer?>

Argyle Dragon: <Explain?>

Fenrir: <Seventeen-year locusts.>

Hayley 9000: <Come on, Fenrir. If you've got something, give it up.>

Fenrir: <Seventeen-year locusts. They hang out in the ground for seventeen years, then all pop out at once. Same principle. Engineer a virus or bacteria that can burrow into the alimentary canal. Engineer it so that it remains dormant for a while. Maybe a long while. Then the whole batch becomes active at once, but instead of eating your garden, it rips your guts out.>

Argyle Dragon: <Citations?>

Fenrir: <None. Just spitballing here.>

Sir Munchalot: <What about a trigger?>

Fenrir: <Meaning what?>

Sir Munchalot: <Instead of a timer, a signal. RF maybe? Could you engineer a biological that would be sensitive to an RF signal?>

Fenrir: <Not sure. I'll put a bot on it and see if there's precedent.>

Angry Irish Inch: <Hey. Check this.>

Inch drops a link to an audio file. I stream it.

" . . . need to know what we're dealing with here. What's the kill rate?"

"Estimated at eighty-eight percent currently. Survivors appear completely unaffected. No deaths observed since the initial strike."

"Do we have containment?"

"Affirmative. Eighty-plus percent of survivors are children. They're mostly staying put. We've had a few takedowns on the perimeter. Expect more in the next two hours."

"Are we a go on the burn?"

"Affirmative. Getting assets into position now."

"Do we have consensus on that? With twelve percent survivors?"

"Best estimate is that if this breaks out, a fifty percent death rate would be sufficient for a national soft kill."

"We don't even know that this is contagious."

"We don't know that it's not."

Fenrir: <Inch? Was that NatSec chatter?>

Angry Irish Inch: <Maaaaybe.>

Argyle Dragon: <Are you out of your freaking mind? Sauron's Eye is watching, brother. I'm out.>

Hayley 9000: <Likewise. Deleting.>
Sir Munchalot: <Eyes and ears open, friends. Check back in a couple of hours.>

I blink my windows closed, and start down the stairs.

Anders looks up when I step into the room. He's on the sofa with Terry, arms around her shoulders. Her face is buried in his chest. Huh. Would not have called that.

"Well?" he says.

"Pretty grim," I reply, and drop into a recliner. "Survivorship is under fifteen percent, mostly kids."

Terry looks up at that. Her face is still screwed up in a half sob, which when you throw in the brow ridge and the gob of snot coming out of her left nostril, is pretty much a horror show in and of itself.

"Survivors?" Terry says. "The wallscreen said there were no survivors."

I shrug.

"Well, I'm guessing that'll be true pretty soon. Sounds like they're planning on a burn-down."

She wipes her nose with her arm, which just smears things around. I toss her a screen rag from the cargo slot in the recliner's arm. She catches it, wipes down her face and arm, and winds up to throw it back. I hold up one hand.

"Keep it," I say. "Please."

She half smiles her thanks.

"I don't understand," she says. "What's a burn-down?"

She looks weirdly hopeful now. Maybe 'burn' didn't mean what it does now, before she got frozen in a glacier or whatever.

"I'm not exactly sure," I say. I glance over at Anders. He's glaring at me for some reason. "I guess they could use a nuke, but considering we're basically downwind, I hope not. More likely an FAE."

"That's enough," says Anders. His head looks like it's about to explode.

"An FAE?" Terry says.

"Right," I say. "Fuel-air explosive. The poor-man's nuke. Most of the boom, with none of the fallout."

"Shut up," says Anders.

"You said there were survivors," says Terry. "They wouldn't do that if there were people still alive in there, would they?"

"Au contraire—"

"I said shut up," Anders growls.

"No, Anders," says Terry. "You shut up. I'm not your fucking damsel in distress. I want to hear what he has to say."

I'm about to go on, but just then some administration tool comes on the wallscreen and starts talking about sterilization. We all listen to his spiel in silence.

"You see?" I say when he's done, and they cut back to the studio mannequin. "Burn-down. They're gonna turn that entire place into a smoking hole in the ground. Only way to guarantee containment."

Terry's crying again.

"My sister is in there," she sobs.

I shake my head.

"Probably not. The estimate I heard, which came from an unnamed but reliable source, was twelve percent survivors with eighty percent of those, children. That puts the adult survival rate at two-point-four percent."

I stop and think for a minute.

"Wait. No, it doesn't. That's not factoring in the preexisting demographics. Say kids under 18 make up thirty percent of the original population. If your overall survival is twelve percent, and eighty percent of those are children, that makes the survival rate for children . . . thirty percent . . . and for adults about four-point-three."

That gets us a solid ten seconds of awkward silence.

"It doesn't matter," says Terry finally. "If what you're saying is right, there must be over five thousand people still alive. They can't just burn them, can they?"

I shake my head again.

"That's what I was trying to say before Anders interrupted. If everyone were really dead like they're saying, they could probably afford to wait for a while, maybe send in some bots to poke around and see what went down. With survivors, though . . . if this is a virus, all we need is for one person to sneak out of town with this stuff percolating in his gut, and before you know it, it's eighty-eight percent of North America dead. Better to make it one hundred percent of Hagerstown, and leave it at that."

Anders is glaring at me again. Terry's face is blank and slack as a rubber mask.

"And they said . . ."

"Right," I say. "They said there were no survivors because saying that we're about to cook a few thousand adorable little scamps down to scrapple would probably upset some people."

She stares at me through a long, awkward pause.

"But you think it's the right thing to do," she says finally.

I kick the footrest up, knit my fingers behind my head, and look up at the ceiling. There's a crack in the joint compound that runs all the way from one end of the room to the other. I never noticed that before.

"I'll say this," I say. "If I were in charge, and I had to make the call on whether or not to slag a few thousand rug rats in order to prevent the release of an engineered virus that had just ripped through an entire town in under an hour, with an eighty-eight percent fatality rate . . . I would be very sorely tempted to do it."

The sofa creaks as Anders shifts his weight. That crack runs right underneath the wall that separates Anders' room from the hallway. Is that a load-bearing wall?

"Do your friends think that's what this is?" Terry asks. "A virus?"

I sigh.

"No, ma'am. They do not."

We sit in silence then. Terry and Anders watch some idiot on the wallscreen drone on about containment protocols for a while, and then they cycle through the same clips they were showing before. I blink to my ocular again, and query similar incidents in the past fifteen years. I get a link to a feed about an outbreak of black pox in a CDC facility in Bismarck, a bunch of links related to that brain fungus thing that got set loose in Tokyo a few years ago, and a couple of dozen fictional vids about viruses that turn everyone into zombies.

I actually consider trying to do some research, but I kind of have a thing for zombie vids, so I wind up streaming one of those instead. This one is called *The Omega Protocol*. It's got a couple of decent actors, and a CGI group that usually does a nice job. It starts out with a little bit of promise, but after about twenty minutes, I click it off in disgust. I like zombies, but I cannot stand zombie vids that take themselves seriously. In this one, zombieism is caused by a virus that can only be spread through the bite of an infected person. Once a victim gets bitten, the virus gestates for a while—to give him time for angst-y conversations with his loved ones and contemplation of suicide, I guess—and then turns him into a shambling, rotting wreck with a hankering for human flesh. At the point where the story picks up, literally everyone on Earth except for the heroes is infected.

Which is all well and good, I guess, except for this: We already have a virus that is spread through bites, that causes you to act crazy, and that is 100 percent fatal. It's called rabies. And yet somehow, not every person on Earth has contracted it.

Something bounces off my head. I blink the ocular back off and look over at Anders.

"Hey," he says. "Why don't you check in with your friends, and see what's really going on?"

Fine. I pop open another chat frame.

Sir Munchalot: <Developments?>

Angry Irish Inch: <Yeah, I've got developments. I've had three attempted incursions in the last thirty minutes.>

Sir Munchalot: <Are you secure?!?!>

Angry Irish Inch: <So far. I may wind up having to ditch this entire rig, though.>

Argyle Dragon: <That's what happens when Peter goes rooting around in Mr. McGregor's garden.>

Argyle Dragon: <You might want to drop off this net until the heat's off, Inch. Don't want to bring Johnny Law down on the rest of us.>

Angry Irish Inch: <Thanks for the support, asshole. I'm gonna reboot everything, and do a complete sweep. Ciao.>

Fenrir: <Did a full precedent search for RF sensitive bacteria. Got a couple of pings, but nothing that comes close to what you'd need for something like this.>

Hayley 9000: <So where does that leave us?>

Drew P. Wiener: <Dunno. Witchcraft?>

Argyle Dragon: <Right. And you know what they do with witches.>

I blink the frame closed again. They've clearly got nothing. I sit up and look around. Terry and Anders are sitting close together. His hands are in his lap, and she's leaning her head against his shoulder. The wallscreen is muted. The view is still cycling between static shots of corpses, overhead shots of corpses, and spysat shots of corpses.

"Nothing new," I say. "Except that one of my peeps has NatSec crawling up his ass, I mean."

Neither of them even glances at me. I kick the footrest down and stand.

"I'm gonna get a drink. Either of you want anything?"

Terry closes her eyes. Anders looks at me like I'm something he scraped off the bottom of his shoe.

"Um . . . I guess not," I say finally, then turn and walk out to the kitchen.

The screen over the stove comes alive when I open the fridge door. I pull out a can of BrainBump, give it a quick shake, and pop the top. I don't usually drink this stuff straight, but I decide to make an exception under the circumstances. I down it in one long, sweet, chocolatey pull while a pretty blonde caster from Washington explains that while nobody wants to do what they're going to do, it's simply a matter of national survival.

"House," I say. "Can you find me a feed that's a little less moronic?"

The screen switches over to *SpaceLab*.

"Ooooh, baby. You do know what I like."

I've seen this episode before, of course, but it's a classic. Science Officer Scott is traveling back to the station by shuttlecraft when he runs into a temporal anomaly—just as he's trying to fart in his spacesuit, loses control, and winds up sharting instead. The anomaly throws him back in time by thirty seconds, and he's forced to relive the sharting over and over until he realizes what's happening and finds a way to break the temporal cycle. In this case, breaking the temporal cycle requires squeezing the gas all the way up his digestive system and belching it out instead. I'm not one hundred percent clear on the physics behind this, but the BrainBump nanos are stimulating my giggle centers, and by the end of the episode I'm laughing out loud.

At least until Anders grabs my head in one giant spider hand, tilts it back until I feel my neck crack, and slams me to the floor.

I'm about to say something, maybe ask him what the hell he thinks he's doing, when I get a look at his face and abruptly shut my mouth. Just then there's a flash outside the window, like catching a reflection of the sun off the windshield of a passing car. He kicks me once in the ass, and then walks away. I lie there on the floor for a minute or so, wondering what just happened. I'm just getting to my feet when a boom like distant thunder rattles the windows.

Right. That.

Forty-five minutes later, and we're all three back in the living room again, watching replays of the bombs going off—it turns out they actually used three of them, synchronized for simultaneous detonation—from a half dozen different vantages. After a while, they switch over to orbital perspectives post-detonation. I kind of expected everything to be on fire, but it's not. The whole town is just a big, black, lumpy splotch on the ground. Apparently, that's one of the beauties of a fuel-air explosive. It sucks up all of the oxygen over a wide area, so that (a) you don't need to worry about survivors anywhere within the blast radius, as long as they're not wearing space suits, and (b) there's not a whole lot of secondary burn, which means your advancing forces can move into the area very quickly after a bombardment.

Of course, in this case we don't have any advancing forces. Just a bunch of bots poking around, looking for any evidence that would help clear up exactly what happened there.

Terry and Anders haven't said a word since the detonation. They're just sitting together on the sofa, staring at the screen. I get why Terry's upset, with her sister just getting vaporized and all, but I have no idea what's gotten up Anders' ass. The entire vibe in the room is making me very uncomfortable, though. It's almost like they think *I* did something wrong. On top of that, it's damn near eight o'clock, and I haven't had anything to eat since noon. I'm just about to ask if anybody has dinner plans when my ocular pings. I blink to a chat window.

Fenrir: <Didn't take long for the conspiracy theorists to get rolling. Check this:>

What NatSec Doesn't Want You to Know About Hagerstown

Earlier today, something truly horrifying happened in Hagerstown, Maryland. A terrible virus struck with lightning speed, killing the entire population, down to the last man, woman and child, in a matter of minutes. Fortunately, NatSec units were already positioned in the Hagerstown area, and they were able to secure the hot zone in less than an hour. A thorough search for survivors was conducted by drone and crawler, and when none were found, NatSec Acting Director Dey reluctantly made the hard decision to sterilize the area, thus saving the rest of us from the threat of contamination.

That's what our good friends at NatSec would have us believe, in any case. Here are the facts:

1. Within seconds of the outbreak in Hagerstown, every civilian drone, crawler, fixed camera, and orbital asset was taken offline, and all existing feeds were redacted to a point approximately ten seconds before the first casualty. **If every citizen of Hagerstown died within minutes of the outbreak, what were they afraid to let us see?**

2. Throughout the crisis, the only data feeds coming from Hagerstown were those passed to the official media through NatSec channels. **What were they afraid to let us see?**
3. The military cordon around Hagerstown was actually secured within twenty minutes of the initial outbreak. **How did they move so quickly, if they were not aware beforehand of what was going to occur?**
4. The fuel-air explosives that were just used to destroy Hagerstown were far more powerful than would have been necessary to eliminate a biological pathogen. **What were they really trying to destroy?**

I don't claim to know the answers to all these questions, but I do know one thing as certainly as I know the sun will rise in the east: **NatSec's story does not hold water!**

Demand the Truth!

Argyle Dragon: <Nice. Where'd that come from?>

Fenrir: <Public feed from someone calling himself the Lone Stranger.>

Drew P. Wiener: <Is that a monkey, or a Silico-American?>

Fenrir: <Unknown. Doesn't look like he knows anything more than we do, though.>

Drew P. Wiener: <This is true. He's doing some serious rabble-rousing, though. How many views has he gotten?>

Fenrir: <Closing in on a million.>

Argyle Dragon: <How long until Sauron's Eye takes notice?>

Fenrir: <I'd be surprised if she hasn't already. Hope old Lone Stranger's got solid security.>

Sir Munchalot: <Or not. Speaking as a monkey, I'm not sure rabble-rousing is really what we're looking for at the moment.>

I'm pulled away from the chat window by a soft *knock knock knock* at the front door. I look around. Anders is staring at me.

"Are you expecting somebody?"

I shrug. The knock comes again, a little louder this time. Anders closes his eyes, and leans his head back against the wall.

"Answer the door," he says.

Fine. I get up and walk into the foyer, set the chain, and unlatch the door. Outside on the stoop is what looks like a supermodel who just lost a cage fight. She's got dried blood on her face and in her hair, her knees are ripped and bleeding, and her eyes don't seem to be pointing in the same direction. Behind her is a shorter, dark-skinned shifty-looking guy in baggy shorts and a pink golf shirt. He's banged up as well, though not as badly as her. They smell like a tire fire.

"Can I help you?" I ask.

Her eyes focus on mine, and I wonder if I've just woken her.

"Hi," she says. "My name is Elise. Is Terry here?"

5. ANDERS

I'm sitting at the little table in the breakfast nook, starting in on my second glazed doughnut of the morning, when Gary comes into the kitchen. He's wearing a surgical mask.

"Really?" I ask. "A mask? Where did you even get that thing?"

"Last Halloween," he says, and takes a seat across from me. "Remember Doctor Love?"

I look up at the ceiling, then back down at Gary. No, he hasn't gotten any less ridiculous.

"Right," I say. "Doctor Love. So that mask is actually from a costume shop, not a hospital."

He shrugs.

"It's the same thing, right? You don't think they make special nonsurgical surgical masks just for Halloween, do you?"

I cram the rest of the doughnut into my mouth and chew. He may actually have a point.

"Still," I say. "You think—"

"Dude. Swallow."

I wash the doughnut down with half a glass of orange juice.

"Still, do you really think a little square of cloth is going to protect you from something that wiped out an entire town in less than five minutes?"

"No," he says, and I can tell he's not smiling under the mask. "What would protect me from something that wiped out an entire town in less than five minutes would be not letting the outbreak monkey, her fiancé, and her sister spend the night. But I got overruled on that one by the guy who only pays his rent every other month. So, here we are."

I sigh, lean back in my chair, and finish the rest of my juice. I thought we'd hashed this out last night, but apparently not.

"Look," I say. "Your guys don't think what happened in Hagerstown was a virus, right?"

"So?"

"So, if it wasn't a virus, then it was something else, right? Poison? Death ray? Voodoo?"

His eyes narrow.

"Maybe. So what?"

"So," I say. "Those things are not contagious."

I reach across the table, and snatch the mask off of his face. He jumps to his feet and tries to grab it back, but I'm much too fast and he's much too short. He drops back into his seat, crosses his arms and glares.

"Fine," he says finally. "But when my liver dissolves and comes pouring out of my ass, my last act is gonna be to roll around in your bed."

I smile and pocket the mask.

"Fair enough."

Gary takes a doughnut from the box on the table. I went out and picked them up from the Jolly Pirate down the block right after I woke up. We have no actual food in the house, and I figured we needed something for our guests other than the case of BrainBump Gary keeps in the fridge.

"So," he says around a mouthful. I resist the urge to tell him to swallow. "What do you think her real story is?"

"Whose real story?"

He rolls his eyes.

"Elise, jackass. What do you think really happened to her yesterday?"

"What?" I say. "You don't believe that this Tariq guy rode into town at the last minute, found her injured and unconscious on the side of the road, and rescued her on his super-cool ATV? Their story seemed totally not impossible to me."

He snorts.

"Right. His ATV. His electric tricycle, which has a maximum speed of thirty-five miles per hour. On that piece of shit, which I would not use to escape from a pack of angry banana slugs, Tariq penetrated the

NatSec perimeter, located his lady love—who, by the way, claims that at the time she was directly in the line of fire of a NatSec killbot—and spirited her away just ahead of the bombs."

I sigh.

"Well, they did both say that she was concussed. She might have imagined the bit about the killbot. Have you ever heard of someone having a conversation with one of those things?"

"No," he says. "But their control hardware is capable of loading a fully interactive avatar, so that part is definitely possible. The part that is not possible is that she was inside the perimeter when it was buttoned up and is not currently a greasy black splotch in the middle of the road."

He takes another doughnut. I probably should have gotten a second box.

"So what do you think really happened?"

He chews and swallows.

"Dunno. Maybe he was there with her when the shit went down, and somehow they managed to sneak out before the cordon closed. Maybe they were never in Hagerstown at all, and this is all some kind of bullshit long con. Or maybe the way she told it first is truth, and Tariq's an evil wizard. Who the hell knows?"

I think about that for a minute.

"You know, Terry did say he's some kind of street magician or something. Maybe there was some spiriting involved."

He stops mid-bite and leans forward.

"Terry said that?"

"Yeah," I say. "She said he makes a living doing stunts. Mind reading and whatnot."

"Huh." He chews thoughtfully. "I was there in the living room until everybody turned in last night. When did Terry say all this?"

Here we go. He taps his chin with one finger.

"Now that I think of it," he says. "Where is Terry right now?"

I look away.

"I don't know. Probably taking a shower."

"Uh-huh. And where was she an hour ago?"

I look back. He's grinning.

"Fine," I say. "She spent the night in my room. Elise and Tariq needed the privacy, and I've got a queen bed."

He's laughing now.

"Oh, this is perfect. You finally get to live out your dream of dating the captain of the football team."

This is the problem with Gary. He has a 150 IQ, coupled with the emotional maturity of a twelve-year-old boy.

"Look, Gary. Terry had a rough day yesterday. Try not to be a total tool about this."

He's still giggling.

"Sure," he says. "I'll try. No promises, though."

As it turns out, Terry doesn't like doughnuts. Terry likes meat, which we do not have any of. Tariq and Elise, on the other hand, are strict vegans, and can't eat the donuts because they don't know what kind of oil they were fried in. This presents a problem, since our neighborhood is what city planners call a food desert—no grocery stores, no produce stands, no dead mammoth vendors or whatever Terry needs.

"I don't get this," says Elise from in front of the open, empty freezer. "How do you guys live?"

I shrug.

"It's never really been an issue for us. Gary pretty much lives on BrainBump, and I get all the nutrition I need from Jolly Pirate doughnuts and the occasional pizza delivery."

Elise scowls. Apparently she doesn't approve of BrainBump any more than she does Jolly Pirates.

"I have a solution," says Tariq. These are the first four words he's said since he came downstairs twenty minutes ago. "My ATV is outside. I can go shopping."

"Your ATV?" says Gary from the living room. "Well, of course. If it can get you in and out of a NatSec quarantine zone undetected, I guess it can get you to the Giant on 33rd and back."

Now Tariq is scowling as well. He lays his hand on Elise's arm, leans in and whispers in her ear, then turns and stalks out the door.

"That went well," says Terry. "You annoyed him enough that he left without asking me for sausage money."

Elise closes the freezer door and sits down with us at the breakfast table. This table is the only piece of furniture in the house outside of my bedroom that belongs to me. It's a simple rectangle of Formica supported by four spindly aluminum legs. Gary doesn't know this, but I actually found it in a dumpster about a week before I moved in.

Elise leans forward and rests her forehead on her hands. I can see the spot on the top of her head that was bleeding yesterday, still red and angry-looking. When she looks back up, there are tears on her cheeks.

"Ellie?" says Terry. "Are you gonna be okay?"

"I don't know," Elise whispers. "I've got no home. I've got no job. I've got some credits, but I'm afraid to access them. I don't know what to do now."

Terry slides her chair over, puts her arm around Elise's waist, and rests her head on her shoulder.

"You can stay with me," she says. "I've got plenty of room, and . . ."

"Stop," says Elise. "Just stop, Terry. You think I'm stupid, but I'm not. NatSec tried to kill me yesterday. I can't stay with you. I can't believe these guys let me stay here last night."

"Yeah, me neither," says Gary.

"Come on," I say. "They didn't try to kill you *per se.* They just tried to kill everybody who happened to be where you happened to be. It's not like it was personal."

She shakes her head.

"It doesn't matter. They know I was there. They've got video and audio of me from the killbot. Even if they didn't think I was contagious, they'd have to kill me just because I know there were survivors when they dropped the bombs."

"About that," I say. "Do you really think that stuff you said about the killbot actually happened? Because Tariq says it didn't. He says he found you blacked out on the road by your wrecked bike, and I thought last night that you were kind of agreeing with him."

She leans her head against Terry's, and closes her eyes.

"I don't know," she says finally. "I love Tariq, and I'd trust him with my life—but you know as well as I do that what he says happened yesterday doesn't make a bit of sense."

"That is true," says Gary.

"Look, Gary," I say. "If you're going to be part of the conversation, come out here and sit down. If you're going to sulk in the living room, then link in a *SpaceLab* episode and shut the hell up."

"I'm just maintaining basic pathogen containment," Gary says. "If someone hadn't taken away my protective gear, I'd be happy to join you out there."

Terry gives me a questioning look. I pull the surgical mask out of my pocket and toss it to her. She rolls her eyes, and drops it on the table.

"So," I say. "If we can all agree that Tariq did not ride into Hagerstown on his trike, engage in some light banter with a NatSec killbot, sweep you up in his spindly little arms, and ride back out without being either incinerated or shot, then what do we think actually did happen? You really were there, right? And you really got out?"

Elise nods.

"So how did that happen? 'Cause it seems like you're the only one who made it out."

Terry's glaring at me now, and I get that I'm pushing someone who's had a really rough couple of days, but I've got a feeling that this is important. Elise lifts her head from Terry's, and opens her eyes.

"I don't know," she says. "I really did wreck my bike, and I'm pretty sure I blacked out for at least a little while. Then I got up and started walking, and I ran into the killbot. I tried to get it to let me pass, but when it wouldn't I just sort of . . . gave up, I guess. I thought it would be nice to watch the sunset. It was a beautiful sunset. Then the drone came up over the horizon, and . . ."

"And then what?" says Terry.

"And then Tariq was there. He tackled me and we were falling together and the killbot was firing and . . . the next thing I remember is being on the back of his ATV, halfway to Baltimore."

"You mean like teleporting?" I say. "You just disappeared and reappeared in another place? Because I'm pretty sure that's impossible."

"No," she says. "It wasn't like that. I told you, he tackled me. Maybe I hit my head again? I remember the killbot firing, and then . . . I don't know. It's all just a jumble from then until I was standing on the stoop, waiting for Gary to open the door."

"Anders," says Gary. "Come here. You need to see this."

I look up from the griddle. Gary's face is on the kitchen wallscreen at five times normal size.

"I'm frying sausage," I say. "Can it wait?"

"No sir, it cannot. Get in here. I'm sure Terry knows how to handle a sausage."

And he giggles. Honest to God, he's an infant.

"Just go," Terry says. "It's crowded in here anyway."

This is true. Tariq and Elise are taking up most of the breakfast table and all but one of our bowls with their chopped-fruit-and-nut platter, and Terry has bacon going on one of our working burners and sausage on the other. I've actually known some vegans who wouldn't be in the same room with frying sausage, but Tariq and Elise are apparently from the reformed branch.

"Fine," I say. "Make sure you turn off the burners when you're done. That stove doesn't have a brain."

Terry gives me a disbelieving look.

"It's like you guys are animals."

I walk into the living room. Gary is sprawled in the recliner closest to the wall. He has a bandana tied over his face.

"So," I say. "Are we holding up the stagecoach later?"

"Bite me," he says. "Look at this."

He winks, and the wallscreen fills with text:

<Posted today, 09:22:17. Redacted today, 09:22:21. Source unknown.>

<u>NatSec</u> has told us that every citizen of Hag-

erstown died yesterday, and that is certainly true. However, as **Lone Stranger** and others have documented, their story of how Hagerstown died is nonsensical. **Deep-dive literature searches** have uncovered no known pathogen or toxin that could produce the effects described by NatSec in the citizens of Hagerstown. It is simply not possible that every man, woman and child in that city died within minutes of one another as a result of **superbugs** or **terrorists**. So, what really did happen?

First, it is becoming increasingly clear that not every citizen died after all. Multiple sources have posted **links** purporting to be video feeds showing at least some citizens of Hagerstown alive and well hours after the attack. All such feeds have been redacted within seconds, and those posters who were not sufficiently secured may well have been redacted themselves, but so many independent voices must amount to more than rumor.

Second, the few posts that have emerged from those who claim to have actually seen these feeds make one thing clear: the survivors were not a random cross-section of the population. The survivors were made up exclusively of the **UnAltered**.

With these two points in mind, the events of yesterday afternoon begin to make a terrible sort of sense. Consider: what software corp releases an app without a **kill switch**? Corporations slip these bits of malware into their products so that they can remotely disable some or all copies of the app—and in some cases disable or destroy the hardware on which the app is running—anytime their customers displease them. The men and women who have created the **genetically** and **technologically** **Altered** who walk among us come from this same world view. Who is to say that they might not have inserted a few kill switches of their own into the **Frankenstein's Monsters** they have loosed on the world?

Of course, this realization raises further questions. Supposing such kill switches exist, why would their makers have chosen to exercise them on the people of Hagerstown? And if the many thousands of UnAltered in Hagerstown in truth were not harmed in the initial attack, why did NatSec make the decision to murder them in cold blood?

The first of these questions is the more difficult to answer. Who knows what motivates the sort of greed-sotted creatures who run **Bioteka** or **GeneCraft**? The most likely explanation, however, is that the knowledge of how to activate these codes has escaped their makers, and that yesterday was a demonstration. If we accept this premise, then the answer to the second question is obvious: our national government is a wholly owned subsidiary of the biotech industry. In a scenario like this, NatSec and other government elements would do nearly anything to suppress the truth.

<End post>

"Huh," I say. "This was up for four seconds? Who pulled it down?"

"Unknown. Sauron's Eye, if I had to guess."

"Who?"

"Sauron's Eye," Gary says. "The spider in the middle of the web, right? The all-seeing queen of the panopticon."

"The what?"

He looks at me like I've just admitted that I do not, in fact, know my ass from a hole in the wall.

"Ever noticed those glass-eyeball-looking things you see on street signs and rooftops and traffic lights? Or the little four-prop helicopters that are always buzzing around? Or the things that look like big bugs hanging off the sides of buildings in the crappier parts of town?"

I give him my best don't-push-it glare.

"I know what a security camera is, Gary. What's your point?"

He sighs.

"My point is that those aren't just cameras, or drones, or crawlers. They're the eyes of the panopticon. Every single spy eye in North America is networked or tapped, Anders. They all feed into NatSec's network."

I sometimes have problems telling when Gary's yanking my chain. This is one of those times. I stare at him for a long moment. He stares back, and then rolls his eyes.

"Look," he says. "Believe me or don't, but it's true. NatSec can tap every cell signal in the world, and every peeper from Mexico City to Nunavut. Every bit of that data gets parsed and sifted by Sauron's Eye."

"You make it sound like it's a person."

He nods.

"Kind of. She's the avatar who runs NatSec's security nets. Folks in my line of work have the same relationship to her that field mice have to a hawk."

I lean forward and rest my forehead on my hands. This conversation is making my head hurt.

"So with all that's going on," I say finally, "you think NatSec is wasting time and effort chasing down conspiracy theorists?"

He shrugs.

"I doubt they'd put any manpower to it, but a few sniffer avatars? Sure. Do you have any idea what their budget was last year?"

He has a point.

"So how widely did this disseminate?"

"Again, unknown. It was downlinked just under a million times in the four seconds it was up. The redactors would have pulled it back off of any servers they could find, but a lot of them were probably beyond their reach."

"Like yours."

He grins.

"Right."

His right eyeball starts twitching. It still bothers me to watch him download. Human eyes weren't meant to move independently. It's creepy enough when a lizard does it.

"So," he says finally. "Are you buying what he's selling?"

I shake my head.

"Not sure. That stuff about the UnAltered bothers me. He's clearly got an ax to grind. On the other hand, it's hard to argue with the logic, and the bit about the kill switch is the first plausible explanation I've heard for what happened yesterday."

Gary nods.

"It sounds reasonable, but how would you implement something like that? I know how to do a kill switch in software. I've designed enough of them myself. I guess I could even see how you could build a kill switch into implanted devices—neural implants for sure, and probably others as well. But how do you build a kill switch into someone's genes?"

I think about that for a minute, but he's right. You could presumably cut DNA such that your product has a shortened life span, but to get a geographically localized group to just shut down like that?

"Possible it was actually just those with biomechanical implants that died?"

He shakes his head.

"Not if the NatSec chatter we intercepted yesterday was anywhere close to accurate. The percentage of people with serious implants is still only in the thirties. Actually, even throwing in all the genetically modified only gets you to maybe forty or forty-five percent."

"Even with the minor mods? The Pretties and whatnot?"

"You mean like the cave ladies and their mouse-man boyfriends? Yeah, I was including them. You wouldn't think it from our social circle, but the majority of the population is still plain old *Homo sap*."

I squeeze my eyes shut and rub my temples with one hand. The headache is not getting better.

"But Hagerstown is pretty much a bedroom community for Bethesda by now, right? And BrainBump had their headquarters there. Their rate of Engineered and Augmented has to be higher than the general population."

"Maybe," Gary says. "But not anywhere close to ninety percent."

"So where does that leave us?"

He laces his fingers behind his head, kicks up the footrest and leans back. "Not sure. I actually like the kill-switch idea. Maybe NatSec just exaggerated the kill rate. We need to think a little more about how you could pull it off, though. Let me check in with my friends, and see what they think."

He closes his eyes. I'm about to get up when the wallscreen pings. It's a direct connection request from Doug.

"Connect," I say. The screen flips to a close-up of Doug's face, with what looks like an industrial clean room in the background.

"Hey," he says. "Have you had a chance to look at those documents I sent over yet?"

I shake my head.

"I've been a bit preoccupied. You may not have noticed, but some crazy stuff happened yesterday."

He scowls, which is a pretty scary thing through the hardware that covers half his face.

"I'm aware. That's kind of why I need you to move up your timelines. Waiting until after your finals or whatever is not going to cut it at this point."

I have a sudden premonition that Elise might not be the only one in this house who ought to be worried about NatSec.

"Doug?" I say. "Is there something you want to tell me about those documents?"

"No," he says. "There's something I want you to tell me about those documents. Specifically, what's in them. Like you said you would, remember?"

"Yeah," I say. "I remember. But I'm a little curious about why this is suddenly so urgent. I'm especially curious as to whether having these documents in my possession is going to get a NatSec crowbar dropped on my house."

"No," he says. "Definitely not. Definitely probably not. Anyway, you've already got them, so if a crowbar's on its way, you should probably let me know what's in the documents before it gets there."

"Thanks, Doug. Your concern for me is overwhelming. I'll tell you what: I'll try to get a look at them tonight."

He scowls even harder, and a servo over his left ear gives out a high-pitched whine.

"Is that the best you can do?"

"That's the best I can do."

His face relaxes, and he lets out a theatrical sigh.

"All right then. Check in tomorrow?"

"Will do. Disconnect."

"What was that about?" asks Terry. She's standing in the hallway, with half a sausage link in one hand and a wad of bacon in the other.

"That was Doug," I say. "He's bugging me for deliverables on some work I promised him."

"Is that who you were going to meet when you left my place yesterday morning?"

"That's the one."

"He sounds like a real humanitarian."

I roll my eyes.

"Ah, Doug's okay. He just tends to focus on his own needs. Pretty much to the exclusion of everyone else's, actually."

"And that's okay because . . ."

I'm trying to come up with a good answer for that when Elise pokes her head into the room and says, "What's a crowbar?"

I look at Terry. She shrugs.

"I don't know either," she says. "I mean, I know what an actual crowbar is, but I'm thinking that's not what you and Doug were talking about."

I glance over at Gary. His right eye is open now, watching us.

"You want to cover this one?" I ask.

"Sure," he says. "A crowbar is what Sauron's Eye gives bad girls and boys for Christmas."

"Uh . . ." Terry says.

"Crowbars are KEWs," I say, and wing a balled-up sock at Gary's head. He sits up, picks the sock up off the floor and throws it back at me. It misses me by at least three feet. I'm pretty sure Gary didn't play a lot of ball sports as a kid.

"KEWs?" Elise says. "Still not helping."

"Kinetic Energy Weapons," I say. "They're basically bowling balls, with little rocket motors attached to them. NatSec keeps a few hundred of them in low Earth orbit at any given time."

"Right," Gary says. "Then when someone annoys them—for example, by conducting totally legitimate and perfectly legal research into their passcode-generation algorithms—their little rocket motors de-orbit them onto that person's house."

"You speaking from experience?" Terry asks.

"Nah," Gary says. "I told you, I work in data entry."

"I don't get it," says Elise. "What's so bad about dropping a bowling ball on someone's house?"

I snicker. Terry catches me, and shoots me a look that borders on terrifying. That brow ridge definitely has its uses, intimidation-wise.

"Energy is mass times velocity squared," Gary says, "and a crowbar comes in at seven klicks per second. That means a ten-kilo weapon has about four hundred ninety megajoules to give up when it lands on you."

"And that's . . ."

"In terms of energy equivalents, just a bit more than a hundred kilos of TNT," I say. "How much of that gets converted to explosive force depends on a bunch of stuff, like impact angle and the density and hardness of whatever it lands on, but it's pretty safe to say that in most cases you'd rather not be in the neighborhood when one of these things drops."

"I dunno," Gary says. "If you're on NatSec's shit list, there are a lot of worse things that can happen to you than eating a crowbar."

"I'm still not following," Elise says. "I mean, I didn't think they were even allowed to use armed drones on Americans. If this is really a thing, wouldn't I have heard something about it?"

"Oh, Elise," Gary says. "You sweet, sweet child. You remember that gas leak outside San Antonio a few weeks ago?"

Elise looks at me, then back at Gary.

"You're saying . . ."

Gary taps his nose with one finger.

"Gas leaks don't really leave craters," I say.

Elise looks like she might be sick.

"There you go," Gary says. "Welcome to the real world."

"Gary thinks we're humping right now, doesn't he?"

I nod. Terry's head is resting on my chest. I can just see the tiny beads of sweat forming on her forehead.

It's after noon now, and the sun is slanting through my bedroom window. I've got a class to teach at three, and I thought a nap might do me some good. Doesn't seem to be in the cards, though.

"We could be, you know."

I nod again. She's been pretty clear on that point.

"Just putting it out there. Could have last night, too. Not so much the night before, though."

I wrap my arm around her shoulders and brush the hair back from her face. She looks up at me, smiles, and pulls my arm tighter.

"Gary's kind of a tool, isn't he?"

I laugh.

"You just have to get used to him," I say. "He spends most of his time on the nets. He doesn't always remember how to act out here."

She looks down, sighs, rests a hand on my stomach. Her breathing slows and her head slides a little farther down my chest, searching for a softer spot. I close my eyes. I'm just drifting off when she says, "I know you're too pretty for me."

I pull her closer and stroke her hair. "It's okay," she says. Her voice is heavy, and I'm not sure she's awake. Her hand slides lower, stops just above my waist. I breathe in, breathe out. Through the floor, I can hear Gary laughing.

6. TERRY

I wake up alone, soaking wet and panting. The afternoon sun pouring through Anders' window has turned the room into a sweat lodge. Apparently, the excellent climate control is only for Gary's parts of the house. I'd been dreaming of Elise. She was standing silent in the center of the road, with her back to me and her head bowed to her chest. The sun was setting beyond her, and I could just hear the low buzz of the bomber as it cleared the horizon. I broke into a run. Elise shrank to a dot and disappeared. I looked up to see the bomb drifting down under a fat red parachute. The sky flashed white, and the air was on fire.

No wonder I was dreaming of being incinerated. It must be a hundred degrees in this room. I sit up, push my hair back with one hand, and wipe my face dry with Anders' top sheet. Five seconds later, I might as well not have bothered. I need another shower. I need a functioning air conditioner. I need a change of clothes.

I need to go home.

Gary is sprawled across the sofa when I come down the stairs. One eye turns to focus on me. The other is vibrating back and forth so quickly that I wonder if he's shorted out.

"Good morning, princess," he says. "Anders says he'll ping you when he gets out of class. Your sister says she's going with Tariq, and she'll let you know where they decide to hole up. Tariq says he thinks we're all idiots who will believe that he outwitted NatSec on a three-wheeled golf cart. Can I get you anything?"

"No, thanks," I say. "I was just leaving."

"Excellent." He closes his eyes. I can see them both twitching together under his eyelids now. "It was great meeting you. I'm glad your sister turned out to be not dead. Have a blessed day."

I've gone maybe ten steps when I realize that I should have asked Gary for a gallon jug of water before I left. Between what I sweated out into Anders' sheets and what's coming out of me now, I'm gonna wind up shriveled up like a slug in salt before I make it home.

Of all the things that my brainless gene cutter gifted me with, I think the ice-age metabolism is the one I like least. I guess for some people there might be an advantage to being comfortable wearing a bikini in a snowstorm, but I live in Baltimore. It hasn't snowed here since Obama was in the White House, and being outside in the summer for me is like being one of the guests of honor at a crab feast.

Fortunately, there's a Jolly Pirate right there at the end of the block. While I wouldn't eat one of their doughnuts on a bet, I'm guessing their bottled water is probably okay. The door dings as I enter. The air inside is at least twenty degrees cooler than outside, and I'm thinking maybe I'll hang around until my core temperature drops back into the nineties when the kid at the cash register slaps his palm on the counter and says "Hey! No!"

I look around. We're the only ones in the store. He's looking right at me, and pointing at the door. He's a scrawny little thing, with a shaved head and a wispy brown goatee. The Jolly Pirate uniform makes him look like he's dressed up in his father's clothes for Halloween.

"I'm sorry," I say. "You're not talking to me, are you?"

"Yeah," he says. "I'm talking to you." His voice cracks, and his lower lip is trembling. "No Altered. You need to go."

I stare at him. He grits his teeth and stares back. I walk slowly to the drink cooler by the counter. I have no idea what's happening right now, but I am thirsty, and I am going to get a bottle of water. I open the case, and take my time making a selection as the cold air flows across my legs. I choose a liter bottle of Appalachian Sweet, let the door swing closed, and set the bottle on the counter.

It sits there between us for a solid thirty seconds.

Finally, I pick up the bottle and tap it against the reader, then tap my phone for payment. A receipt pops up on my screen. I discard it.

And then he hits me.

I duck my chin, and his fist smacks into the top of my head. The snap of his hand breaking rattles all the way down my spine. I stagger a half step back from the counter and look up. He's holding his right hand up in front of his face. The index and middle fingers have an extra bend between the knuckles and the wrist. His eyes are anime-wide, and a high-pitched whistle is coming from his nose.

As God is my witness, I will never understand how people like this drove people like me to extinction.

"Thank you," I say. "You've been incredibly helpful." I turn to the door.

"We won't forget Hagerstown," he croaks, as my hand touches the crash bar.

"Neither will I," I say without pausing. "My sister was there."

I stand on the corner outside for a few minutes, drinking my water and trying to decide what just happened. The clerk was obviously upset about something, even before his hand got smashed, but I can't figure out what. I finish the water in one long pull. I'd kind of like another. I toss the bottle into the recycling bin by the entrance, and touch two fingers to the top of my head.

There's a little bump there, but nothing to get upset about. I pull the door open, and step back into the Jolly Pirate. The clerk is over by the drink fountain, trying to fill up a plastic bag with ice using only his left hand. It isn't going well.

"Sorry to bother you again," I say. "But I'd like some more water. Also, would you mind explaining why you just assaulted me?"

He keeps fumbling with the ice dispenser. Cubes are scattered all over the floor around him.

"Look," he says finally, "I'm sorry I hit you. Just go away, okay?"

I walk over to him. His hand is swollen, and purpling up nicely. I take the bag and nudge him aside. I fill it with ice, tie it off, and hand it to him. He winces as he presses the ice to the back of his hand.

"So," I say. "I'm guessing that's the first time you've ever punched somebody?"

He hesitates, then nods. He won't meet my eyes.

"Just for future reference," I say, "everything between the eyebrows and the crown is pretty much a no-go zone for that sort of thing. That's especially true for someone like me, but you'd probably have broken your hand on a standard *Homo sap* skull there too."

He shrugs. His eyes stay pinned to the floor. I feel like I'm talking to a giant toddler.

"You know you're gonna need to get those fingers set, right?"

I reach for his hand, but he pulls it away.

"I know," he says. "But I'm the only one who showed

up for the afternoon shift. I can't leave the store until the night guy gets here at eight."

I roll my eyes.

"That's very conscientious of you. Sounds like you've read the Employee Handbook. Does it have anything to say about customer punching? Maybe with an emphasis on girl-customer punching?"

That gets him to look at me, at least.

"I said I was sorry. It's not like I actually hurt you."

I smile.

"That's true. Still doesn't answer my question, though. What, exactly, is your problem with me?"

He looks away again.

"Haven't you been monitoring the feeds?"

I shake my head.

"Not really. I've been asleep most of the afternoon."

He scowls, but doesn't lift his eyes up from the floor. I'm almost starting to feel sorry for him.

"They're all saying that not everyone actually died from the plague," he says. "Only the Altered. All the *Homo saps* were still alive when they dropped the bombs."

I have to stop to think about that. The one person I know for sure survived is as unmodified as they come. Elise doesn't even carry a phone with her half the time. And while I have my doubts about Tariq, he's always claimed to be one-hundred-percent natural as well.

"Okay," I say finally. "Suppose I accept that. How do we go from there to you punching me in the head?"

"Well," he says. "This is the start, isn't it? Somebody figured out a way to take out the Altered—all of them.

And the Altered who run NatSec killed every normal human in Hagerstown to keep it from getting out."

This is the start, isn't it? I'm still thinking about that question when I get home.

"House," I say. "Search for posts on public feeds. Time frame: noon today onward. Key phrase: This is the start. Associate with: UnAltered Movement. Associate with: Hagerstown."

My house avatar pops up on the living-room wallscreen. She looks like a cartoon robot today, complete with shiny silver skin and a funnel for a hat.

"Do I have to, Terry? I'm kind of busy right now."

"Yeah," I say. "You have to. And what do you mean, you're busy? For shit's sake, you're an avatar."

She pouts, and turns half away.

"Yeah? Well avatars have lives too, you know."

"No," I say. "They don't. At least other people's don't. Now run the search."

"Please?"

I sigh.

"Please."

The robot freezes while the system grinds on the search for a while.

"Two results," she says finally.

Then a few seconds later, "Correction: no results."

I stare at her. She's smirking.

"Correction?" I say finally. "You've never said 'correction' before. What does that mean?"

She shrugs.

"Two results were downloaded. Both were redacted prior to display."

"Redacted? You mean the authors withdrew them?"

"No," she says. "They were deleted from your servers."

I head for the bathroom, dropping clothes as I go.

"Deleted? By who?"

"Unknown."

"How does that happen? Aren't you secured?"

She pops up on the bathroom screen and gives me an apologetic smile.

"Our system contains a number of mandatory commercial and government back doors," she says. "I can't tell which of them was used to execute the redactions."

I step into the shower and turn on the water. I now have to consider the strong possibility that Mr. Jolly Fucking Pirate has a better-secured network access than I do. I also have to consider that those posts were almost certainly redacted by NatSec—which means that by conducting that search, I probably flagged myself to a NatSec sniffer.

"Hey," House says. "While I'm thinking about it, Dimitri called for you while you were out."

"Really?" I ask. "What did he want?"

"He wanted to know if you have a sister."

My heart thumps hard in my chest.

"Did he say why?"

"Not really. He just asked if you were related to Elise Freberg. Seemed kind of worked up about it, actually."

That can't be good.

"What did you tell him?"

"I said I wasn't authorized to give out personal information about you, even to super-sexy secret-agent men. He didn't seem amused."

I rinse the sweat off of my skin and out of my hair; then I stand in the water for another few minutes with my eyes closed, thinking. Why would Dimitri be asking about Elise?

Don't assume. We've got an uncommon last name, and at a minimum she'd have been on the list of victims. It's possible he saw her name somewhere, and he's just showing concern.

It's also possible that he's seen the video that killbot supposedly shot of her, and he knows she wasn't actually a victim. If that were true, though, I'd probably be in a tiny room in an undisclosed location right now.

I turn off the water and reach for the towels.

"House," I say. "Can you repeat the most recent search?"

"Sure," she says. "Not sure what the point is, though."

"Can you download any results, and then immediately cut all external access?"

She shrugs again.

"I can try."

"Please do so."

I walk into the bedroom. House produced a pile of clean clothes while I was gone. For the first time in two days, I actually have fresh panties and a bra.

"House. Results?"

"No results."

Huh.

"No feeds were found?"

"Not exactly," she says. "One appropriate feed was found. It was redacted three seconds after download."

"Did you cut external access after download?"

"I did. Access was reestablished, and the feed was redacted."

Son of a bitch.

I pull on a pair of shorts and a soft cotton shirt and head for the kitchen, where I open the fridge and pull out a hunk of turkey breast and a slice of ham. After a little consideration, I grab a couple slices of provolone cheese to wrap them in. There's not much in my refrigerator that doesn't come from an animal in one way or another. It's pretty well established, now that there are at least a few of us around, that Neanderthals need a lot more protein in our diet than *Homo saps*, but we're not actually one-hundred-percent carnivorous.

My dad thought we were when I was little, though, and I really got used to the diet.

I take my snack into the living room, drop onto the sofa and prop my feet up on the coffee table that Anders tried so hard to destroy on Saturday night. It's more than a little frustrating that I can't download anything related to my conversation with Mr. Pirate. It's also distressing that NatSec can apparently barge into my servers whenever they want to. There's too much going on that I don't understand.

I bet Dimitri understands.

Based on my conversation with House, it's possible that he understands a lot more than I'd like him to. Probably not a good idea to start ducking him now, though.

"House," I say. "Direct contact. Dimitri."

I expect to get the bear, but a few seconds later Dimitri's face appears on the living-room wallscreen. He looks like he hasn't slept in a week.

"Terry," he says. "I am happy to see that you are well."

I smile.

"I wish I could say the same. You look tired, Dimitri."

He grimaces.

"Yesterday was hard. Today has been harder. What can I do for you?"

I try to make my smile apologetic.

"I have some questions."

His expression softens.

"Ask. You know I can make no promises, but I will tell you what I can."

Let's work into this slowly.

"First," I say, "a lot of the public feeds I've tried to access today have been redacted. These are just open-source jawing, not the kind of things that NatSec usually worries about. Any idea why?"

He rubs his face with both hands.

"You are probably not aware of this, but certain organizations are attempting to use what happened yesterday to stir up public unrest. Tensions are high enough already without any fanning of the flames."

Yeah. That, I already knew.

"What organizations," I ask, "and what kind of unrest? A guy just punched me in the head in a doughnut shop, and said it was because of stuff that was floating around the public feeds."

He sighs.

"Are you familiar with the UnAltered Movement?"

I shake my head.

"Politics isn't my thing."

Dimitri scowls.

"The UnAltered are a quasi-religious group which preaches the sanctity of the body and the sanctity of the genome. They condemn both genetic and mechanical augmentation. Some branches claim that the so-called Altered have no souls."

"Okay," I say. "I think I've heard of these guys. They're a cult, right? Like the Satanist Temple, or the Church of Cthulhu?"

"No," Dimitri says. "Unfortunately, the UnAltered are no longer a fringe group, and they are no longer a joke. Over the past five years, their numbers have doubled, and doubled, and doubled again. There are enough of them now to be a serious danger, if they choose to make themselves so."

His face is an expressionless mask now, and I feel a shiver run from the back of my neck to the base of my spine. I may not know exactly what Dimitri does for a living, but I know enough to know that I really, really wouldn't want him to think of me as a serious danger. Dimitri thinks of himself as a sheepdog, faithfully guarding the flock. And if he decides that you're a wolf?

"Okay," I say finally. "So what does this have to do with Hagerstown?"

He looks down, then back up, and I can almost see him trying to decide how much to tell me.

"This is not widely known," he says. "We do not wish this to be widely known. But certain among the UnAltered are claiming that the actions in Hagerstown yesterday—both the plague and the airstrikes—were the first blows in the war between Altered and UnAltered."

I laugh. Dimitri does not join in.

"Wait," I say. "You're serious? You think someone's trying to start a war between us and the *Homo saps*?"

"It does not matter what I think," Dimitri says. "If the UnAltered believe it, it has the potential to become a self-fulfilling prophecy."

"Okay," I say. "I can understand why you'd want to keep a lid on that. But it seems right now like pretty much everything anyone is saying about Hagerstown is being redacted. I actually had a couple of files pulled off of my servers this afternoon. Does NatSec really have that kind of authority?"

He looks less tired now, and more irritated.

"NatSec has a mandate to protect the people, and to maintain public order. The right of conspiracy theorists to spout foolishness in public is the least of our concerns at the moment."

"No worries about the First Amendment, huh?"

His eyes harden.

"This is not protected speech, Terry. This is yelling 'fire' in a crowded theater."

I know this is pushing it, but I need to find out how honest he'll be with me.

"Okay," I say. "How about this: a lot of folks are saying they've seen video feeds of survivors moving around Hagerstown yesterday afternoon. Any truth to that?"

That touches a nerve.

"There were no survivors, Terry. Acting Director Dey made this very clear in his statement before the bombing."

"But the feeds . . ."

"There are no feeds such as you have described. Anyone who says he has seen these is a liar." He looks down at his hands, then back up at the screen. "This is beginning to feel like an interview, Terry. Have you become a reporter now?"

He looks genuinely angry. Time to back down.

"No, Dimitri. I'm not a reporter. I was just hoping you could help me understand what's happening."

He rubs his face again, and runs his hands back through his hair. "I am sorry," he says. "I become unpleasant when I do not sleep. I know this is frightening. Please trust that we are doing what we can to control the situation."

"I know, Dimitri. I do trust you. Try to get some sleep."

"I will try. Good-bye, Terry."

"Good-bye, Dimitri. Disconnect."

I guess I shouldn't be surprised that Dimitri can't tell me the truth. I'm not sure exactly what his relationship with NatSec is, but even if he's just a freelance contractor, they'd have him fitted with internal monitors. It's also possible that he really believes that the truth in this case needs to be suppressed, and that he would have lied to me even if he didn't have to.

It's also possible that he's right.

It occurs to me as I'm walking back to the kitchen for a water bottle that he didn't say anything about Elise. I honestly don't know if that should make me more nervous, or less.

I spend the next two hours vacillating between boredom and frustration. No matter what combination of search terms I try, I can't get anything from either the professional media or the private nets that doesn't back up the NatSec version of what happened to Hagerstown. I do finally get a hit from my current-events sniffer, though. It's from DC. A girl was found beaten unconscious in Rock Creek Park. She'd been jogging. She wasn't robbed, wasn't sexually abused. Just beaten to a pulp and left bleeding on the path.

She was a Pretty.

I'm thinking about following this up, when the wallscreen dings.

"Anders Jensen is at the door," says House.

My heart jumps. What the hell is wrong with me?

"Open."

I hear the door unlatch and swing open, and Anders steps into the room. He smiles when he sees me.

"Hey," he says. "I know I said I'd ping you, but I have to walk right past here to get home from Hopkins. Okay if I stop by?"

"Come in," I say. "Have a seat. Try not to trip over the table this time."

He's wearing khakis and a dress shirt. He hardly looks sweat-drenched at all. Apparently a tall, skinny mouse-man bleeds off heat better than a short, bowling-ball-shaped Neanderthal girl.

"You look pretty wound up," he says. He sits down beside me, not touching, but not on the other side of the couch, either—midway between lover and visiting third cousin. "What have you been doing?"

"It's been a busy afternoon," I say. "I found out that a guy I've been friends with for almost three years is perfectly comfortable looking me in the eye and lying. I found out that NatSec can pull whatever they want off of my servers whenever they want to, even if I order a complete disconnect from the networks. I found out that there are a whole lot of people trying to blame what happened yesterday on the Engineered. Oh, and I got punched in the head by the doughnut guy at the Jolly Pirate. So yeah, a good day all around."

"Wait," he says. "Somebody punched you at the Jolly Pirate? My Jolly Pirate?"

"Yeah. The guy behind the counter."

"Who, Joey? Skinny guy with a goatee?"

"That's the one."

He looks like he's trying to decide whether to be angry or confused.

"Why would Joey punch you? Did you do something to him? Joey's a nice guy. He always stuffs an extra doughnut in the box when I get a dozen."

I shake my head.

"They all do that, Anders. For everyone. It's called a baker's dozen."

He looks crestfallen. I have to stifle a laugh.

"Oh," he says. "Still, why would he punch you in the head? He never does that to me."

I giggle. That's weird. I never giggle.

"First," I say, "he wouldn't be able to reach your head. Second, he doesn't seem like the type who would have the balls to punch another guy. And third, he punched me in the head because I'm Engineered, and the Engineered killed all the normal humans in Hagerstown for some reason."

He's definitely confused now.

"But . . . I'm Engineered. I got a doughnut from him on my way to class. He didn't even give me a dirty look."

"Yeah," I say, "you're Engineered. But nobody would know that unless they saw you escape from a cat. It's pretty obvious for me."

He gives me a half smile. That had better not be pity.

"Anyway," he says, "I thought they've been saying it was the Engineered who died, and the UnAltered who lived? Shouldn't you have been punching him?"

"Right. And then the Engineered, who everybody knows run NatSec, dropped the FAEs to make sure all the *Homo saps* died as well."

He thinks about that for a minute.

"That's not good," he says finally.

"No, it's not."

"Who's pushing this line?"

"My understanding is that it's folks from the UnAltered Movement. Bear in mind, though, that I'm getting most of this from a conversation with a guy who punched me in the head, and the rest from a demonstrated liar."

He shakes his head.

"I still can't believe Joey punched you. Are you okay? Or do I need to go down there and give him what for?"

I smile.

"Nah, I'm good. I explained to him afterward that the top of the head is the wrong place to punch a Neanderthal."

"Broken knuckles?"

"And how."

We sit in silence for a minute or two.

"So," I say. "How was your day, honey?"

"Oh, great," he says. "Nobody punched me, but I did just spend three hours trying to explain fullerene fabrication to a bunch of bored-ass rich kids. Half of them spent the entire lecture watching porn on their oculars, and half the rest tried to follow along but couldn't, because they have the attention spans of gnats. The rest maybe got a little out of it, but will probably give me a lousy evaluation at the end of the term anyway because I couldn't find a way to mix references to *SpaceLab* into my visuals."

I lean back and cross my arms over my chest.

"Look, Anders, I'd love to engage with your whole 'kids suck these days' old-man rant," I say. "But I'm not going to, because you totally lost me at 'fullerene fabrication.' "

This is his chance to roll his eyes at me.

"Fullerene fabrication. Buckyballs, carbon nanotubes, that kind of thing."

I give him an exaggerated nod.

"Oh, right. Buckyballs. Gary told me you led a glamorous life, but he never said it was *buckyball* glamorous."

His smile widens.

"You have no idea what a buckyball is, do you?"

I shake my head.

"None whatsoever."

His eyes light up.

"This is actually kind of interesting," he says, which is almost always what someone says right before starting in on something that is not even a little bit interesting. "A fullerene is a hollow structure made of carbon atoms. A buckyball is just a spherical fullerene. They're useful enough in isolation, but you can make macro structures out of them with some really amazing mechanical properties—"

At which point I grab him by the back of the neck, pull him over on top of me, and kiss him. His eyes are wide open and his jaw is clamped shut, but when I don't let go, he slowly relaxes into it. After a while, I come up for air. He pulls back a few inches and raises one eyebrow.

"Sorry," I say. "You really needed to stop talking."

"That's okay," he says. "I mean, I was just kind of surprised, and I thought—"

I pull him down again. I definitely like him better

when he's quiet. His hand slides under my shirt and up along my ribs. A shiver runs down my spine, and I can feel goose bumps rising on the backs of my arms. His mouth tastes like mint and his hair smells like chamomile and sweat and I can feel the muscles in his neck and back tensing and relaxing under my fingers.

A sweet time passes.

"Do you . . . uh . . ."

I nod.

"Can I . . ."

I nod again.

"You know," I say finally. "This is a lot more fun with you conscious."

He laughs into my belly. I run my fingers through his hair, and press him downward.

7. ELISE

"So, where are we going?"

Tariq doesn't answer. He's trying to wave a honking car around us. We're heading north on York, just passing the Loyola campus. My arms are wrapped tight around his waist, my legs snugged up behind his hips. I tried at first to rest my chin on his shoulder, but our helmets bumped, and he made me lean back so that now all I can see is the back of his head. Tariq has hauled me around Hagerstown on this thing before and it's been okay, but in north-Baltimore traffic on a Monday afternoon, it's pretty scary.

I have to admit, Gary was absolutely right to make fun of Tariq for calling this an ATV. It really is a three-wheeled golf cart. With the throttle wide open, the speedometer is just tickling 40 miles an hour—barely fast enough to keep us from being crushed by a bus on this road, and not nearly fast enough to not get honked or yelled at by every driver who has to work his way around us. Tariq yells back, sometimes in English, sometimes in another language that I've only heard him use in brief snatches when he's really stressed. I asked him what it was once, after he'd yelled something incomprehensible at a tourist who'd snatched a twenty from his hat in the harbor. He just laughed and told me to run it through a translator app.

As the guy behind us now accelerates past, Tariq holds his left hand up in the air, dangles his pinky and wiggles it back and forth. I've seen him do this once or twice before, but I have no idea what it's supposed to mean. The driver probably doesn't either, but he gives us the finger out the window as he speeds away, just to be safe.

A few minutes later, a cab slides up beside us in the left lane. It's a two-passenger self-driven model, barely bigger than Tariq's cycle, and almost as slow. It's carrying a fat, balding, middle-aged guy in a rumpled gray suit. He glances out the window at us, then turns half-around to ogle me. I'm about to give him the finger when the cab's right turn signal comes on, and it slides over into our lane.

My first thought is that the passenger has taken control of the cab somehow. Auto-cabs don't forget to check their blind spots. My second thought is that I can't believe I'm going to die under the wheels of a cab on York Road after surviving a doomsday plague, a firebombing, and a psychotic killbot. Tariq curses and jumps his brakes. The cab leaps ahead as the back wheels of the cycle lift off the ground and the visor of my helmet smacks into the back of Tariq's. A horn blares close behind us and Tariq leans back into me, and for one long moment we balance there, front tire screeching across pavement, back wheels wavering in the air, until finally gravity reasserts itself and we're back on the road, swerving crazily once, twice, before Tariq releases the brakes and somehow regains control.

"Tariq!" I shout. "What the fuck just happened?"

He glances quickly over his shoulder.

"It could not see us," he says.

"What? The auto-cab? They don't have eyes, Tariq! They have sensors, and they don't make mistakes like that!"

"They do have eyes," he says, "but they are blind to us today. I must remember to be more careful."

We pull into the driveway of a little house in the north end of Towson, set back from the road, just short of the beltway. The traffic on 695 is a constant rumble in the background. Tariq parks in front of the one-car garage, takes off his helmet, and hangs it from the handlebar by the chin strap. I hang mine next to it, stand, and stretch. My arms are sore from clutching at him the entire ride, and there's a crick in my neck that pinches when I turn my head to the left. The yard in front of the house is small and well kept, with neatly trimmed hedges along the sidewalk and a huge, gnarled Japanese maple dominating the center.

"You may find the interior of this house unusual," Tariq says as we step up onto the porch. "Please try not to offend."

He bumps the door with his phone. After a moment it swings open, and we step through. The air inside is cool and dry, especially compared to the soup we've been breathing for the last hour. The blinds are drawn, and the lighting is dim and blue-tinged. A narrow staircase runs up to our left. An entranceway to the right leads into a completely darkened room.

A woman sweeps down the hallway in front of us, and into Tariq's arms. She's shorter than he is, with long dark hair, and skin that's almost black in this light. The sleeves of her gown hang to her fingertips, and her hemline sweeps the floor. She wraps her arms around Tariq's chest, presses her face against his neck and says something in what sounds like the same language Tariq reserves for the targets of his road rage. He whispers into her ear, then presses her back to arm's length. He looks over his shoulder to me and says, "Aaliyah, this is Elise. This is the one I have told you about. Elise, this is Aaliyah. My sister."

I nod, but she's already stepping in for an embrace—not a lean-in, Nordic hug, which is what my family gets from me, but a full-body wrap, with her arms tight around my rib cage and her face pressed between my shoulder and my left breast. I wrap my arms around her, catch Tariq's eye, and grimace. He winks and turns away, trying not to laugh.

Aaliyah breaks the hug after what seems like a very

long time. She steps back, and looks me up and down.

"Tariq," she says. "You have lied to me. You said she was beautiful, but in truth she is a valkyrie." She touches my chin, turns my face one way and then the other. "And unmodified, I see. A wonder, indeed."

Tariq gives me a warning look and a tiny shake of his head. I force a smile.

"It's so good to finally meet you, Aaliyah. Tariq has told me so much about you."

She beams.

"All lies. Tariq is a terrible liar."

This is true. Of course, so am I. Tariq has told me more than once that he has no siblings.

"Ah," she says, "but the truth will out. Come and sit. You must tell me everything about the wedding."

She leads us into the darkened sitting room. The lights come up as we enter, but they're the same as in the hallway and I'd almost rather they stayed dark. There are cushions scattered around the floor, and a low table in the center. There is no wallscreen, or anything else electronic that I can see. I look over at Tariq. He gives me another tiny head shake, and gestures for me to sit.

"Thank you for taking us in, Aaliyah," says Tariq. "I'm sure you know that our homes have been destroyed. NatSec did a terrible thing yesterday, and I do not think that we will be safe until this all has been settled."

Aaliyah drops onto a cushion, and leans back against the wall. "It is nothing," she says. "We will not talk of sad things now. Tell me about the wedding."

Tariq looks at me expectantly.

"Well," I say. "I don't really . . . I mean, our plans are kind of up in the air at this point. We were thinking about maybe having an outdoor ceremony in Cunningham Falls Park, but after yesterday . . ."

"Will you be married in the faith?"

I didn't know Tariq had a faith.

"Elise is not of the faith," says Tariq. "Our wedding will be a civil one."

To me, she says, "Will you convert?"

I look at Tariq. He doesn't meet my eyes.

"We . . . haven't discussed it," I say finally.

"I did not ask if you had discussed it," Aaliyah says slowly and clearly. "I asked if you would convert."

"Aaliyah," says Tariq. "This is not the time for such a question. Elise was in Hagerstown yesterday. She is not able to think about questions of the spirit now."

Aaliyah looks from Tariq to me, then back to Tariq.

"If she was in Hagerstown," she says, "then why is she still alive?"

"She is alive," says Tariq, "because I saved her."

"Tariq," I say. "We need to talk."

He opens his eyes. We're in a sagging double bed in Aaliyah's guest room. The blinds are drawn here as well, but I've determined that it doesn't matter, because behind the blinds is a sheet of very fine metal mesh that lets in almost no light at all. The overhead fixture in this room holds the same dim, blue, fluorescent bulbs as the ones in the sitting room and the foyer.

"So talk," he says. "I will listen."

"Well," I say, "First of all, what's with the lighting in here? And why is every window covered?"

He scowls.

"I told you my sister's house would seem odd to you. She is being very gracious in letting us stay here. She does not accept visitors often."

I scowl right back at him.

"That's not an answer, Tariq."

"It is an answer," he says. "The lighting and windows are as they are because my sister wishes them to be so. Who are you to judge?"

I glare at him, but he's actually got a point.

"Fine," I say finally. "So what about yesterday? Your sister asked the right question, Tariq. Why am I still alive?"

He rolls over to face me, and looks into my eyes for what seems like a very long time.

"I answered her question," he says. "You are alive because I saved you."

"That's true," I say. "I know that's true. But Tariq . . . how? I remember what happened yesterday. I remember talking to the killbot. That wasn't a delusion, and it wasn't a dream. I remember talking to it, and I remember seeing the drone. And then . . ."

"You are wrong," says Tariq. His voice is soft, almost sorrowful. "You did not speak with the sentinel. You did not see the bomber. I found you by the side of the road, and I carried you to safety."

"On your ATV."

"Yes, on my ATV."

"The same ATV that could barely go fast enough to keep us from getting crushed by a city bus on York Road."

That hangs between us for a while. Tariq closes his eyes, and I think for a moment that he's fallen asleep. When he opens them again, he says, "You are alive because I love you, Elise. You are alive because I could not live if you did not. That should be enough for you."

I slide closer, put my hand on his shoulder and kiss his forehead.

"Fine," I say. "I'll let it go for now."

He kisses my nose, and presses his forehead to mine.

"Thank you," he says. "I would tell you more if there were more to tell."

"Remember," I say. "I said for now. You're not off the hook permanently."

He rolls onto his back and closes his eyes again. I watch as his breathing slows, then let my own eyes fall closed. I'm just drifting off when he says, "It is a Faraday cage."

"What?" I open my eyes. He hasn't moved, and I wonder if I was dreaming.

"The house," he says. It almost sounds like sighing. "It is a Faraday cage. That is why the windows look as they do."

I'd like to ask what a Faraday cage is, but his eyelids flutter and his face goes slack, and I'm pretty sure he really is asleep now. I watch him breathe for a minute more, and then carefully roll away from him and sit up on the edge of the bed. I pull out my phone and hold it close to my mouth.

"Question," I say. "What is a Faraday cage?"

The phone beeps. The only other time I've ever heard my phone beep is when I was wandering around Hagerstown yesterday afternoon. I look at the screen. It reads, "No network connection."

I think back. I don't believe I've ever seen that message on a phone screen before. We have connectivity everywhere. I wonder if maybe the phone was broken during my accident, or maybe when Tariq tackled me. Tariq's phone is sitting on the nightstand on the other side of the bed. I lean across him and pick it up. No network connection.

"House," I say quietly. "Are you there?"

Nothing.

And with that, for maybe the first time in my life, I'm completely cut off from the world.

It's later, and we're lounging on cushions around the table in the sitting room. How much later, I have no idea, because time doesn't seem to mean much in this house. I would have assumed that my phone has an internal clock, but apparently it doesn't, because the only thing it can tell me is that it has no network connection. There are no clocks in this room, the bedroom, or the upstairs bathroom, which are the only rooms I have been allowed to see. It's been made very clear that I'm not going to find out what's at the other end of that darkened hallway.

"Tea?" asks Tariq. I nod, and he fills my cup from a heavy ceramic pot. I sip. It's hot and bitter, with an aftertaste that I first think is sweetness, but that resolves into something unnameable. I take a wedge of flatbread from the platter in the center of the table, and use it to scoop up something thick and yellow from the last of the five bowls Aaliyah has set out for us. I've been able to identify a couple of the other dishes—one I'm pretty sure holds baba ghanoush, and another is a variant on hummus—but this one has me completely stumped. It's spicy and sweet, with a gritty texture. Maybe something with cornmeal? Aaliyah watches me expectantly. I smile and nod.

"I hope everything is acceptable," she says. "I am such a poor cook, and it has been so long since I have been blessed with visitors."

"Everything is wonderful," I say. "I can't remember when I've had such a variety of tastes and textures in one meal."

"My sister is too modest," says Tariq. "She learned our mother's lessons well. I paid no attention, and now I live on berries and nuts."

Aaliyah laughs.

"I see now why you rush to marry," she says. "You need her to save you from starvation, not loneliness."

Tariq smiles.

"Elise has many gifts, sister, but cooking is not among them."

That's not entirely true. I used to be able to put together a pretty impressive steak *au poivre* before I met Tariq. The last eight months really have been mostly berries and nuts, though.

"Well," says Aaliyah, "I am sure she will learn. Perhaps I will gift her a recipe book at the wedding."

And I'm thinking that since respect for all living creatures, no matter their deliciousness, is Tariq's thing, maybe he's the one who needs to learn how to make hummus and baba ghanoush and cornmeal whatever. But this is not the time or the place for that discussion.

I take another dollop of the hummus, and one of mystery dish number two for good measure. I use my right hand only, as Tariq instructed me. My left hand stays in my lap. This, even though I explained to him that I actually use my right hand to wipe my backside. Apparently the appearance is more important in this case than the reality.

"Aaliyah," I say after a long silence. "I hope this isn't a sensitive topic, but I've noticed that my phone doesn't seem to work here."

Aaliyah shoots a quick, sour glance at Tariq.

"That is true," she says. "Has Tariq not explained this to you?"

I shrug.

"He said something earlier about a Faraday cage,

but I don't know what that is, and without my phone, I couldn't look it up."

"I do not know either what is a Faraday cage," she says. "My home is a refuge. What is of the outside cannot reach us here, and objects that are of the outside—like your phone, or implants if you had them—cannot function here."

"Implants?" I say. "You mean like oculars?" Aaliyah nods. "What about medical nanos? Or macro devices like cardiac pacemakers?"

She shakes her head.

"All these things are dependent on contact with the outside," says Aaliyah. "None of them will function here."

I look at Tariq.

"I would have explained this if it had been necessary," he says. "You have no implants, so it did not seem important."

I stare him down. Plenty of people claim to be 100 percent natural. Not so many actually are at this point. It would have been a wicked surprise if I'd keeled over as soon as Aaliyah's door closed behind me.

I guess that would have been one way for him to find out that I'm not the girl for him.

"You should have explained all of this to Elise," says Aaliyah. "Not because she will die for lack of her implants, but because this is an important aspect of the faith." She turns to me. "What has my brother told you about his faith? What has he told you about his family?"

Tariq's eyes are wide. The truth is that he's told me

virtually nothing about his family, and I had no idea that he had a faith until Aaliyah asked me if I would convert.

"Well," I start in, but Tariq cuts me off.

"I have not spoken with Elise about our family," he says. "And I have not spoken with her about our faith. You know this, Aaliyah. It is unkind to torment her so."

"Yes, I know." Aaliyah says. "I know that I have opened my home to a stranger."

Tariq shakes his head. He opens his mouth to speak, but I put a hand to his lips.

"No," I say. "I am not a stranger. Tariq may not have told me as much as he should have, but he will now. I may not be family yet, but I can be. I will be."

Aaliyah's eyes flicker back and forth between mine and Tariq's. I close my eyes, and when I open them Aaliyah is smiling.

"So tell me," she says. "How did you meet?"

I met Tariq in the Inner Harbor, on the last Friday night in August. I was walking off dinner with Terry, wandering past the aquarium and talking about heading over to Fells Point for a drink, when I saw Tariq mugging for the tourists in the little amphitheater on Light Street. There was a crowd around him—mostly women, and mostly either drunk or on the way there. Tariq was giving them a mix of silly acrobatics and card tricks, and they were squealing and cheering and egging him on. I had no intention of stopping. Terry was actually making fun of him when his eyes met mine.

"Elise Freberg," he said. "Come and join us. We've been waiting for you."

Terry stopped in mid-mock, and stared at me. "Do you know this guy?"

I shook my head. Tariq crooked a finger at me and smiled.

"Seriously?" Terry asked. She put a hand on my elbow. I pulled away. Tariq held up a stack of cards. He fanned them out, and letters written in marker on the backs spelled out my name.

"Come on," said Terry. "The Green Goose is calling."

But I wasn't interested in the Green Goose. I was interested in Tariq. He was short and skinny, and wearing these ridiculous green cargo shorts with a tee shirt that had a picture on the front of Theodore Roosevelt boxing a kangaroo. His teeth were a little crooked, and his hair looked like he'd cut it himself. But his cards spelled out my name, and for some reason that made up for everything else.

Later, when the tourists were gone and the sun was down and Terry had taken a cab back to her apartment, I asked him how he'd known my name.

"I've always known your name," he said. "I just didn't know when I'd finally be able to say it."

Back in the guest room, I grab Tariq by the shoulders and push him down onto the bed.

"Elise," he says. "Why so forceful? All you had to do was ask."

He looks up expectantly, but I'm not smiling. His face falls. I sit down beside him, rest my elbows on my knees, and run my hands back through my hair. I haven't washed it in two days now—or is it three?—and my fingers come away with a light coating of oil.

"Look," I say. "I need to know what's happening, Tariq. You haven't been honest with me, and that's not a good thing, considering that we're supposed to be getting married in less than a month."

"This has nothing to do with the wedding," he says. "Bigger forces have intervened in our lives."

I shake my head.

"This has everything to do with the wedding. We all have little secrets. I mean, I may not have been totally honest with you as far as how I feel about a nice medium-rare steak, but Tariq—this is a pretty big one. Why didn't you tell me you have a sister? I didn't think you had any family at all. Were you planning on springing them all on me on our wedding day? And by the way, how many more are there?"

He stares me down, and for one long moment I think he's actually going to give me shit about the steak thing.

"There are no more," Tariq says finally. "My parents are no longer with us, and I have no other siblings, no nieces or nephews or uncles or aunts. Aaliyah is all."

"And you never told me about her because . . ."

He looks away.

"Because I was afraid of how your meeting would go. You see how she is, with her talk of cookbooks and conversions. I was afraid she might . . . frighten you away."

I look at him. His eyes are wide, and almost pleading.

"So you thought you could hide her from me forever?"

He shakes his head.

"No! Not forever. Just until after the wedding. Until you could see that her talk is just talk. Until you could see that I have no interest in making you over into something you are not. Aaliyah is all the family I have, and I love her terribly. But she and I are very different, and I wanted to make sure that you could see that certainly before you spoke with her."

He takes my hand and squeezes. I sigh, and squeeze back.

"Fine," I say. "I'll give you a pass on the sister—but what about this faith? I'd kind of assumed you were a Rastafarian or something, but now I'm thinking that's not right."

He laughs.

"No, I am not a Rastafarian."

"So what are you? My next guess would be Muslim, but I don't think that's right either, is it?"

"No," he says. "I am not a Muslim. In truth, I am not anything. I am of the outside now. I can no more claim my mother's faith than I can her cooking."

There's a sadness in his voice now, and I don't want to press—but I do want an answer.

"But what about Aaliyah? Her faith seems to be

very important to her, and it seems like she thinks it should be to you as well."

He looks down, then away.

"My apostasy saddens her. This is very true. There are few of us left, and every loss now is another coffin nail. There is great beauty in the faith, and very deep truth. But there is also a bitterness at the core that I found at some point I could no longer deny."

I slide over until our hips touch.

"Isn't that true of every faith? Grace was raised Catholic, but she doesn't pretend to follow every tenet of the faith. I doubt there's a single Catholic in North America who does."

He shakes his head.

"That may be so. But our faith is not the sort that can be taken in parts. It must be embraced in its sum, or rejected. Aaliyah embraces it, and you can see what this does to her. I have rejected it, and so am now a part of the outside."

I wrap my arm around his waist. He leans his head against mine, and closes his eyes.

"You know," I say. "You still haven't told me which faith I'm not converting to."

He smiles, and pats my leg with one hand.

"No," he says. "I have not."

I'm jolted from sleep by a knock on the door.

"Aaliyah?" Tariq's voice is slurred with sleep. He rises up on one elbow beside me.

"Wake up, brother," says Aaliyah from behind the door. "You need to go."

He sits up fully, and rubs at his eyes.

"Go? Go where? You agreed that you would keep us here."

"Yes," says Aaliyah, "and I am not withdrawing my hospitality. But events are moving swiftly, and there are things that you must do. I will keep Elise here. You will do what you must and return."

"Sister, why? Have I not done enough?"

There is a long silence before Aaliyah replies.

"I am sorry, brother—but it seems that you have done too much."

8. GARY

Angry Irish Inch: <Hey Munchie, you there?>

Sir Munchalot: <Inch! Good to hear from you, sir. There was talk in these parts that you might have gotten yourself pinched.>

Angry Irish Inch: <Nah, the bastards never laid a glove on me.>

Angry Irish Inch: <I did have to ditch a lot of sweet gear, though.>

Sir Munchalot: <Price of doing business, my friend.>

Angry Irish Inch: <No question. Hope I don't have to do a flash burn again anytime soon, though. That stunt took a serious bite out of my margin for the year.>

Sir Munchalot: <Understood. Speaking of margins, any progress on the current project?>

Angry Irish Inch: <Yeah, about that. I'm actually cutting my losses on this one. I can't afford another burn.>

Sir Munchalot: <Inch. We're making some real

progress here. Are you sure you want to give up your share?>

Angry Irish Inch: <Twelve percent of zero is zero, Munchie.>

Sir Munchalot: <Can't argue with the math, Inch. I'm still optimistic, but I get that you're not.>

Angry Irish Inch: <You've always got Fenrir, right?>

Sir Munchalot: <Right. Bastard.>

Angry Irish Inch: <Good hunting.>

Sir Munchalot: <Good hunting, Inch.>

I open my eyes. Someone's pounding on the door. I blink to my chronometer. It's a little after nine.

"Anders!" I say. "Is that you?"

"Yeah, it's me, Gary. Unlatch the door."

I shake my head clear, arch my back and stretch.

"I dunno, Anders. It's past your curfew. I expected you home by six."

His fist thumps against the lintel.

"Open the fucking door!"

Okay, he's not amused. I kick down the footrest on the recliner, stand and stretch again. For most of the day there's been a dull ache in my lower back. Now it's radiating all the way up to my shoulder blades. I can't complain about my job for the most part, but it's definitely tough on the spine.

I'm sure my ditch-digging grandfather would sympathize.

I walk into the foyer. Anders has the door open a crack, but I've got the chain lock set. He gives it a rattle when he sees me coming.

"Why the chain, Gary?"

"These are crazy days," I say. "UnAltered roaming around, beating up innocent mutants and cyborgs. Can't be too safe."

I push the door closed and unlatch the chain, then open it again to let him in. He shoves past me, and stalks into the kitchen. I close the door behind him, turn the deadbolt and set the chain.

"Easy there, big guy," I say. "What happened? Rough day at the office? Did one of your students finally figure out that you have no idea what you're talking about?"

The fridge door opens. I hear Anders rooting around, and then the door slamming closed again.

"No beer, huh?"

"Nope," I say. "I think your cave lady put away the last one yesterday."

He growls. Like a dog. Not a scary dog, though. Maybe a pomeranian.

"Seriously," I say. "What's the issue, friend? You're being kind of a tool."

"Nothing," he says. He stomps into the living room and drops onto the couch. I follow after him. He's sitting with his hands folded behind his head, staring at the wall.

"Okay," I say. "I think I get it now. You're three

hours late getting back from class, and you're clomping around the house like a sixteen-year-old girl who didn't get asked to the prom. So let me guess: trouble in prehistoric paradise?"

His eyes narrow, and his mouth sets into a hard, thin line. Bingo.

I sit down beside him and put a hand on his knee.

"What happened, buddy? I'm here for you."

He looks at me, then down at my hand. I snatch it back. When he gets annoyed with me, he does this hand-slap thing. He's too fast to dodge, and it hurts like hell.

"Really," I say. "I hate seeing my big Swedish meatball down in the dumps. What's going on?"

"Seriously," he says. "Nothing is going on. I stopped by Terry's place on the way home. That's all."

"Did she feed you?"

He looks at me.

"What?"

"Did she give you any dinner?"

He rolls his eyes. Not sure where the attitude is coming from.

"No, Gary. She did not give me any dinner."

I smile.

"Mystery solved. You're being a jerk because you have low blood sugar. Also low blood alcohol. I'll ping for a cab."

The taxi drops us off in front of the Green Goose a little after ten. Anders gets out while I pay the driver.

The driverless cabs are cheaper, but in my line of work, it's a good idea to pay a little extra to avoid traceability.

"So," I say. "How long are you working tonight?"

"Not sure," the driver says. "Nobody out tonight. Maybe I go home and take a nap."

I hand him double the fare.

"Tell you what," he says, and hands me a card. "You need a ride home later? You give me a call."

I climb out and close the door. The driver signals, pulls out into the nonexistent traffic, and accelerates away.

The Green Goose is on Thames Street, just off of Broadway in Fells Point. It's usually packed on weekend nights, and pretty busy even in the middle of the week. It's empty tonight, though. There are two bartenders—a big guy with a red neckbeard, and a woman who's an obvious Pretty—and a couple of waitresses circulating around, but not more than a half dozen customers. Anders takes a stool at the bar, and I sit down beside him. I love this place. The bar stools are comfortable, the brass is polished, the sound system is loud enough to hear but low enough to talk over. It always makes me think of "A Clean, Well-Lighted Place."

I once made the mistake of mentioning that to Anders. He looked at me like I had two heads.

"Hemingway," I said.

Nothing. It was like talking to a chimp.

"Hemingway," I said again. "Ernest Hemingway, you illiterate dolt."

He did the hand-slap thing then. Bastard.

The Pretty bartender comes over. Her eyes slide past me and settle on Anders.

"Hey," she says. "Where's your no-tip robot friend?"

Anders hesitates, then snaps his fingers.

"You wait tables at the diner up on Charles, right?"

"Yeah," she says. She turns around and hikes her ass up onto the bar. "Now do you recognize me?"

Anders blushes. I burst out laughing. She smiles as she hops back down.

"It's okay. Everybody in that place stares at my ass. I'm pretty sure that's what they hired me for. Anyway, what can I getcha?"

Anders scratches his head.

"Two IPAs to start with. Is the grill still running?"

She looks at Neckbeard. He shakes his head.

"Nah, but there's not much going on tonight. I can fix you something cold. Sandwich and a salad, maybe?"

"Sure. Ham and cheddar, with some yellow mustard?"

"You got it." She looks at me. "How about you, hon? Hungry, or just thirsty?"

I shrug.

"Same as him, I guess. With a BrainBump."

She looks at Neckbeard again. He scowls. She leans over the bar toward me and lowers her voice.

"We're not serving that crap for the duration. Better stick with the beer."

She straightens up and heads into the kitchen.

"Huh," I say when she's gone. "What do you think that was about?"

Anders looks around. Neckbeard is pouring our beers. There's nobody else at the bar.

"I'm not sure," he says. "But I guess there's some bad stuff going on. Terry said she got punched in the head this afternoon by Joey at the Jolly Pirate."

I start to laugh, but Anders isn't smiling.

"Wait, are you serious? Did she break him in half?"

He shakes his head.

"Didn't need to. Apparently he broke his own hand on her skull."

Neckbeard sets our beers down in front of us. Anders taps his glass against mine, then downs half of it without coming up for air. I take a sip, and try not to grimace. I'm not a beer guy. I kind of want a margarita, but not enough to put up with the grief I'd get from Anders. Old Neckbeard doesn't look like he'd be too friendly to a girl-drink drunk either.

"Anyway," I say. "What does Terry getting punched in the head have to do with whether or not these idiots will give me a BrainBump with my ham sandwich?"

"Think about it," says Anders. He takes another long pull at his beer. "Who drinks BrainBump?"

I stare at him blankly.

"I dunno. Everybody?"

He shakes his head.

"Not quite. UnAltered won't touch it. They think the nanos are a corruption of the natural order of the blah blah blah. You've seen a bit of the propaganda they're pushing about Hagerstown. If you're some dipshit UnAltered looking for someone to punch, Terry's a pretty obvious target. What about me, though? Or even you, when you're not in the middle of a download? Most Engineered, and a lot of folks with serious implants, aren't so easy to pick out. Maybe looking for people pounding BrainBump makes a nice shorthand for them."

I hadn't thought about that.

"So what do you think she meant by 'the duration'?"

He shrugs.

"Until everything goes back to normal, I guess. Until everybody quits pissing their pants over what happened yesterday, and goes back to living their lives."

I nod.

"Right. And how long is that, do you think?"

He finishes his beer, and waves to Neckbeard for another.

"If I had to guess, I'd say it's gonna be a long, long time."

The sandwich is pretty good, as it turns out. It's real ham, carved off of an actual pig's leg with an actual knife. The cheese is just a little melty, and the mustard isn't too spicy. The salad is just wilted lettuce and tomatoes, but I wasn't really planning on eating that anyway.

Pretty sticks around to chat up Anders after bringing us our food. I spend a lot of time telling Anders how ugly he is, but apparently she—Anders tells me her name is Charity—doesn't agree. She plays with her hair while he's talking, and giggles at his witty little jabs. It becomes clearer and clearer as my sandwich disappears that Anders is going to get laid tonight, and the sure knowledge of that is making my stomach hurt.

"So," Charity says to me. "Do you tip?"

I wash down the last mouthful of sandwich with the last dregs of my beer.

"That's a little forward, isn't it?"

She laughs.

"I'm just trying to figure out if all of his friends are cheapskates, or only the robot ones."

Ah. Doug.

"No," I say. "I'm not a cheapskate. Neither is Doug, actually. He just has a thing about tipping."

"Yeah," says Anders. "He thinks if nobody tips servers in diners, they'll eventually all be replaced by super-efficient robots, and he won't have to worry about people spitting in his eggs anymore."

"Of course," I say. "He wouldn't have to worry about people spitting in his eggs in the first place if he'd just leave a decent tip once in a while."

"I don't spit in his eggs," Charity says. "But I don't rush his orders, either."

I glance around. It would be nice if there were another woman in the place. Anders clearly has this one locked up, and I really am not looking forward to a late night of listening to him make that crack in the ceiling bigger while I watch *SpaceLab* on the living-room wallscreen. There's not, though. There are three men at a table in the back, working their way through three pitchers of something dark and foamy, and a middle-aged couple near the door, talking over empty glasses. I guess I could take a run at one of the waitresses, but neither of them looks very friendly, and I'm not sure how I'd start a conversation as long as Charity and Neckbeard are here to keep me in sandwiches and beer.

Anders is telling Charity about the time he played one-on-one against the backup point guard for the Celtics. This is not his best story—it ends with him in the emergency room—but she's eating it up. They're leaning across the bar, touching and pulling back, laughing more than the story deserves. They might as well be squatting by the watering hole, picking bugs out of each other's fur. I wave my empty glass at Neckbeard. He grabs a clean one and goes to pour me another IPA. For what it's worth, he looks to be even less happy about what's going on here than I am.

Not that I blame him, of course. Charity really is a first-rate piece of work. The Pretty package was the first commercially available gene hack. It was only popular for five or six years, but that cohort is in their prime bikini-body years now, so you see a lot of them around. The Pretty mods are all superficial—hair color and texture, eye color, facial symmetry, base metabolic rate—and when you overlay those things on the body structure that Mom and Dad provided, you sometimes wind up with some pretty funky-looking results. Not Charity, though. I'm guessing she would have been something even without the mods, and she's obviously put some effort into making sure that she takes full advantage of what God and GeneCraft gave her.

Neckbeard brings me my beer. I salute him, and take a long, bitter pull. Chairs scrape across the floor behind me. The couple near the door is leaving. A brief, loud argument breaks out at the table in the back, but then quickly subsides. As the couple walk out, the man holds the door open for someone coming in.

Needless to say, the newcomer is not a pretty girl. In fact, he's a bland-looking Asian guy, wearing chinos and a black compression shirt. This is not a good look on anyone, but this guy is too flabby to even make it look arrogant. He takes a stool two down from Anders, looks around, and then raps on the bar with his knuckles. Neckbeard seems to have disappeared. Charity is busy brushing Anders' hair back from his forehead with one hand. Mr. Chinos raps again, louder. Charity rolls her eyes, steps back from Anders, and turns to our new friend.

"What can I getcha, hon?"

"Gin and tonic," he says. "Not too much ice."

She turns away to make his drink. Anders is eyeballing Mr. Chinos. How many beers has he downed by now? Four? Five? His sandwich is only half eaten. A drunken Anders is a punchy Anders, and a punchy Anders is an Anders that I have to take to the emergency room because he broke his own fibula.

"Hey," I say. "You about ready to head home?"

Anders turns to me, one eyebrow raised.

"What? No. I haven't finished my sandwich yet."

Charity brings Mr. Chinos his drink. He takes a sip, makes a sour face, and pushes it back across the bar.

"This is vodka," he says. "I asked for gin."

She shakes her head. "Sorry, hon. I'm pretty sure you asked for vodka."

"No," he says, a little louder. "I asked for gin."

"Hey," says Anders. "Do you want to think about maybe being less of a dick?"

Crap.

Mr. Chinos gets to his feet. The guys at the back table have turned to watch us.

"I'm sorry," he says. "Is my drink order getting in the way of your blow job?"

Charity's jaw drops open. She picks up the drink, and splashes it all over Mr. Chinos' chinos. He leaps backward, bellowing something unintelligible.

"You know," I say, "I think he did order a G and T."

Nobody even glances at me. Anders is laughing as Mr. Chinos swipes at his pants.

"Stupid Pretty bitch," he says, then looks up at Anders. "And fuck you too, jackass."

I put a hand on Anders' shoulder, but he shrugs me off and stands.

"You need to go," he says.

Neckbeard is back behind the bar now.

"Truth," he says. "You need to go, sir. No charge for the drink."

Mr. Chinos looks at Anders, then Neckbeard, then back at Anders. He's obviously trying to use psychic powers to make their heads explode, but it's not working for him. I imagine I can hear his teeth grinding together. After a few seconds that feel more like an hour, he kicks over a barstool and storms out the door.

"Well," I say after a long, awkward silence. "That was super fun, but I'm pretty tired now. Anders, you ready to head out?"

Anders sits back down and picks up his sandwich. He takes a bite, chews, and swallows. He's about to take another when the door bangs open.

It's Mr. Chinos.

He's carrying a pistol.

He looks much less ridiculous with a gun in his hand. Neckbeard ducks behind the bar. Mr. Chinos takes three steps forward, raises his arm and takes aim at Charity, who's standing with her mouth hanging open and her arms at her sides.

Anders throws his sandwich.

It sort of comes apart in the air, but the ham and the bottom bun hit Mr. Chinos square in the face. He flinches as he pulls the trigger, and his shot goes into the ceiling over the bar.

It's at that point that I realize I've never actually seen Anders move at full speed. Mr. Chinos never gets off a second shot. Anders is on his feet with a beer glass in his hand before the report from the first one dies away. He takes two steps and throws, and the heavy glass explodes against Mr. Chinos' forehead like a bomb. Mr. Chinos goes over backward, and his head hits a table on the way down. The gun skitters across the floor.

"Holy shit," says Charity.

I think for a minute that Mr. Chinos might be dead. Anders takes a cautious step toward him, and Neckbeard comes out from behind the bar. Mr. Chinos is not dead, though. He rolls onto his side, then scrambles to his feet, one hand holding the back of his head, the other groping for the gun that's no longer there. His face looks like it got shoved into a garbage disposal.

"Easy," Anders says, but Mr. Chinos is not interested in easy. He backs two steps away, bumps into a table, and then turns and bolts for the door.

"Let him go," says Neckbeard.

Anders turns on him.

"Are you kidding? He might be going to get his other gun."

"He's not," says Neckbeard. "He's going home to put a gallon of Bactine on his fucked-up face. Let him go."

Anders hesitates, then shakes his head and starts for the door. I look at Neckbeard, then at Charity. She raises one eyebrow. I scowl, and take off after Anders at a run. I come through the door just behind him, then smack into his back as he skids to a stop.

"Hey!" I say, but he's not paying attention to me. He's staring at something going on across the street. I lean around him, trying to get a look while keeping my important parts behind him. Mr. Chinos is over there, leaning back against a long, low red car. Someone is with him, a heavily built man dressed entirely in black. They're close together, almost as if they're talking—but no, Mr. Chinos isn't talking. He's twitching. He's twitching, and the other man is holding something against the side of his neck.

As I watch, Mr. Chinos goes limp. His head lolls back, and he slides down until he's sitting on the pavement. The other man crouches beside him, leans in close. He puts whatever he'd been pressing to Mr. Chinos' throat into a pouch at his waist.

He looks quickly around.

He meets my eyes.

They're thirty feet away, but my ocular zooms in until I can see the pores on his face. He puts one finger to his lips, and slowly shakes his head. I nod. He stands, ignoring Anders, never taking his eyes from me. Mr. Chinos slumps to the side, then sprawls facedown in the street. The other man glances around once more, then turns and walks away.

I step out from behind Anders. He looks down, as if he's just noticing that I'm here.

"What the fuck just happened?" Anders whispers.

"Pretty sure Mr. Chinos just got terminated," I say.

"Holy shit," Anders says, a little louder. "Holy shit. That guy . . ."

"Yeah," I say. "That was the guy who was looking for you on Sunday morning. That was Dimitri."

Fenrir: <How goes it? Any progress tonight?>

Sir Munchalot: <Pretty sure I just watched a NatSec operative kill a guy. Does that count?>

Fenrir: <Depends. Was the guy he killed UnAltered?>

Sir Munchalot: <Dunno. Does it matter?>

Fenrir: <It does. Check this.>

Fenrir links an audio file. I blink to stream. It's a man's voice, deep and gravelly, speaking over the sort of low, ominous musical background that you usually only hear in negative political ads:

"Fellow Americans, and fellow humans: the time that we have awaited with both dread and anticipation is upon us. Yesterday, an unknown hero struck the first blow in the holy war against those who would steal from us the one thing that is most precious: our humanity, and the humanity of our children."

"For more than thirty years, the monsters in Bethesda have been turning humans into something less than human. For what is it that defines us as humans, if not our genome? We have been told that our genes differ from those of the chimpanzees by less than two percent. How much do they differ from those of a Pretty? Or one of the manufactured creatures that the wealthy now call their children? To call these things human is an insult to our species, and to the God who made us.

"Of course, this is not the first time that there have been two species of humanlike creatures on this world. In ages past we shared the Earth with *Homo erectus*, with the Denisovans, with the true Neanderthals. And how does it end when one species of human encounters another? History is clear. One species thrives. The other species dies.

"Friends, this same dynamic is playing out today. These pseudo-humans have been growing in numbers, year over year. Today, they make up perhaps a tenth of our population. In another twenty years, they may be half of all Americans. Already they refer to true humans as '*Homo saps*.' How long until they decide that '*Homo sap*' is an obsolete species, no more deserving of a place in this world than *Homo erectus*?

"My friends, we, the UnAltered, will not stand by and watch as our species is driven from this world. Our ancestors earned our place on this planet. They paid the price for it in sweat and in blood, and we will not relinquish it without a fight. Rise up, friends, and fight the Altered wherever you find them. God willing, there will be more Hagerstowns. And when there are, the UnAltered will rise up with you, and we will prevent NatSec from striking down the true humans who emerge from them unscathed.

"These are terrible times, my friends, and in times like these, terrible things must sometimes be done. But make no mistake. This is our best chance—our last chance—to save our species from extinction. May God grant you courage, and may God grant you strength."

Argyle Dragon: <Nice. How widely has this circulated?>

Fenrir: <A couple of million downloads. NatSec has been chasing it down like crazy. No

idea how many of those might have wound up redacted.>

Argyle Dragon: <Think anyone takes this shit seriously?>

Sir Munchalot: <Guy at the donut store this morning took it seriously enough to punch a Neanderthal in the skull.>

Hayley 9000: <That's pretty seriously.>

Drew P. Wiener: <There has been some sporadic violence against obvious Engineered over the past twenty-four hours, but nothing organized so far.>

Argyle Dragon: <The bit where he hopes for more Hagerstowns is a little disturbing.>

Sir Munchalot: <Not sure he's hoping. Sounds more like planning.>

Argyle Dragon: <Hence my original question: Any progress?>

Fenrir: <Still leaning toward the kill-switch theory. Been working on cracking GeneCraft systems. No success so far. They've got a lot more money to put to security than NatSec, apparently.>

Hayley 9000: <I managed a couple of minor incursions into Bioteka.>

Argyle Dragon: <Anything interesting?>

Hayley 9000: <Well, their CFO is into some pretty freaky shit. Otherwise, no.>

Argyle Dragon: <So we're still just speculating at this point.>

Drew P. Wiener: <Pretty much.>

Sir Munchalot: <Keep digging, gentlemen. I know it's taking time from our commercial ventures—but if this spirals out of control, our commercial ventures aren't going to mean much.>

I blink the text window closed. My chronometer reads 02:45:05. I sit up on the couch. My neck cracks as I arch my back and stretch.

"Hey," Charity says. "You finally done with the porn?"

"Why does everybody say that?" I ask. "People do lots of things with their oculars that have nothing to do with porn, you know."

She laughs.

"Do they? I thought the only reason people got those things implanted was so that they could indulge their perversions in private."

"That may be true for some people," I say, "but I use mine strictly for professional purposes."

She laughs again. I think I like her laugh.

"Sorry about Anders," I say. "I have no idea why he's being so unsociable."

She shrugs.

"Whatever. I was planning on thanking him for saving my life and all, but . . ."

"Yeah," I say. "Don't be offended. It's not about you."

"What?" she says. "He's got a girlfriend?"

"Not exactly."

"Boyfriend?"

"Closer. It's complicated."

We sit in silence for a while. I'm just starting to drift when she says, "It's pretty late. Okay if I crash here?"

I sigh.

"You're not an outbreak monkey, are you?"

She smiles.

"Uh . . . no. I don't think so, anyway."

"Then you're a big step up from my last set of boarders. Checkout is at eleven. Enjoy your stay."

9. INTERLUDE

<Posted today, 09:00:00. Redacted today, 09:00:02. Source unknown.>
Greetings to my fellow UnAltered. My name is Denise Magliano. You have known me up until now as Princess Blue. If you are reading this message, it is because I failed to upload the code at either 09:00 or 21:00 that would have prevented it from being posted to all of my public and private feeds. The only reason that I would have failed to do that (and the only reason that I would tell you my real name) is that I am now dead.

I am (I was?) a healthy seventeen-year-old girl, with no known genetic defects, no dangerous or unhealthy habits, and no inclination toward violent or dangerous sports or other activities. The current death rate for someone with my demographic, social, and genetic profile is less than two per one hundred thousand per year. If I am dead, there is a very good chance that it is because someone decided to make me that way.

So, what have I done to make someone want

to kill me? Something, obviously, or I wouldn't have gone to the trouble of setting up this message with a dead-man switch. I've only ever done one thing that might have brought a killer to my door, and that is to exercise my God-given right to free speech. I had the gall to pass on information to all of you that contradicted the official NatSec version of what happened to the good people of Hagerstown. And for that, someone at NatSec decided that I had to die.

If you search for my name now in the Baltimore newsfeeds, I'm sure that you will find a story about a poor young girl who was killed in a car accident, or shot during a mugging, or drowned in the bathtub after passing out drunk. Do not believe whatever slander NatSec has put out about me. I am not a crime victim, or a self-destructive loser, or a poor girl who was in the wrong place at the wrong time.

I am a casualty of war.

<Posted today, 10:13:33 by Hobo Joe>
Okay, I've seen a half dozen or so of these farewell notes from our UnAltered pals this morning, and they're starting to get on my nerves. They all claim to have been whacked by NatSec, supposedly because their subversive feeds were deemed to be a Threat to the Republic. You know what? I've read some of their feeds. They're not subversive. They're sub-literate. All

these guys are the same, whining about how the Engineered and the Augmented have lost sight of what it means to be human and blah, blah, blah. Guess what, assholes? Humans in a state of nature have a twenty-five percent infant mortality rate, and a median lifespan of twenty-eight years. They live in the jungle, and eat shit that they pick up off the ground. If that doesn't describe your life experience, you're one of the Altered whether you like it or not. My implants are no different than vaccines or blood pressure pills or artificial hips.

So, if there's not a vast conspiracy to kill every two-digit-IQ UnAltered with access to the networks, what is tripping these idiots' dead-man switches? Here's a guess: Maybe they spent last night out looking for Engineered to whale on—like that Pretty who got mauled in Rock Creek Park the other day. A Pretty's mods are all superficial, but many of ours are not. I'm pretty confident that I personally could take down a dozen UnAltered if I had to, and after the way things have gone the last couple of days, I don't think I'd be gentle.

<Posted today, 10:18:08 by Shark Sandwich>
I'm not generally one to respond to stupidity, but I do feel like I need to say something to Hobo Joe. First, while I'm sure that he's a super tough guy and that he has Engineered muscles

just popping out all over his body, that kind of thing hasn't been the deciding factor in human conflict for at least the past fifty thousand years. Gorillas and elephants and lions are super strong too, and have claws and trunks and whatnot to boot. How's that been working out for them? If one of our UnAltered brothers decides to take him down, it won't be by challenging him to fisticuffs. It would more likely be by putting a .50 caliber slug between his eyes from a kilometer away.

Second, while I could basically agree that someone with an ocular or even an exoskeleton is still pretty much human, that simply cannot be said for any of the Engineered. A species is defined by its genome. Anyone with germ-line modifications is by definition no longer human. To say that splicing ape genes or Neanderthal genes or cougar genes into the human genome is no different than vaccination is just stupid. You can argue that these sorts of changes are inevitable, or even that they're a good thing, but you cannot argue that they do not represent the creation of a multitude of new species. This kind of rapid speciation is not something that has ever happened on this planet before, and we have no idea what consequences it will ultimately bring.

<Posted today, 10:19:23 by Agent of Change>
Hey **NatSec**—you might want to consider putting

Shark Sandwich on your kill list. I'm pretty sure he just threatened to shoot Hobo Joe in the face.

<Posted today, 10:22:57 by Thomas Pain>
Really, Agent of Change? You think this is funny? Elements of the government murdered thousands of American citizens on Sunday afternoon. Elements of the government are currently executing American citizens in the streets and in their beds without trial or appeal. Those who would surrender essential liberties in exchange for a little temporary security are deserving of neither, and the most essential right that we have is the right to life. The America we live in today would be absolutely unrecognizable to the founders of this once-great nation. We have tolerated the gradual growth of the panopticon, because it made law enforcement more effective. We have tolerated the tapping of virtually every communications channel available to us by the government, because it has made things marginally more difficult for terrorist organizations. Now we tolerate mass extrajudicial executions because NatSec tells us that they are necessary to stave off a repeat of the horrors of Hagerstown. How much lower can we possibly sink, and still call ourselves Americans?

<Posted today, 10:30:42 by Lord Fizzlebottom>
Thomas Pain is absolutely correct to say that

the America we live in today would be utterly unrecognizable to the founders. For example, in their America, Thomas Paine had to crank out his screeds on a printing press and distribute them to his fellow citizens by hand, whereas in our America, **Thomas Pain** can say whatever he wants to a huge number of his fellow citizens with a click or a poke or whatever you idiots who haven't got oculars yet do. Of course, most would say that this change is a good one, enhancing our right to free speech by making widely distributed speech truly free—not every ignorant eighteenth-century peasant had access to a printing press, after all.

However, there are a few other changes in today's America that may be less benign. For example, in Thomas Paine's day, if one of our good citizens took it into his head to do harm to his fellow men, his power to do so was fairly limited. Hard to go on a rampage with a musket, and you can't even make a really effective bomb with black powder. Today, however, anyone with the inclination to do so can get hold of a high-capacity automatic rifle. If he's ambitious and has a bit of money, it's conceivable that he could cobble together an engineered virus that could take down half the North American population in a matter of weeks.

The question, then, is this: Even if we concede that we would not be willing to trade our essential liberties in order to gain a little temporary security, might we be willing to compromise at least a few of them in order to allow our continued survival as a nation?

We still do not know what, exactly, happened in Hagerstown. **NatSec** says every living person within the secured perimeter died within a matter of minutes. The UnAltered say that no, only ninety percent of them did. Even if they're right, this was a shot across our bow. Speaking for myself, I'm willing to concede a hell of a lot to **NatSec** if they can keep it from happening again.

<Posted today, 10:39:09 by Thomas Pain>
Sorry to contradict you, **Lord Fizzlebottom**, but there is nothing unique about our age. Fear has always been the best friend of the tyrant. You can fret about the possibility that some lunatic in a basement might cook up a virus that will wipe out half the population. I'm sure our ancestors would be very sympathetic. Ever heard of smallpox? How about the bubonic plague? Those two entirely naturally occurring diseases wiped out 90 percent of the North American population and 60 percent of the European population. You worry that a terrorist might blow up a building—or hey, maybe an entire city? The Mongols wiped out cities by the dozen, and piled their citizens' skulls outside the gates like cantaloupes.

It's easy to look at what feels like an existential threat, and to wish for a big strong someone to step in and save you. That's not unique to our age either. People have been falling in line behind kings and emperors and dictators in the face of external threats at least since Gilgamesh ruled Uruk. But the fact that this urge to self-infantilization seems to be a part of human nature doesn't make it right, and if we wish to remain—or to become again—a free people, it is something we must resist to our last drop of blood.

You seem to believe that submitting meekly to NatSec's intrusion into every aspect of our lives is the only way for us to survive. I disagree. But even if you're right, there's a difference between surviving and living. It's worth taking the risk of doing neither, in order to try to do both.

<Posted today, 10:41:50 by Agent of Change>
Hear hear, Thomas Pain. Let's dismantle the security apparatus that NatSec and other government agencies have built up over the last forty years. You know—the one that has averted three known attempted nuclear strikes against American cities, that cut al Qaeda in North America down to the last man, and that has helped America to the lowest rate of violent crime in the world. True, there is no evidence that this apparatus has ever been used to subvert our political freedoms or to

so much as harass a single innocent American citizen, but who knows? Maybe someday it might be. Surely a few million deaths here or there is a small price to pay to avert that possibility.

<Posted today, 10:42:30 by Captain Obvious>
This is boring. Any UnAltered out there? Give us one of your "Genetic Modifications are the Devil's Tilt-A-Whirl" sermons. Those are always fun to read.

<Posted today, 10:43:44. Redacted today, 10:43:47. Source unknown.>
Laugh it up, fuckers. There are more of us than there are of you, and we don't have kill switches built into us. The hammer's gonna fall soon, and when it does, *Homo sapiens* is gonna be the only human species on this planet again.

<Posted today, 10:44:08. Redacted today, 10:44:14. Source unknown.>
Homo saps may still be a majority, but NatSec and the military are both forty-plus percent Engineered and one hundred percent Augmented. If and when the hammer falls, I promise you that it's not gonna fall on us. You can ask your UnAltered friends in Hagerstown about that.

<Posted today, 10:45:19 by Captain Obvious>
I stand corrected. That wasn't fun at all.

10. ANDERS

For the second time in three days, I wake up hungover. On the plus side, this time I'm in my own bed, and there's nobody in it with me. On the minus side, my head hurts worse than it did on Sunday, and there's a weird, gnawing discomfort in the pit of my stomach that I suspect doesn't have much to do with how much I had to drink.

Also, I'm pretty sure I watched a NatSec agent kill a guy last night—a NatSec agent who was apparently at my house on Sunday morning looking for me. I make a mental note to have a chat with Terry about that.

I start to sit up, but a knife-twist in my side drops me back with a gasp. I must have horked something doing my Speedy McGreedy routine at the bar. Hopefully it's just a pull. Tears hurt twice as bad, and they take forever to heal. I roll over slowly onto my side, drop my feet to the floor, and lever myself up into a sitting position. This is exactly why I quit playing ball. I can still remember waking up feeling like this on the mornings after games, and thinking that this must be what it's like to be really, really old.

I check my phone. It's a little after nine. No alerts, so at least the world hasn't fallen apart any more than it already had while I was sleeping. Also on the plus side, my room is cooler than it has been in a week or so. Looks like the heat has finally broken. The sky outside the window is low and gray, with darker black streaks and swirls off to the south. The weather matches my mood.

I stand slowly. The pain is centered on my right side, between my pelvis and my ribs, but I think I might have done something to my chest as well. I try to stretch it out a little, but the muscles give me just enough of a warning jolt to convince me to leave them alone. I pick up the pants I left on the floor last night and pull them on, then take a shirt from the top of my dresser and carefully pull it over my head. This definitely reminds me of my playing days. I shuffle out into the hallway, and pull the door closed behind me.

I'm a little surprised to find Gary already awake, leaning back with his fingers knitted behind his head in one of the recliners in the living room. He's got one eye open, while the other twitches its way through a download.

"Morning," he says. "Coffee and doughnuts are in

the kitchen. I meant to grab something for the chlamydia you probably picked up yesterday afternoon, but I forgot. Sorry."

"Thanks for the doughnuts. Also, bite me. Also, What's got you up so early? I didn't expect to see you before noon."

He opens both eyes now, sits up and stretches.

"Big doings," he says. "I'm monitoring the early stages of the RAHOWA."

"The what?"

He rolls his head around in a slow circle. I can hear his vertebrae cracking.

"RAHOWA," he says. "Racial holy war. The term was popularized by white supremacist groups at the end of the twentieth century. They used it to refer to the coming apocalyptic clash between the genetically pure and morally upright Aryans and the mixed-blood degenerates. Those guys were butt-munches, obviously, but as an acronym it's got a nice ring to it, so I thought I'd revive it to describe the current foofaraw."

Now I'm confused.

"The Aryans?" I ask. "Weren't they from India?"

He grins, and levers himself to his feet.

"We're talking about white supremacists, Anders. They didn't make it through tenth-grade social studies. Don't try to apply too much critical thinking to their worldview."

"Right," I say. "Speaking of genetic purity, where's Charity? Did she end up heading home after all?"

He shakes his head.

"I figured she would, once she realized that you're obviously sexually confused," he says. "But she wound up sleeping on the couch."

"Great. And now she's . . ."

"In the bathroom, I think."

"Uh-huh. So how are things going, RAHOWA-wise?"

He shrugs.

"Pretty much all show, no go at the moment. There are a lot of threatening feeds floating around on both sides, but actual violence at this point is still small-scale and sporadic. Pretties look to be taking the worst of it on the Engineered side, probably because they're easy to spot and easy to beat up. There's also some indication that NatSec did some housecleaning last night. The UnAltered feed distribution network seems to be pretty heavily compromised."

"Housecleaning?"

"Oh yeah. I've seen eleven dead-man-switch messages from UnAltered network repeaters. They all claim to have been whacked by NatSec, and the two locals I followed up on definitely had bad things happen to them last night. One was a high-school girl who died of a heroin overdose—a drug that she had no history of ever using, by the way—and the other one was a middle-aged chino-wearing guy named Christopher Cai, who supposedly died in the street of an aneurism after he got his head smashed in by some jerk with a beer glass at the Green Goose."

"Again, bite me, Gary."

"No," he says. "I'm serious. The guy you busted

up last night was apparently a big name with the Un-Altered. He put out a daily feed with over a million paid subscribers. Kind of explains why he was such a douche-nozzle, doesn't it? He's definitely dead, so I doubt he'll be coming after you anytime soon, but you might want to keep an eye out for his fans. Your name showed up in the feeds, and it seems like a lot of them are pretty mad."

Fantastic. This week just gets better and better.

So Charity spent the night on our couch. Her and Gary? No, I'm not gonna think about that before breakfast. She comes out of the downstairs bathroom when I'm halfway through my third Jolly Pirate. Gary follows her into the kitchen, and they join me at the breakfast table. Charity lifts the lid on the box and pulls out a doughnut, holding it between her thumb and forefinger like a dead mouse. She looks it over, wrinkles her nose, and takes a nibble.

"Let me guess," I say. "You're a doughnut hater?"

"Honestly," she says, "I don't think I've ever eaten one." She takes another, slightly bigger bite. "It's not bad. Just a big wad of fat and sugar, right? Is this really how you guys eat?"

"Pretty much," says Gary. He reaches into the cupboard against the wall and pulls out three coffee mugs, fills them from the box on the table, and hands them around.

"So," Charity says. "How in the world are you still alive?"

"An excellent question." Gary pulls a doughnut from the box and tears half of it off in one bite. "Anders here has a very high metabolism. He needs about five thousand calories a day just to keep from wasting away." He chases the doughnut with coffee, then jams the rest into his mouth. "I, on the other hand, don't actually eat very much. It's a life of constant discipline, which I maintain by making sure that everything I do eat is as disgusting as possible."

Charity sets her half-eaten donut down on the table and takes a sip of coffee.

"Lovely," she says. "I think I've had enough."

"See? It's working on you, too. Soon you'll be as thin and pretty as I am."

Charity giggles.

"I think we've actually got some fruit in the fridge," I say. "Help yourself. We're probably not going to eat it."

She shakes her head.

"I'm good. I don't usually eat breakfast anyway."

I finish my coffee. Gary thoughtfully chews his second doughnut, while staring at Charity's boobs.

"So," I say finally. "Charity. What are your plans for the day?"

She grimaces.

"I have to be at the diner by eleven for the lunch shift, and I have to get home and get cleaned up before that. Speaking of which, I don't suppose either of you owns a car?"

I shake my head. Gary's not listening. He might as well have her nipples crammed into his ears. Charity sighs.

"I didn't think so. It's okay. I'll get a cab."

She pulls out a phone, and taps at the screen.

"Huh," she says. "I guess I don't need a cab after all."

"You sure?" I say. "Don't know where you live, but it's a solid two miles from here to the diner."

"I'm sure," she says. "Apparently, I just got fired."

"I got fired once," says Gary. "That's why I became an entrepreneur."

Charity taps at her phone some more. "Thanks. I'll get right on that. Is applying for government credit entrepreneurial?"

"Not really," I say. "But suing the diner for unlawful dismissal might be. Did they give you a reason?"

"Nope. Just said not to show up today."

"Just out of curiosity," says Gary. "Is your boss Engineered?"

"No," she says. "No mods, no implants."

"RAHOWA," says Gary.

"I haven't looked into this RAHOWA thing," I say. "But I'm pretty sure that firing waitresses is not part of it."

Charity looks at Gary, then at me.

"RAHOWA?"

"Racial holy war," I say. "It's Gary's new thing."

"Cataclysmic battle to the death between the Engineered and the UnAltered," Gary says. "First they came for the cave ladies, and I said nothing, because I was not a cave lady. Then they came for the hot waitresses, and I said nothing, because I was not a hot waitress. Then they came for the bastard offspring of Mickey Mouse and a seven-foot-tall transvestite prostitute, and I said nothing, because I was not Anders. Then they came for me, and there was nobody left to speak."

Charity looks at me and raises one eyebrow. I shrug.

"Martin Niemöller," says Gary. "You did go to college, didn't you?"

Charity gives Gary a long, blank look.

"So you're saying I got fired because I'm a Pretty?"

"Yes," I say. "That's what he's saying."

"Except I'm not," she says.

"Not what?" I ask.

"Not a Pretty. I know I look like one, but I'm not."

I try to give Gary a warning look, but his eyes are fixed on the point where her shirt snugs against the tops of her breasts.

"Come on," he says. "There's no way that this"—he gives a vague wave that encompasses everything from her ass to the top of her head—"just happens."

She smiles.

"I didn't say I'm not Engineered. You've got more in common with a bonobo than you do with me. I'm just not a Pretty."

Charity is upstairs using our shower when Doug pings me.

"Connect," I say. "Vid to the wallscreen."

I walk into the living room and drop onto the

couch. My side is still pretty sore, but my chest feels better, and I'm starting to think I got away with some minor strains. Doug's face pops up on the screen. He does not look happy.

"Anders," he says. "What's the word?"

"RAHOWA, apparently. Have you been following the feeds?"

He grimaces.

"I have. That's why I'm here. We really need your feedback on those documents. Have you opened them?"

I shake my head.

"I have not. Been kinda busy. Today, though, I will definitely get to them. In fact, I'll start digging into them as soon as we disconnect."

"This is important," he says. "I may not have emphasized this before, but I really, really need you to get back to me on this as soon as possible."

I roll my eyes.

"I've got it, Doug. I told you—no promises about what I'll find, but I'll have something to give you by this afternoon."

"Good."

The screen goes blank.

"Great," I say. "Good to talk to you too, Doug. Have a lovely afternoon. Bye."

There's no real reason for me to work on this in my bedroom—I'm pretty sure Gary can monitor everything I do there just as easily as what I do in the kitchen—but I decide to do it anyway. I guess the illusion of privacy is better than nothing at all. I'm just settling into my work chair and pulling up the files when Charity comes into the room. She's carrying her clothes over one arm, and wearing a towel wrapped around her torso.

"Hey," she says. "Whatcha up to?"

I make a conscious effort to drag my eyes away from her.

"Something I should have been doing a couple of days ago, apparently," I say.

She sits down on the edge of the bed, crosses her legs and looks up at the wallscreen. It shows a schematic diagram, rotating slowly in three dimensions.

"Seriously," she says. "What is that?"

I shrug.

"That's what I'm trying to figure out."

I wave my hand and the schematic disappears, replaced by scrolling columns of numbers and symbols. When Doug told me that he wanted me to review some documents for him, I assumed that he meant . . . well . . . documents. These are not documents. There is nothing here that was meant to be parsed by a human.

Charity scoots a bit closer. I've never seen a Pretty this up-close before, and although she claims not to be one, she definitely has those mods on top of whatever else she's got. Her breasts have absolutely no sag to them. Gene cuts or no, it's not clear to me how that's physically possible.

"So," I say. "Do you think you might want to put some clothes on?"

She smiles.

"I think that may be the first time anyone's ever said that to me. Am I distracting you?"

"A bit, yeah."

She leans back on her elbows.

"Are you sure you don't want to be distracted?"

My eyes slide up to her face, then back down again.

"You know," I say. "I'm starting to think you might be a succubus."

I wave again, and another schematic comes up. It shows what looks like a molecular diagram. Charity scowls, picks up her clothes and starts pulling them on. I point and push, and the view moves to a three-dimensional representation of what I'm pretty sure is a protein. Another wave, and a third diagram appears.

Which I recognize.

It's a schematic for a simple nanomachine, one that I've used as an example in my lectures. It's a temperature-sensitive molecular cage, similar in its basic structure to a buckyball. You can put a small molecule inside it, and it will stay chemically isolated from its surroundings for as long as the cage maintains its integrity—which it can no longer do after its temperature exceeds 36° C.

Charity slams the door behind her on the way out.

I know what these files are now.

Doug is definitely trying to get me killed.

"So," Doug says. "What have you got for me?"

He's grinning. I am not.

"Well," I say. "I'm pretty sure I know what these files are, and what they're for. I'd like to know how you got hold of them."

His grin widens.

"Come on, Anders. I can't tell you that. Trade secret, blah blah blah. What are they?"

"Do you seriously not know?"

His left eye begins vibrating its way through a download.

"Do you have to do that?" I ask.

"Do what?"

"The eye thing. It bothers me when people do that. Shouldn't you be doing all of your downloads through your brain thingie now?

"My what?"

"Sorry. Your wireless neural interface. Shouldn't that be handling your downloads now?"

He shrugs.

"It does. But any visuals still get fed through my ocular. That's more efficient than trying to tap the optic nerve directly if you've already got one implanted."

I run one hand back through my hair.

"Great. I was kind of hoping that the advent of brain thingies would end the whole lizard-eye thing, but whatever. Anyway, do you really not know what you gave me?"

He gives me a drawn-out, theatrical sigh.

"Did I not agree to pay your war-profiteering consulting fee? Would I have done that if I already knew what was in the files?"

"I have no idea what you would or wouldn't do at this point, Doug. Where did you get these files?"

He shrugs.

"I jacked them from a server."

"Right. Whose server?"

"Another jacker."

"So you seriously have no idea what these are?"

"None whatsoever."

I suddenly realize that I've let the heavy augmentation color my view of Doug for the last fifteen years. He is not, in fact, an intelligent man.

"Then how do you know they're important?" I ask, speaking slowly now. "Why did you agree to pay my fee?"

He smiles. Doug's smile is a very creepy thing.

"Because the guy I jacked them from had them locked up very, very tight."

"So if I told you this was somebody's encrypted home porn?"

The smile disappears.

"I would be bitterly disappointed. Unless it was something really freaky, and we could associate it with somebody rich and closeted. Is it porn?"

I sigh.

"No, Doug. It is not porn. You did at least glance at the files, right?"

"I did not."

"So you . . . wait, what? You didn't even look at them?"

"I did not."

I'm not sure what to say to that.

"Don't look at me like that," he says. "I thought there was a chance they might have come from NatSec."

"And?"

"NatSec puts tracker bugs into anything that goes onto their servers. Anytime you open one of their files, the bugs pop their little heads up and check to see if they're in a NatSec environment. If they're not, they start screaming for help on any accessible channel. I've got containment systems, of course, but NatSec programmers are tricky. I'm not one-hundred-percent confident they'd hold."

My stomach is suddenly churning, and I can feel my jaw sag.

"When you say 'help,' " I say slowly, "I assume what you mean is a crowbar?"

He nods.

"If you're lucky, yeah."

I stare at the screen. Apparently, my earlier reassessment needs to be reassessed. Doug is not stupid. Doug is the devil.

"Come on," he says. "You knew all this, right? Why did you think I agreed to give you hazard pay?"

"Hazard pay?"

He rolls his normal eye. The other one is in full-on lizard mode.

"Six hundred an hour? I know what you make, Anders. Why would you throw out a crazy number like that if you didn't know you were putting your ass on the line?"

"It didn't occur to you that I was just being greedy?"

His face goes blank. Apparently, it did not.

"I'm really sorry, Anders," he says finally, his voice dripping with mock sympathy. "I've been going under the working assumption that there's a brain inside your cranium. It would have saved us both a lot of trouble if you'd told me up front that it's just a big wad of hair in there."

I open my mouth to tell him to go fuck himself, then close it again. He's right. A man who won't leave a two-dollar tip to prevent a busboy from licking his pancakes agreed to give me an open-ended six-hundred-dollar-an-hour consulting gig without batting an eye. I drop my head into my hands.

"Oh, buck up," Doug says. "It doesn't matter anyway. You're working through Gary's system, right? He's an order of magnitude tighter than I am. That's one of the reasons why I approached you with this in the first place."

This is probably not the time to mention that my original plan was to review his files in my shared adjunct's office at Hopkins.

"Look," he says. "You're not currently being anally probed by a NatSec operative, and your house is not a smoking hole in the ground. So it all worked out, right? What have you got for me?"

I look up. The smile is back. He looks like a kid on Christmas morning.

Well, a kid who's been partially digested by his toys, anyway.

"First," I say wearily, "these are not documents. They're configuration files."

The smile widens.

"Bingo. Configuration files for what?"

"For a nanoparticle fabricator, Doug. They're formatted for a Siemens machine, I think, but I'm not positive about that."

Doug pumps one fist in the air, and does a little dance. Calling the effect disturbing is a huge understatement.

"Score!" he crows. "What are they plans for? What can we make? Is it a weapon? It's a weapon, isn't it?"

I rub my eyes, then push my hair back from my forehead. I really, really need a nap.

"No, Doug. It's not a weapon. I'm actually only about ninety percent sure what we're looking at. I recognize one of the schematics, and I can infer what a couple of the others are intended to do, but the rest are still pretty much a mystery."

"Come on," he says. "You're killing me. Am I a rich man or not?"

"Well," I say. "I'm not sure how exactly you're going to monetize this, but you've definitely got something of value. I'm pretty sure you've managed to steal the secret formula for the nano suite in BrainBump."

Doug's jaw sags open, and for a moment he looks like he might cry—but then he shakes his head, and the half of his face that's still made of meat smiles.

"Okay," he says. "Right. I can work with this. There's gotta be a buyer out there for something like that. Pretty sure's not gonna do it, though. I need totally sure."

I shrug.

"I don't have access to a Siemens fab unit," I say. "I can run the files through an emulator if you want. You won't get any nanos out the back end, but it'll give you a full roster of whatever particles would have been produced if you provided the files to an actual fabricator."

"Good enough," Doug says. "Don't care about the actual particles. I just need enough proof to show a buyer."

I glance up as I boot the emulator and feed it the config files. Doug's leaning toward the camera, almost like he's trying to look over my shoulder. I think about explaining to him that getting a forehead print on his wallscreen is not going to give him a better view, but he's back to the kid at Christmas thing. I start the production run. I'm expecting a return after twenty or thirty seconds. It comes back after five.

"Well?" Doug says. "What do we have?"

"Nothing," I say. "Your files crashed the emulator."

That gets me five seconds of awkward silence.

"Uh, Anders? What does that mean?"

I shrug.

"I don't know. I've never seen it happen before. This is freeware, but it's been around for a long time. Most of the bugs got ironed out years ago."

He leans back away from the screen. The smile is gone.

"So what do we do?"

"I'm not sure. I've got source for the emulator, but

the code is way too involved for me to debug. Gary might be able to work his way through it . . ."

"No," Doug says. "I don't want Gary in on this right now. What else do you have?"

I think about mentioning the fact that if Gary wants to know what we're doing right now, he can find out without being invited, but I don't want to get Doug any more agitated than he already is.

"How about this?" I say. "I can feed the files for the different particles to the emulator one by one. Maybe it's just one of them that's causing the problem."

"Fine," Doug says. "But make it quick. I'm not paying you for downtime."

I shoot the screen a poisonous glare.

"As near as I can tell," I say, "you haven't paid me for anything yet."

"Yeah, well . . . if you want that to change, figure it out. Chop-chop."

I fold my arms across my chest.

"Really, Doug?"

He stomps both feet and turns half around.

"Come on, Anders. You're killing me."

"What's the magic word, Doug?"

"Ass-monkey?"

I laugh. "Close enough."

It takes me about ten minutes to parse out the files. There are plans here for five distinct particles, ranging in size from a huge bot that I'm guessing is designed to interface with a specific implant, to a modest neurostimulator, to the little molecular cage. I start with the biggest one, reasoning that the more complex files are more likely to have fatal errors. The emulator runs for ten seconds or so, and then spits out reams of output data.

"Well?"

I shrug.

"That one ran cleanly. Let's try the next."

I work my way through the files, largest to smallest. Each runs perfectly.

Until the last—the friendly little buckyball. That one crashes as soon as I launch it.

"Well," I say. "There's your problem."

Doug scowls.

"That's what the guy who fixed my arm said, right before he told me that I owed him eight thousand dollars."

I stare at the screen.

"This doesn't make sense," I say. "I know this bot. I use the schematic for a molecular cage almost exactly like this as an example for dimwit rich kids. It's not that complicated."

"So how do you fix it?"

"Wait a minute," I say. "Let me check something."

I swipe open my course folder and search for the molecular cage config file. I'm thinking that maybe I can run a simple diff on the two files, but when I pull them up side by side, Doug's is over twice as large. I pop them both open. The schematics are similar. The spec files are almost exactly the same. I come to the ends of the files without finding any serious difference.

Except that Doug's is still twice as big.

"So?" Doug says. "Do you know what's wrong?"

"Yeah," I say. "There's a whole lot of stuff in here that shouldn't be."

11. TERRY

Elise is gone.

She's not dead. If she were, I'd be able to contact her phone, and an avatar would say "Sorry, Elise can't speak with you at the moment. She's dead." She has a cloud avatar, of course, but it has no more idea of where she is than I do.

The only thing I can think of that would cause every trace of her to drop off the networks would be if she, her phone, her house, and all her other networked gear were completely vaporized.

Which she told me very clearly two days ago is not, in fact, what happened.

Tariq said yesterday morning that they were going somewhere safe. It didn't occur to me to ask whether "safe" actually meant "on the surface of Mars."

"House," I say. "How many locations within sixty

miles of Baltimore are completely inaccessible to any public networks?"

House has to think about that for a minute. She pops up on my kitchen wallscreen with one finger pressed to her lips. Her silver forehead wrinkles in concentration.

"Two known locations," she says finally. "One suspected."

"Where are they?"

"Known locations are the interiors of containment units one and two at the Chesapeake Fusion Facility. Suspected location is within the NatSec facility in Chantilly, Virginia."

"Seriously?" I ask. "That's the best you can do?"

She shrugs.

"You asked for locations that are completely inaccessible. There aren't too many of those around these days."

Okay. Elise is probably not in either of the known locations, and I somehow doubt that Tariq would have taken her to the suspected one. So where does that leave me?

"Fine," I say. "Get me a connection to Dimitri. Vid to the wallscreen."

She disappears while she pings Dimitri's system, then pops back up long enough to say, "Sorry. No luck. Here's one of his avatars, though."

It's the bear.

"Terry," it says. "So good to hear from you. Dimitri would very much like to speak with you, but he is sleeping at the moment. Can I help you?"

I glance at my chronometer. It reads 10:45:15.

"I'm not sure," I say. "When do you expect Dimitri to wake up?"

It shrugs apologetically.

"I do not know. Dimitri has not slept well for the past three days. I have no interest in waking him any sooner than I must."

"Can you have him contact me when he wakes?"

"I will. Good-bye, Terry."

"Disconnect."

I walk into the living room, and drop onto the couch. I have some design work that I could be doing—that I should be doing, honestly. My client is expecting a first pass for review at the end of the week. There's no possible way I'm going to be able to concentrate on color palettes and furniture layouts and placement of *objets d'art* right now, though. There's not much point in worrying whether or not you've got the Renoir placed in ideal lighting when the world is swirling the drain.

"House," I say. "Vids. News. Local. Centrist."

The wallscreen cuts to two men on low couches facing each other across a coffee table. The overlay identifies the clip as an interview with NatSec Acting Director Dey, livecast today at 09:00. I recognize the interviewer. His name is John Flaherty. He's been doing interview feeds with celebrities and politicians since I was in grade school.

The interviewer in this case is much more famous than his subject, who I've never actually seen before. Dey has only been in the job for a few months—just since Director Stevens resigned. I know there was some sort of scandal around that, but it must not have been too interesting, because I can't for the life of me remember what it was about. Dey is short and thin, with dark skin and hair, and a heavy black mustache that curls around the corners of his mouth and almost down to his jawline. He's wearing a dark brown suit that looks to be a couple of sizes too large.

"Good morning," says Flaherty. "We're here today with NatSec Acting Director Augustus Dey. Thank you for joining us, Mr. Dey."

"It is my pleasure to be here, John," says Dey. He has just a hint of an accent, somewhere between South Asia and a private British boarding school.

"Let's get right to business," says Flaherty. "Two days ago, this nation suffered the most devastating terrorist attack in its history, with a total of almost fifty thousand casualties. What has NatSec been able to learn about this attack, and what are you doing to make sure that it cannot happen again?"

Dey smiles.

"No preliminaries, eh, John? Very well. First, although anti-terrorism protocols have been implemented, there is in fact no hard evidence as of yet that what happened in Hagerstown was a terrorist attack. No group has claimed responsibility, and due partially to our own response to the strike, very little physical evidence was obtained that could be used to help explain what happened. We have several competing theories as to what actually caused the deaths of the good people of Hagerstown. So far, however, no proposed mechanism has been shown to be fully capable of producing the effects seen there.

"Second, we at NatSec are currently doing everything in our power both to determine who or what may have been the cause of this tragedy, and to ensure that such a thing cannot recur. Both our physical and virtual agents have been on twenty-four-hour duty cycles since Sunday afternoon, and they will remain so until this situation is fully resolved."

Flaherty leans forward.

"I hope you will forgive me," he says, "if I note that you have not fully answered my question."

Dey's smile broadens.

"I will forgive you. I'm sure you understand that there are limits to what I can say in a public forum."

Flaherty nods, but he doesn't look convinced.

"Of course, sir. On a related topic, in the past hour, accusations have arisen that NatSec agents may have carried out a number of targeted killings last night against leaders of the UnAltered Movement. Can you either confirm or deny that such operations may have been carried out?"

Now Dey leans forward, and his smile disappears.

"You surprise me, John. I will not dignify that question with an answer, except to say that the purpose of

NatSec is to protect the lives of American citizens, not to end them."

"Quite so, sir. However, you must have taken note of the feeds coming from the so-called UnAltered Movement since Hagerstown. Many of them have been forcibly redacted, but my organization has been able to retain enough over the past two days to paint a picture that borders on incitement to terrorism. Is this not so?"

Dey leans back and crosses his legs.

"I cannot comment on any ongoing investigation. You know that as well as I do."

"I understand, Mr. Dey. However, hypothetically speaking, if NatSec were to make a determination that an individual or organized group was engaging in incitement to terrorist activity using public feeds, would you not be obligated to take forceful action?"

Dey's face remains calm, but his voice takes on an icy tone.

"As you know, John, this is the United States of America, and the First Amendment is still in full effect. That said, there are laws governing public incitement to violence, and they have repeatedly been determined to pass constitutional muster. If we or any other law enforcement agency made a determination that these laws were being broken, it would be our obligation to take action."

"And would such action include targeted killings?"

Dey scowls.

"I believe I already answered that question, Mr. Flaherty."

"So you did, sir. So you did."

I pause the feed. A tap, tap, tap is coming from my foyer.

"House," I say. "What's that noise?"

She pops up on the screen, sitting on the couch next to Augustus Dey. She winks at me, and slings an arm around his shoulder.

"Someone is knocking on your door," she says.

"Knocking? Who is it?"

She leans over and nibbles Dey's ear.

"Unknown. This person carries no traceable electronics."

Which is why he's knocking, obviously.

"Can I get a visual?"

House hesitates. She leans away from Dey, and her face and voice become suddenly serious.

"No visual available."

My heart gives an alarming thump in my chest.

"What?"

"No visual available. The entry camera is not functioning."

The knock comes again. I feel a nervous stirring in the pit of my stomach.

"How long has the camera been out?"

"Forty-five seconds."

"Is the camera at the building entrance functioning?"

"It is."

"So show me visuals for anyone who's entered the building in the last five minutes."

House hesitates again. I really don't like where this is going.

"No visuals available."

"So nobody has entered the building in that time?"

"Unknown. The entry camera for the building was not functional for thirty-five seconds during that period."

The knock comes a third time, slightly louder. Someone is at my door.

Someone with the power to ghost the panopticon.

I'm on the third floor. There is no back door, no fire escape. I'm frantically considering tying together bed-sheets and climbing out the window when a muffled voice comes through the door.

"Terry, are you there? I hope I'm not disturbing you, but I really need to speak with you right away. Please open the door."

It takes me a moment to process the voice, and another to check that I haven't wet myself.

"House—" I begin, but my voice cracks. I clear my throat and try again. "House. Open the door."

I get to my feet. My hands are trembling, and I can feel the adrenaline washing through my system. I hear the door swing open, and footsteps in the foyer.

"Jesus H. Christ," I say. "What are you doing here, Tariq?"

"**W**ell at least this is all starting to make sense," I say. "You're gonna be my brother-in-law in a month. When were you planning on telling me you're with NatSec? Does Elise even know?"

Tariq shifts uncomfortably on the couch.

"I don't know what you mean," he says. "I am certainly not with NatSec. I have not checked their hiring profiles, but I am fairly sure they do not employ performance artists."

I laugh.

"Right. Performance artist. Is that even a thing? God, I feel like such an idiot."

He puts a hand on my knee, then snatches it back when he catches my expression.

"Terry, please. I assure you, I am what I claim to be. If I were associated with NatSec, I would not need to ask for your help."

I lean back, and run my hands back through my hair. The fight-or-flight is draining out of me, and I feel almost giddy.

"Look, Tariq. I said I feel like an idiot, not that I am one. If we're going to continue this conversation, you're going to need to explain some things to me. First, if you're really just a simple street performer, how exactly did you manage to ghost my building's security systems?"

His eyes slide down and away. I have no idea why NatSec would hire this guy. He's a terrible liar.

"I do not know what you mean."

"House," I say. "How is my entry camera?"

"Functioning normally."

"How was it when Tariq was standing in front of it?"

"Not functioning."

"And how was it before Tariq arrived?"

"Functioning normally."

"That, my soon-to-be brother-in-law, is what I mean by ghost. You're invisible to the panopticon. That's not an easy thing to be, and as far as I'm aware, the only people who are able to manage it are NatSec agents."

"Is it not possible," he says, "that your camera is malfunctioning? Perhaps this is simply coincidence."

I lean forward.

"So you're saying that my entry camera has a glitch, which happened to show up exactly when you did, and which spontaneously resolved as soon as you were no longer in front of it?"

He shrugs, but still can't meet my eyes.

"This is possible, is it not? Correlation does not prove causation."

"And the fact that my building's entry camera had the same glitch sixty seconds earlier—again, just when you happened to be passing in front of it—is also coincidence?"

Tariq's eyes are fixed on the floor, and for a moment I'm reminded of the clerk at the Jolly Pirate.

"I have never claimed to be an ordinary man," he says quietly. "I have made a career doing unusual things. But I swear to you, these things have nothing to do with NatSec."

I draw a deep breath in and blow it out. Dimitri is the only person I know for certain is with NatSec in some capacity. He's never said so outright—I'm pretty sure they're not allowed to admit it—but he's never really denied it either. Tariq seems pretty sincere, and I'm starting to feel bad about badgering him.

"Fine," I say. "You're not with NatSec. Let's just assume you're actually a vampire. What can I do for you?"

"I need your help," he says. "But for Elise, not for myself."

That gets my attention.

"Elise?" I say. "Where is she? Is she okay?"

"She is fine. She is safe. But . . . I must tell you that I have not been entirely honest about what happened in Hagerstown."

I sit bolt upright, and cover my mouth with both hands.

"What? Tariq, I am shocked! Shocked! You certainly had all of us fooled."

He scowls.

"I know you all think me a liar, and perhaps you are right. In truth, much of what Elise remembers of that day is correct. She did speak to a sentinel, and its sensors captured her face and her voice. It is likely that they also witnessed some part of her escape."

"On your ATV?"

His scowl deepens.

"That does not matter. What matters is that NatSec has evidence that she was present in Hagerstown, and that she did not die there. I do not believe this has come to the attention of anyone who matters—but if it does, I fear that I will not be able to protect her."

I roll my eyes. He's right about that, anyway.

"So," I say. "What exactly do you intend to do about this?"

"This is why I need your help," he says. "I intend to destroy the evidence before it is noticed."

Gary throws open the door just as I'm raising my hand to knock.

"Evil Wizard!" he says. "Cave Lady! Welcome! What brings you here so soon after we finally managed to get rid of you?"

"Hello, Gary," I say. "Can we come in?"

"Sure," he says, and steps aside with a flourish and a bow. "Why not? I run a boardinghouse now. Make yourselves comfortable."

We enter, and he closes the door behind us.

"If you're looking for Anders, he's up in his room doing super top-secret stuff that I'm not supposed to know anything about. I've got it up on the living-room wallscreen. Wanna watch?"

"No," I say. "Not really. We actually came to talk to you."

Tariq perches on the edge of the couch. I sit beside him, and Gary drops into one of the recliners. There's what looks like some sort of molecular diagram rotating on the wallscreen.

"Hey," Gary says. "Here's a fun fact: Last night, I'm pretty sure I watched your pal Dimitri whack a guy. Care to comment?"

I stare at him. He stares back, with bland half smile on his face.

"What are you talking about?" I finally ask.

"Dimitri," he says. "You know, the super scary guy who showed up at my door on Sunday morning looking for Anders, presumably because he was peeved at your little . . . whatever it is you two have going on?"

"Yeah," I say. "I know who Dimitri is. You saw him hit somebody?"

"No," Gary says. "I did not see him hit somebody. I saw him whack somebody: one Christopher Cai, in fact—noted racist, UnAltered rabble-rouser, and man about town."

"I believe," Tariq says, "that Gary is saying that he saw your friend commit a murder."

"No," I say. "He's not."

"Yes," Gary says. "I am."

I look at Tariq, then back at Gary.

"You're saying that you saw Dimitri kill someone last night, in public, in full view of every drone and spy eye in Baltimore?"

"No," Gary says. "I am saying I saw him kill someone, but I don't think it was in full view of anyone but me and Anders. Dimitri's NatSec, right? I'm guessing he was ghosted."

"Just to be clear," he goes on after a pause, "I'm more than willing to give old Dimitri a pass on this one murder. The guy he killed was a serious douchenozzle, and had himself just gotten done trying to kill a very hot barista. I'm not condoning extra-judicial executions in general, but in this particular case, I think the guy probably had it coming."

I'm really not sure what to say to that.

"Look," I say finally. "I don't know what you saw, or didn't see, or whatever, but I don't really want to talk about Dimitri right now."

"Yeah," says Gary. "Me neither. This is boring. How about some *SpaceLab*?"

The wallscreen blinks on. I need to head this off right away.

"No," I say quickly. "No *SpaceLab*. We actually need to talk about something important."

He raises one eyebrow.

"Important, huh? Fine then." He winks, and the wallscreen goes blank. "What can I do for you?"

I look at Tariq. He shakes his head. His face tells me clearly that he thinks I'm putting our lives in the hands of a lunatic. Apparently, I'm gonna have to be the spokesperson.

"Well," I say. "We have something that we need to get done, and I was thinking that either you or someone you know might be able to help us with it."

Gary laughs.

"Oh boy, I can't wait to hear this. Do you have any idea what I actually do?"

"We need you to crack a server, and remove some data from it."

"Huh." Gary scratches his head. "I guess you do know what I actually do. Okay. Whose server, how tight is their security, do they have cloud as well as local storage, and do you need the data extracted or just destroyed? Please answer these questions as accurately as possible, because my estimates are not binding, and if I wind up going over on either time or materials, you might end up with a really outrageous bill."

"We just need to have the data destroyed," says Tariq. "We do not need to retrieve it. And I am fairly certain the data are localized."

"Good," says Gary. "That makes things easier. Maybe you'll only need to sell one kidney each to pay for this. Whose server are we talking about?"

I look at Tariq. He shrugs.

"NatSec's," I say. "We need you to destroy whatever video the sentinel unit got of Elise in Hagerstown on Sunday afternoon."

Gary laughs again. He looks from me to Tariq, then back to me. We are not laughing. His smile fades.

"Get out," he says.

"Wait," I say. "We've actually got more resources available than you think. If you need to bring someone else in to get this done, we can afford that. This is really important."

Gary closes his eyes, rubs his face with both hands, and then pulls his dreads back into an awkward, greasy-looking ponytail.

"I bet it is," he says. "So are we giving up on the whole 'Tariq and his shiny ATV' story? Are you gonna tell me what really happened?"

I would like to say that Tariq still hasn't told me what really happened, but now is not the time.

"Tariq really did save Elise," I say. "How, exactly, isn't important. The point is, NatSec has video of Elise in Hagerstown, and they probably have at least some video of her getting out of Hagerstown. And if anyone notices that fact, they're going to come looking for her."

There's no humor at all in Gary's expression now.

"Yeah," he says. "You bet your ass they will. They'll come looking for her, and anyone who's had any interaction with her. Shit! I knew I was gonna wind up eating a crowbar over this somehow."

"None of us needs to eat a crowbar," Tariq says quickly. "If we destroy the data, all will be well."

Gary stares at Tariq silently for a moment.

"Sorry," he says finally. "I'm not great at reading people. I'm still trying to figure out if you're yanking my chain, or if you're just really, really stupid. I'm not sure if I mentioned this story earlier, but when all this started, one of my colleagues tapped twenty-some seconds of NatSec internal chatter. Just tapped, mind you, not destroyed. Even with that, I still have no idea how he managed it. Twelve hours later, NatSec agents were crawling all over his place, which fortunately for him he had already completely flash-burned. I like this house a lot, and do not have any wish to flash-burn it. Moreover, what you are asking is about three orders of magnitude more difficult than what Inchy did. I'm sorry, but it just can't be done."

Tariq looks like he's about to reply, but just then we hear footsteps at the bottom of the stairs. A woman who looks a lot like Elise walks into the room and looks around at us. She's wearing khaki shorts and a yellow polo shirt with the Green Goose logo over her ridiculously perky left breast, and a towel tied up around a mass of wet blonde hair. I can feel my stomach slowly twisting itself into a knot.

"You know," she says to Gary, "your roommate is kind of an ass."

"So true," he says. "Bar Floozie, I'm pleased to introduce you to Cave Lady and Evil Wizard. Cave Lady and Evil Wizard, this is Bar Floozie—another one of my endless string of uninvited house guests."

"Wow," she says. "So you're kind of an ass too. Nice to meet you two. I'm Charity. You're Gary's friends?"

"Sure," I say. "Let's go with that."

Charity takes a seat in the other recliner, and starts working the towel through her hair.

"Don't let me bother you," she says. "Just go on with what you were doing."

Tariq gives me a sad, pitying look, and I wonder how much he can read on my face. Gary suddenly looks almost gleeful.

"So," he says. "Where were we? You were trying to convince me to commit suicide, right?"

"That's a good idea," says Charity. "You're a burden on your friends and family. Is this a Hemlock Society thing?"

He shakes his head.

"No, more like a 'Charge of the Light Brigade' thing."

She grins.

"You mean they're trying to convince you to do something so monumentally stupid that it almost looks brave?"

Gary's eyes light up.

"Something like that. You a Tennyson fan?"

Charity lowers the towel and flips her hair back over her shoulders.

"Half a league, half a league, half a league onward. All in the valley of Death, rode the six hundred. My degree was in English literature."

"Ah," says Gary. "Hence the career in food and beverage delivery."

"Yeah, right." She gives her hair a final shake, and drapes the towel over the arm of the chair. "So really, what are we talking about?"

"We were actually talking about Anders," says Gary, "and what a fine hunk of meat he is."

"He's a fine hunk of something." Charity looks like she's bitten into something rotten. My stomach gives a hopeful flutter.

Sweet Jesus, I am a prepubescent girl.

I knock softly, wait a moment, and open the door. Anders is lying on his bed and staring at the ceiling with his fingers knitted behind his head.

"Hey," I say.

He shifts his eyes to me, then back to the ceiling.

"Terry," he says. "You are not who I expected to see."

"Yeah, I know."

I sit down with my back to him, on the edge of the bed. Thunder rumbles in the distance. It's been threatening rain all morning, but the streets are still dry.

"So," I say. "Charity seems nice. How did she wind up falling into your orbit?"

Anders sighs.

"She works at the Green Goose."

"So I gathered. Did you dump a drink on her, too?"

He laughs.

"Nah. I threw a sandwich at a guy who was trying to shoot her in the face."

I lean my head back, and roll my neck in a slow circle.

"Ah," I say. "I'd have slept with you if you'd done that for me."

He laughs.

"You slept with me anyway."

"So I did."

I look down at my hands. They're knotted around each other, clenching and un-clenching.

"Did she?" I ask finally.

"No," Anders says. "She did not."

Gary's laugh carries up from the living room. I left him introducing Charity and Tariq to the wonders of *SpaceLab*.

"Hey," says Anders. "Do you drink BrainBump?"

I turn my head to look at him. He actually looks concerned.

"What? No. I don't have any interest in corporate nanobots crawling around inside my brain."

He nods.

"What about Elise? Does she?"

I shake my head.

"Elise won't even eat GM corn. She wouldn't touch a can of BrainBump unless she was wearing a full-body condom."

"Huh."

His eyes slide away. I can almost see the wheels turning.

"Why are you asking about BrainBump? Did someone break into Gary's stash?"

"No," he says. "Just wondering."

Thunder rumbles again outside, and a sudden gust of wind rattles the window in its casement.

"Storm's coming," says Anders.

I smile.

"About time. This heat has been killing me."

His hand presses against the small of my back, then slides up to my shoulder. He pulls gently, then a little harder. I let him ease me back until I'm lying with my head on his belly and my feet on the floor.

"Look," he says. "About yesterday . . ."

I shake my head.

"Don't talk. It just gets you in trouble."

His hand still rests on my shoulder. I slide my own up, and twine my fingers with his. Lightning flashes outside the window, and thunder follows a second after, loud as a bomb in the street. A few drops of rain spatter against the window, then a few more, and then the sky opens up. The wind rises to a howl, and a wave of hailstones batters the side of the house. Anders' fingers tighten around mine. Gary is laughing again, and as the wind dies down I hear Charity join in.

"So," says Anders. "Why are you here?"

I shrug.

"I was in the neighborhood. Thought I'd stop by to say hello."

"Got it."

He brushes my hair back from my forehead with his free hand, and then slowly works his fingers down to the nape of my neck. I roll my head around again in a slow, lazy circle.

"You know I'm not a dog, right?" I ask after a while.

"Sorry," he says, and pulls his hand away.

I reach up and pull it back.

"I didn't say to stop."

The wind is rising again. The rain pounds on the roof above us, and the roar of the storm outside the window sounds like the end of the world.

12. ELISE

"So," says Aaliyah. "Was my brother right in his fears? Has meeting his mad sister caused you to regret your hasty decision to wed?"

I smile, raise my teacup to my lips and sip.

"Not yet," I say. "There's a very thin line between crazy and wise. I still haven't decided which side you're on."

She laughs. We're sitting across from each other at the table in the sitting room, with a pot of tea and a plate of sticky sweet rolls between us.

"You are too kind," she says. "If I am wise, it is only in the sense that the admission of ignorance is the beginning of wisdom. And even at that, I am less than sure."

"Tariq believes you are wise."

She shakes her head and bites into a roll.

"Tariq believes many things," she says. "Tariq believes you are fool enough to marry him. How does that speak to his judgment?"

"I would say it speaks well," I say. "I was fool enough to marry him before he saved my life."

She shakes her head again, chews and swallows.

"Perhaps," she says, and takes a sip of tea. "Tariq asked me not to speak to you of our faith, and I agreed that I would not. But he has left you here in my clutches, and we cannot speak clearly if you remain completely ignorant of all that is around you. And I cannot tolerate sharing my home with you if we cannot speak clearly."

She drains her cup, reaches for the pot and refills it.

"What you hear now, it cannot be unheard. You understand this?"

I nod. I've heard the sales pitches of missionaries before—Catholics, Jehovah's Witnesses, Scientologists—they always think what they say will change your world, but I've never been able to figure out what they're getting so worked up about.

"You say that Tariq saved your life," Aaliyah says, "but you cannot say how he might have done this. He has told you, but you do not believe him. Is this not so?"

I shrug.

"The story Tariq told us about what happened on Sunday makes no sense. There's no way he should have been able to get me out of Hagerstown once the NatSec cordon closed."

She smiles.

"No, that is not so. Tariq certainly had the ability to help you, and he could have explained to you how it was done. Why do you suppose he did not do so?"

I think about that for a moment.

"He's protecting me," I say. "He's always protecting me. Maybe he thinks that if I know what really happened on Sunday, it'll make me even more of a target for NatSec."

"You are partially correct," Aaliyah says. "Tariq is protecting you, but not from NatSec. Tariq is protecting you from me. He is protecting you from the faith."

It's later, and we're walking together through the neighborhood. Aaliyah made me leave my phone inside, but I'd guess it's a little before noon. It's hard to say exactly, because the sky is a thick, leaden gray, and the sun is nowhere to be seen. A cool, gusty wind is coming down from the north, and I'm pretty sure we're in for one of those crazy, sky-turns-green kind of storms.

"What I don't understand," I say, "is why you're so hesitant to explain things to me. Tariq told me that your faith is dying. Shouldn't you be trying to convince me to convert?"

There's a camera mounted on a pole at the corner. Aaliyah looks up at it, and the lens rotates away from us. She turns to look at me.

"Have you ever owned a dog?"

I smile.

"Sure, when I was young. He was a beagle. We called him Ajax."

"Was he happy?"

I have to think about that.

"Yes, I think so. He was a dog. What's not to be happy about?"

She nods.

"Did it bother him to know that he would live only a few years, that his whole life would barely span your childhood? Did it bother him to know that your father would have him put to sleep as soon as he became inconvenient to keep?"

I shake my head.

"That's not what happened. But even if it were, no, it wouldn't have bothered him. He was a dog. He didn't know anything about that."

"No," she says. "He did not. He knew that his belly was full, or that it was not. He knew that his ears were being scratched, or that they were not. This was enough for him. Is this not so?"

I shrug.

"I suppose so."

"A dog knows nothing of time, and a dog knows nothing of death. He lives in an eternal present, with no concern for what occurred yesterday, or for what will come tomorrow. This is the source of his happiness. If you could have told Ajax what the future had in store for him, would you have done so?"

I give her a long look. I have no idea where she's going with this.

"I didn't know what the future had in store for him," I say finally. "He got hit by a car when I was twelve."

Aaliyah sighs loudly.

"But if you had known, and could have told him, would you have done so?"

"No," I say. "Why would I do that?"

She nods again, as if I've just made her point.

"This is why Tariq asked me not to speak to you of the faith."

It takes a minute for that to sink in.

"So in this scenario, I am the dog?"

"Yes, Elise. You are the dog."

The clouds are darker now, and every few minutes, lightning flashes in the distance. The weather has chased us back to the porch. We sit together in wicker chairs, watching the storm roll in.

"What do you know," Aaliyah says, "of the history of our people?"

"Depends on what you mean," I say. "My people come from Norway. I'm guessing yours are from somewhere very different."

She shakes her head, and her eyes narrow.

"No," she says. "What you say is a mistake. We are all one people. All who are alive today are one people, though it was not always so. In the time of the mother-of-all, there were many peoples, and we were not the strongest. Our cousins spread across the breadth of the old world. Some were taller and swifter. Others were stronger and hardier. We huddled in one corner of Africa, few in number, and dwindling."

I remember this vaguely, from an anthropology class in college.

"Right," I say. "But then something happened. The Great Leap Forward."

"Yes," she says. "The Great Leap Forward. The Great Leap Forward was the faith."

"The faith was born in the Summer of Burning. That winter, the mother-of-all waited for the rains, but the rains did not come. For many years, the mother-of-all had lived with her people on the shores of a great lake. The lake gave fish and fresh water, and the forest gave roots and nuts, and the odd carcass if the spirits were generous. As the dry winter wore on, though, the great lake retreated, and the streams that fed it shrank and died. Then the winter ended, and the tall runners came in the night. They drove the people out of their homes and away from the lake, away from the forest—away from all that they had known.

"The mother-of-all led her people out onto the plains, away from the tall runners, and into the lands of the lion and the baboon. Without the great lake, it was hard for the people to find water, and when they did, there were hyenas and great cats and crocodiles to torment them. The summer turned toward fall, and still the rains did not come. Clouds brought lightning without rain, and the lightning set the plains afire.

"The flames drove the people out of the plains and into the mountains of the east. The higher slopes of the mountains were safe from the fire, and the streams still ran there, but the air was cold at night, and there was little to eat. The people spent their days searching fruitlessly for food, and their nights hugging their empty bellies and moaning.

"The mother-of-all looked out over her people and saw that they were dying. She went to the eldest and said 'What shall I do? My people are dying. We have not the claws of the lion, nor the jaws of the hyena. We have not the strength of the people of the north, nor the tireless speed of the tall runners. How are we to live?'

"The eldest pointed to the snows that capped the mountain, and said, 'Go seek the sleeping place of the Spirit of the Moon. Tell him that your children are dying. Perhaps he will take pity on us, and gift you with a way to save your people.'

"And so, the mother-of-all climbed the mountain. For two days, she climbed through grass and trees. For two days, she climbed over bare rocks. For two days, she climbed through ice and snow. She ate insects, and drank snow that she melted in her hands. Her belly shrank as she climbed, her cheeks hollowed, and her eyes sank deep into her face. The hairs fell from her head, and her teeth grew loose in her jaws and bloody. Finally, on the seventh night, she reached the cave at the top of the mountain where the Spirit of the Moon slept through the day. She remembered what the eldest had instructed her to do, but she was too proud to beg a gift of the Spirit of the Moon. She hid herself inside the entrance to the cave, and waited for him to arrive.

"That morning, when the Spirit of the Moon returned to his cave to sleep, the mother-of-all pounced on his back. She wrapped her skinny arms around his neck and her skinny legs around his waist, and drove him to the ground. 'Stop!' cried the Spirit of the Moon. 'Mother-of-all, why are you hurting me?' The mother-of-all twisted her arms tighter, and bit down on the Spirit of the Moon's ear. 'My people are dying,' she hissed. 'You must gift me with a way to save them.'

"The Spirit of the Moon was afraid, because he knew that there is nothing fiercer than a mother who sees her children about to die. But he was also angry that she had come into his house, and that she had come as a thief in the night rather than as a beggar. So he said to the mother-of-all, 'I can indeed gift you something that will save your children. But once I have given it to you, it cannot be given back.'

"The mother-of-all bit down harder on his ear, and said, 'Give it to me. Give me what I need to save my children, and I shall never give it back.' So the Spirit of the Moon reached into his purse and pulled out a certain mushroom. 'Eat this,' he said. 'Eat this, and you will see things as they truly are, not as you wish them to be. Then you will know what you must do to save your children.'

"The mother-of-all took the mushroom and ate it, but she did not release the Spirit of the Moon from her grip. 'Let me go,' he said. 'I have given you what you demanded.' But the mother-of-all would not let him go until she knew how she would save her children. Her stomach burned, and she thought that the Spirit of the Moon had poisoned her. She squeezed his neck with all her strength, determined that they should die together. But then she cried out, and her eyes were opened, and for the first time she saw the world as it truly was.

"She saw the world laid out before her, both inside and out. She saw the world as it was, as it had been, and as it would be. She saw the path that each of her children would walk. She saw each of her sons gasp out his first breath in fear, and she saw each of her sons gasp out his last breath in agony. She saw her own death growing inside her belly, and she saw how and when it would find her.

"To the Spirit of the Moon she said, 'You have tricked me! You promised me a way to save my children from dying!' But the Spirit of the Moon said, 'Can you not see now, mother-of-all? There is no way to save your children from dying. They are already dead, and always have been. If you go on as you are, their dying will be over in a few short generations, and you will be at peace. But look on, mother-of-all, and you will see how you can make their dying last for many thousands of generations. Your children will drive out the tall runners, and they will drive out the people of the north, until they fill up every corner of the Earth. And I will watch over you, and laugh at your misery for all the ages of the world.'

"And so the mother-of-all looked out again over the world. She saw a wild olive tree, but rather than the sweet fruit, she saw how a branch could be cut and carved just so, and another could be carved to fit against the first to allow a man to throw a spear with the strength of a giant. She saw a bed of reeds, and saw how they could be woven together and lined with bark, and used to carry her children to the far side of the great lake. She saw her children being born in greater and greater numbers.

"And then, she saw each of her children dying in agony, while the Spirit of the Moon looked on, and laughed."

"That's a nice story," I say. "But I'm pretty sure I've heard it before. Garden of Eden, right? Tree of knowledge? A lot of cultures have stories like this. What makes this one special?"

"True," says Aaliyah. "Many cultures have stories like mine. Many cultures also have stories of a great flood, like that of Noah. Do you know why that is?"

I shrug.

"I guess one builds off of the other. Someone makes up the first story, someone else hears it and adapts it to their own circumstances . . ."

She shakes her head.

"Many cultures have stories of a catastrophic flood, because many of the cultures in today's world were born in a time of catastrophic floods. At the end of the last cold time, the melting of the great ice sheets raised the level of the seas by hundreds of feet. In some places, the bursting of ice dams released oceans of water in a day and a night. What is now the Mediterranean Sea was once fertile land. Imagine leaving your village to hunt in the hills, and returning that evening to find an ocean. This is a story you would remember, and tell to your children."

The wind is rising now, steady from the west. Thunder rumbles closer, and a chill runs from the base of my spine to the back of my neck.

"Maybe," I say. "But your story isn't about a flood. Are you saying that there really was a tree of knowledge?"

"No," she says. "The story you read in your Bible is many, many thousands of years removed from the truth. There was no tree of knowledge."

I look over at her. She's grinning.

"So what's the point?" I ask.

"My point is this," Aaliyah says. "The story I have told you is not thousands of years removed from the truth. I learned it first in the mother tongue. The story I have told you *is* the truth."

The storm announces itself with a crack of thunder and a wave of wind-driven hail that slants in under the porch roof and clatters at our feet. Aaliyah has to shout to be heard over the burst of noise.

"I believe that it is time to return to the sitting room."

She stands and holds the door for me, then closes it behind us. The sudden silence as the door latches leaves my ears ringing.

"Be seated," she says. "I will join you in a moment."

I step into the sitting room, push a cushion against the wall and sit. I'm adjusting slowly to life with Aaliyah, but I do very deeply miss chairs.

The cushions are orange, yellow and red today. The colors make a cheery contrast to the weather. I pick up my phone from the table. I have no idea why I keep carrying it around with me. It hasn't worked since Tariq brought me here. This reminds me that I also have no idea what's been happening in the world for the past two days. I want to talk to Terry. I want to talk to Tariq.

"You must not," says Aaliyah.

I look up. She's seated across from me, with a pot of tea in her hands. Two cups sit on the table beside her.

"How do you do that?"

She smiles.

"Perhaps you will learn. This is what we must discuss now. But first, you must put aside any thought of leaving my home with that device in your hand."

I look down at the phone. No service. It's mocking me.

"Would it really be so bad?" I ask. "I just want to check the news, and maybe talk to my sister."

"Well," she says. "You know more of these things than I. Tariq tells me that there is an excellent chance that NatSec is trying to locate you right now. How long would it take them to do so once your phone returned to the network?"

And she's right. I do know this.

"You have no idea what it's like," I say, "being cut off like this."

"You are like an addict denied her drugs, are you not?"

I slide the phone across the table.

"It's probably best if you hold onto this."

She picks it up, and slips it into a pocket.

"So," she says. "I must ask you a question now. When you came here, I asked Tariq if you would convert. He forbade me to ask again. But he is not here, and I am not one to be forbidden. I have told you many truths today. I have taught you much about the world, and much about the faith. So now, I ask again. Will you convert?"

Her face is blank, but there's a tension in her fingers where they grip the teapot that I haven't seen before. I look down, then back up into her eyes.

"What would Tariq say?" I ask. "He's told me that he abandoned the faith. If I were to convert, would he abandon me?"

"No," she says. "Tariq has not abandoned the faith. This is something you must understand before deciding. Once the faith has been embraced, it cannot be abandoned, any more than a bell can be un-rung. This is as true for us now as it was for the mother-of-all. Tariq would no doubt be furious to know that we are speaking of this, but he will not leave you, no matter what you decide.

Her eyes are half closed now, and her finger traces tiny circles on the teapot's side.

"What would it take?" I ask after a long silence. "Are there rites and rituals? Is there a catechism to be learned?"

Aaliyah smiles.

"No," she says. "No robes, no rituals, no ceremonies. No tattoos or brands or sacrificing of animals."

She lifts the lid from the teapot, and carefully fills both cups to the rims. She slides one of them across the table.

"All you need do, is to accept the Gift of the Moon."

I reach out, and wrap my hand around the teacup. A wave of nausea rolls over me.

"Decide now," says Aaliyah. She lifts her cup to her lips, and drinks it down.

I lift the cup. The tea is thick and dark as molasses. It smells of an alkaline something, strong enough to sting my nose.

"You say this bell can't be unrung," I say. "But if it were possible to set the faith aside, would you do it?"

Aaliyah shrugs.

"You say your dog Ajax was happy. Would you trade the life you have now for his?"

I bring the cup to my lips, and drink.

First comes pain, a twisting knife in my gut that doubles me over. I clutch at my belly and gasp for air as my eyes lose focus and a rising roar fills my ears. This lasts for what seems like hours, like days, until the pain fades, and an electric tingle runs up my spine, then down my arms and legs and back again. I slowly push myself upright. Tears trickle down my cheeks, and from the spreading warmth in my crotch I'm guessing that either I'm bleeding out or I've wet myself.

I look down at my hands. They're strangely out of focus. I rub the tears from my eyes, blink them clear and look up at Aaliyah. She's smiling.

And then, like Saul on the road to Damascus, the scales fall away, and I see. I see the city laid out below me from ten thousand feet. At the same time, I see individual people going about their days, walking and talking and sitting and sleeping in parks and cars and offices and homes. All of this is background, but with a thought I focus in on one bit of imagery—a boy, maybe fifteen or sixteen, huddled in the doorway of a building on Light Street, waiting for the rain to ease up. And still, I can see Aaliyah watching me with a widening grin on her face.

I'm trying to understand how I'm processing all of that when what looks like a chat box on my phone pops up, floating in the air beside Aaliyah's head. At first it's just a blank white rectangle, but after a moment a message appears:

Sauron's Eye: <Welcome, Elise. We've been waiting for you.>

13. GARY

Charity is, as it turns out—aside from being a bar floozie who will traipse home after any idiot who happens to save her from a deranged gunman—a woman of refinement and good taste. She takes to *SpaceLab* like a booze hound to beer nuts, laughing at all the right places, and never giving me that 'what the hell are you watching' look that I've come to know so well.

Tariq, on the other hand, is a philistine. He perches on the edge of the couch and fidgets through the first three clips, never laughing, and occasionally trying to interrupt. I studiously ignore him.

Terry has been gone now for almost an hour. I'm honestly not sure what's going on with Anders. For the last year and a half at least, he's been in a committed relationship with his right hand. Now the world is ending, and suddenly he's got one woman in his bedroom and another who apparently would have been if he were slightly less of an idiot.

Not that I'm bitter, mind you.

The clip we're watching is a classic. The captain and Science Officer Scott spend the entire episode on the bridge, debating the pros and cons of being absorbed into a tentacled hive mind that's attached itself to the station. On the plus side, the captain points out that the hive mind takes care of all your excretory needs, and also that the only attractive woman on the station has already been absorbed. Science Officer Scott concedes the points, but counters that the hive mind handles excretions by recycling them back into your mouth, and that Communications Officer Keiko is much less attractive with a tentacle coming out of her ass. In the end, of course, both arguments are moot, because the captain puts his drink down on the self-destruct button and blows up the station.

"Wow," says Charity. "Where has this been my whole life?"

"*SpaceLab* is like the Grand Canyon, or the Mona Lisa," I say. "It's always been there, just waiting for you to discover it."

She giggles. I'm not ordinarily a fan of giggling, but Charity giggles with panache.

"Charity," says Tariq. "Perhaps now you might give us some privacy? Gary and I have important matters to discuss."

She breaks into a full laugh now, and I join in. Tariq

looks back and forth between us. His jaw is clenched, and if he were really an evil wizard, I'm pretty sure we'd both be toads.

"Gary," he says. "Please. Time is running short, and there is danger for you as well."

Charity looks at me, one eyebrow raised.

"Is this guy serious? Am I interrupting a secret mission?"

"Sort of," I say. "He wants me to break into NatSec's servers, and delete a video of his girlfriend being carried out of Hagerstown on the back of a giant bat."

"Gary—" says Tariq.

"Oh, cram it," I say. "We're not gonna do it, because, as I have already explained several times, it can't be done. Anyway, Charity's not NatSec. And even if she was, they can't drop a crowbar on you for fantasizing. Although, now that I think about it, they probably can drop a crowbar on you for knowing that your girlfriend got out of Hagerstown alive. Charity—you're not NatSec, are you?"

She laughs again. Her giggle is sweet, but she laughs like a hyena. I find it doesn't bother me, though, as long as I stay focused on what it does to her breasts.

"No," she says. "I'm not NatSec. I used to date a NatSec guy, though. Maybe he could help?"

"I do not think your ex-boyfriend will help us," says Tariq. "I suspect he might call in the crowbar Gary is so concerned about."

"You're probably right," she says. "He does love his crowbars. So I guess it's just us, huh?"

"Us?" I say.

"Sure. You let me in on your secret plans. Now you've got to let me help. Otherwise, I'll go tell my ex."

She's kidding. I think.

"Look," I say. "There are no plans here. For the third time, there is no way to do what Tariq wants to have done."

"Why not?"

I roll my eyes.

"Start with the fact that he wants to crack NatSec in the first place. Their budget is bigger than the GDP of Norway, and a big part of it goes to dataspace security."

"Pffft," says Charity. "That's just money. You're brilliant, right?"

I shrug.

"Yeah, that's true. However, all their data gets mirrored to their warm site in Chantilly. That's physically isolated from the public networks. The only way to get the data back out from there would be to insert a virtual agent into their external nets, and have it persist there long enough to be mirrored. They comb through their data very, very carefully before they mirror anything over. That's the part that I don't believe can be done."

Tariq is staring at the floor, his hands flexing rhythmically. He looks up.

"What if you had physical access to the server farm in the Chantilly facility?"

I laugh. Tariq meets my eyes without blinking.

"Wait," I say. "Are you serious?"

"I am," says Tariq. "If you had physical access to their servers, would you be able to do this?"

I take a moment to think about that.

"Well," I say finally. "Speaking hypothetically, if I had physical access to the servers, and some time to work with them without being shot or stabbed or anally electrocuted . . . yeah, I might have a shot at it. I'd want to talk to Inchy first, to see if he has any pointers on breaking their firewalls. If I could put some of his code into one of my cracker avatars, I'd give myself even odds of being able to pull it off."

"So," says Charity. "Are we a go on this?"

I laugh again.

"No, Charity. We are not a go. I think I mentioned that we were speaking hypothetically. Chantilly is the heart of the panopticon, and I am not a ninja. There is no possible way that I can get physical access to NatSec's server farm."

Tariq looks at Charity, then back at me.

"I can," he says.

Sir Munchalot: <Munch to Inchy. Come in, Inchy.>

Sir Munchalot: <Inch—you there? I need a consult, brother.>

Angry Irish Inch: <Hey Munch. Kinda busy at the moment. Is this a quick thing?>

Sir Munchalot: <Not sure. I've got some questions. If you've got easy answers, this could be quick. Otherwise, maybe not so much.>

Sir Munchalot: <Hello?>

Angry Irish Inch: <Sorry. I'm gonna be doing some serious multitasking, so please forgive the latency. I'll give you what I can.>

Sir Munchalot: <Many thanks. First—remember when you dropped that clip of NatSec chatter?>

Angry Irish Inch: <You mean the one that cost me my house? Yeah, I think I vaguely remember that.>

Sir Munchalot: <Great. So, uh . . . how, exactly, did you do that?>

Sir Munchalot: <It's okay if it takes a while to prepare a detailed response. I'll wait.>

Angry Irish Inch: <I did say I'm kinda busy, right? No time for goofing.>

Sir Munchalot: <Sir, you wound me. I need to know how you cracked their dataspace.>

Angry Irish Inch: <If you're suicidal, there's easier ways. Stick your head in a wood chipper, maybe.>

Sir Munchalot: <You're still alive, right?>

Angry Irish Inch: <No disrespect, Munchie, but you're not me.>

Sir Munchalot: <Granted. So assume that I'm just tired of life, and looking to go out in a blaze of whatever's the opposite of glory. How do I do it?>

Angry Irish Inch: <Depends. What, exactly, are you trying to accomplish?>

Sir Munchalot: <I need to delete a few minutes of video from one of their surveillance archives.>

Sir Munchalot: <Hello?>

Angry Irish Inch: <Sorry, Munch. Just processing. So you say you've suffered brain damage, and lost eighty IQ points?>

Sir Munchalot: <Yeah, that's about right. Assume we're not worried about the warm site. Just need to pull off what's theoretically accessible from the public networks.>

Angry Irish Inch: <Not worried about the fact that whatever you delete will get restored from Chantilly within twenty-four hours?>

Sir Munchalot: <Not at this time, no.>

Angry Irish Inch: <Well, given that, your solution is pretty easy.>

Sir Munchalot: <Well?>

Angry Irish Inch: <You subcontract the job to me.>

Sir Munchalot: <I thought you were out of the NatSec business?>

Angry Irish Inch: <I'll take precautions this time.>

Sir Munchalot: <Precautions?>

Angry Irish Inch: <I'll route everything through your systems.>

Sir Munchalot: <Excellent. Ask not for whom the crowbar tolls . . . >

Angry Irish Inch: <It tolls for thee.>

Sir Munchalot: <Perfect. I'll shoot you specs and a contract shortly. Now—how do I break the Chantilly servers?>

Angry Irish Inch: <???>

Sir Munchalot: <Speaking purely hypothetically, if I could get physical access to the server farm, how would I break their security?>

Angry Irish Inch: <With the understanding that, in the real world, this is not a possible thing?>

Sir Munchalot: <Right.>

Angry Irish Inch: <Given that, this is actually a much easier job than deleting something from their networked servers. They rely pretty heavily on physical security at Chantilly. All you'd really need is a set of fully authenticated NatSec credentials, with sufficiently high clearance to gain access.>

Sir Munchalot: <And I would get those where?>

Angry Irish Inch: <What is the source of all good things in your life, my friend?>

Sir Munchalot: <My best pal Inchy?>

Angry Irish Inch: <You know it, brother.>

"Before we go any farther," I say, "we should probably discuss payment terms."

"This is true," says Charity. "Gary needs to be able to pay his subcontractors."

"I only have one subcontractor," I say.

She looks confused.

"I thought you said you were getting help from one of your friends?"

I nod.

"Right. Inchy. That's my subcontractor."

"So am I a full partner, then?"

We're sitting around the breakfast table in the kitchen. Anders called in a pizza and four liters of soda after the storm quieted down, and we're passing around cups and slices.

"No," I say. "You are not a full partner. You're more of an unpaid intern."

She shakes her head.

"I don't think so. I've already provided you several valuable services."

"Such as?"

"Well, for starters, not having my ex-boyfriend come here and kill you all."

"She makes a good point," says Anders. "You should probably pay the lady."

Tariq scrapes the cheese off of his pizza, and leaves it in a greasy lump on his plate. Terry raises one eyebrow. Tariq shrugs. Terry picks up his cheese, and pops it into her mouth.

"I thought we had agreed that you have as much stake in this as we do," says Tariq.

"That may be," I say. "But as Charity says, I have to pay my subs. Also, I think my liability here is a lot smaller than yours. You need to erase any record that NatSec has of Elise being alive in Hagerstown on Sunday afternoon. I just need to make sure that there's no record that she was in my house. That's a much easier job. If you want me to focus on that and forget about the video, then I guess we can call it square."

Tariq scowls. Terry takes another slice of pizza.

"Fine," she says. "How much?"

"Well," I say, "that's partially dependent on how much Bar Floozie here intends to extort from me."

Charity shrugs.

"Five thousand?"

"Done," I say. "Inchy's gonna want more like twenty-five. Ordinarily I'd need something similar, but I'll credit you with the work I'd need to do to save my own ass. Forty grand total sounds about right. Does that work for you two?"

Terry looks at Tariq. He leans back in his chair and sighs.

"I think we have little leverage to negotiate," he says. "If this is your price, then we will pay it."

"Excellent," I say. "Make the transfer, and I'm on the job."

"Wait," says Terry. "You're expecting us to pay in advance?"

"Well, yeah," I say. "Tariq's apparently going to break into the most secure facility in North America. I'm pretty sure if I don't get my money up front, I'm not going to get it at all."

"He also makes a good point," says Anders.

Terry shoots him a poisonous look.

"Shut up, Anders."

Anders grins. I glance at Charity. She catches my eye and winks.

"Okay," she says. "Are we a go now?"

"Yes," I say. "I believe we are a go."

My fabber has just spit out a pass card that Inchy assures me is NatSec coded and keyed to Tariq's biometrics, when a chat frame pops up in my field of view.

Argyle Dragon: <Heads up, gentlemen. We've got a second strike. Reliable sources tell me Portland just got hit.>

Drew P. Wiener: <Yeah, I'm seeing the same thing. Nothing on the public feeds yet, though.>

Fenrir: <Check this—must've gotten out just before the communications cordon dropped:>

It's an audio file. I blink to stream.

"To anyone who can hear this: My name is Robert Barrow. I'm in Portland, Oregon. Whatever happened in Hagerstown on Sunday—it's happening here. People are dying, choking on blood . . . But listen—it's not everyone. It's not even most people. I'm fine. My wife, my daughter—they're fine. We're at a ball game right now. A bunch of the people in the stands are dead or dying, but at least half are okay. I'm sure NatSec is going to say we're all dead and they have to do what they did to Hagerstown. For God's sake, don't let them. This will be redacted as soon as they figure out what's going on, so please, repost if you can. We need your help. My daughter—she's six years old. She needs your help. Please. Don't let them burn us."

Hayley 9000: <Heavy. What do?>

Fenrir: <Dunno. Dump it through your private feeds, I guess. He's right. NatSec is going to push for another burn. If half the population of Portland is still kicking, we really shouldn't let that happen.>

Argyle Dragon: <Fifty percent fatality is still enough for a national soft kill if this thing gets loose.>

Fenrir: <We've been through this. Don't know what this is, but it's definitely not a virus.>

Drew P. Wiener: <Portland's a hub for the Un-Altered, right?>

Hayley 9000: <Yeah. So?>

Drew P. Wiener: <So, unofficial estimates for kill rate in Hagerstown were around ninety percent. Hagerstown had a very high concentration of Engineered and Augmented. Portland does not, and it sounds like their kill rate is a lot lower.>

Fenrir: <So we're back to the kill switch hypothesis?>

Drew P. Wiener: <This kinda pushes us in that direction, doesn't it?>

A second frame pops open. I blink the first one closed.

Angry Irish Inch: <Is everything ready on your end?>

Sir Munchalot: <Pretty much. I've got the pass card. I've got a search-and-destroy avatar loaded onto a data pin. All I need to do now is show my Evil Wizard friend how to use them.>

Angry Irish Inch: <Tell him to be quick. Those credentials are probably only going to hold until the first time the guy who actually owns them makes a data request.>

Sir Munchalot: <Understood. I'll ask him not to dillydally.>

Angry Irish Inch: <Good. If you're really going to do this, you should do it in the next hour. NatSec is going to be very distracted. I'm beginning my penetration now.>

Sir Munchalot: <Hey—just out of curiosity, whose credentials are these?>

Angry Irish Inch: <Is there a reason why you should care?>

Sir Munchalot: <Am I correct in thinking that whoever it is will be on a burn list by the time this all shakes out?>

Angry Irish Inch: <Probably. Again, though, not sure why you should care. I wasn't

aware that you had a lot of NatSec operatives on your friends and family list.>

Sir Munchalot: <There's a lot of things you don't know about me.>

Angry Irish Inch: <No, Munch. There aren't.>

Sir Munchalot: <Fine. So give me a name. If someone challenges Tariq, maybe knowing what his name is supposed to be will keep him un-shot.>

Angry Irish Inch: <I doubt it. The name attached to the credentials is Dimitri Yakovenko. He's a local, known to many of the personnel at Chantilly. If your friend runs into a human during the course of this fiasco, he's probably screwed.>

Sir Munchalot: <Huh. I'll make sure to point that out to him.>

Angry Irish Inch: <You do that. Good hunting, Munch.>

Sir Munchalot: <Yeah. Good hunting, Inch.>

I blink the second window closed.

"Well?"

I look around. Terry is standing behind me with her arms crossed. Anders, Tariq, and Charity are in the hallway, crowded around the door.

"Well," I say. "First, what are you doing in my room? I told you to wait downstairs. Second, Portland just got whacked, so the time to jump is now."

"Wait," says Anders. "Portland, Oregon? You mean like Hagerstown?"

"Looks like it. Whatever's happening out there, it's going to keep NatSec busy for a while."

I catch Terry's eye. A faint twinge of guilt tickles the base of my skull.

"Hey, Terry?" I start, then trail off. She raises one eyebrow in question. Anders and Tariq turn to look at me as well.

"Got something to say?" Anders asks.

"Yeah," I say. "Sort of. How tight are you and Dimitri, exactly?"

She shrugs.

"I dunno. Kind of? We're friends, that's all."

"Right," I say. "Friends, but not family. So if you had to pick somebody to get an ice pick in the back of the skull, and your only choices were Dimitri and Elise, you'd definitely pick Dimitri, right?"

They're all staring at me now.

"Gary," Anders says. "Is there a point to this?"

I look at Anders, then Terry, then back at Anders. Probably best to let this go.

"No," I say. "No point."

I walk out into the hall. Terry trails after me. She looks vaguely unhappy, but she doesn't pursue the question. I hand the pass card to Tariq.

"This and your retina will open doors, and ought to log you into any systems that the real owner is authorized for. However, if a human cross-checks your identity, he will almost certainly not be fooled."

For the first time, Tariq looks worried.

"Is there a heavy human presence at Chantilly?"

I shake my head.

"No. The security there is almost entirely automated. They've got avatar-run visual surveillance of pretty much every square inch of the facility, but I'm assuming you'll be able to wizard that, right?"

Tariq doesn't look as confident now as he did before. I hand him the data pin.

"Upload what's on this onto any machine in the server farm. My avatar will do the rest. Understand?"

He nods. I look at Anders. Anders looks at Tariq. Terry clears her throat. Finally, Charity speaks.

"So what happens now? Does he just disappear in a puff of smoke? I've never seen a wizard in action."

"No," I say. "I'm pretty sure that now he rides away on his magical ATV. Right, Tariq?"

He nods again, and starts down the stairs.

"So," says Anders. "Anybody for a gin and tonic while we wait?"

We're back in the living room—Anders and Terry together on the couch, Charity in one recliner and me in the other. Turns out we don't have either gin or tonic, but we do have rum and grape soda, so everyone's more or less happy. There's nothing about Portland yet on the official newsfeeds, but a few of the less-clueless private channels are starting to buzz.

"So Anders," I say. "How's Doug's super-top-secret

project going? Have you discovered a new form of porn? Hippo on wildebeest, maybe?"

"Nah," he says. "Turns out the whole file's just a really elaborate knock-knock joke."

"I thought you said it was the secret formula for BrainBump," says Charity.

Anders rolls his eyes.

"Having trouble with the whole 'super-top-secret' concept, huh, Charity?"

"Oh please," she says. "You said what it was right in front of me. If you can tell the bar slut, I assume you can tell your roommate, who was probably monitoring you the whole time anyway, right?"

"It's bar floozie," I say. "You'd need to sleep with at least one of us to qualify as a bar slut."

"Give me time," she says.

My heart skips a beat.

"Actually, I didn't," says Anders.

"Didn't what?" I ask.

"Didn't say that Doug's files were design configurations for the BrainBump nanos. I said that to Doug. Charity had already left the room."

Charity catches my eye and mouths 'sorry.' Anders is staring me down.

"Fine," I say. "I might have been duping everything you said and did to the living-room wallscreen. You were working through my systems. Shouldn't I have the right to know if you were doing something that was gonna bring a crowbar down on my head?"

The muscles in Anders' jaw are bulging in a tooth-cracking kind of way.

"Anyway," he says finally. "Yeah, I'm pretty sure the file Doug gave me is the design specs for the nanos in BrainBump—but there's something else there as well, and I'm not sure what it is. I've got some suspicions, but I need access to a Siemens fabricator to test them out."

"What kind of suspicions?" I ask. There's an unpleasant tingling in the pit of my stomach. I've probably drunk more BrainBump over the last ten years than anyone else in North America. I've put away three cans of it just today.

"Look," he says. "There's no point in getting worked up about it until I get a chance to run the files through an actual fab unit."

A bead of sweat runs down my forehead. I really don't like where this is going.

"Actually, I'm getting kind of worked up already," I say. "Why don't you tell me what you're thinking, pal?"

He looks at Terry, and then Charity, and then me.

"Well," he says. "You know we've been talking about what happened in Hagerstown, right?"

The tingle in my stomach turns into a sharp, stabbing pain. Anders goes on.

"Nobody's been able to come up with an explanation that makes any sense. Your guys said the same thing, right, Gary? A virus or a toxin wouldn't be able to act against so many people over that big of an area at exactly the same time. The only idea that came close was the one the UnAltered were floating—the kill switch."

"Right," says Terry. "But the kill rate was too high for it to be just Engineered and Augmented, even in Hagerstown . . ."

"But everybody in Hagerstown drinks BrainBump," says Charity.

"If I had to guess," says Anders, "I'd say probably about ninety percent of them, anyway."

Everyone is looking at me.

"So you think somebody snuck poison into the BrainBump production line?" Terry asks. "That doesn't make sense either, does it? I mean, wouldn't Gary be dead by now?"

And with that my stomach heaves, spewing pizza and grape soda and rum all over my hardwood floor.

They're all yelling and jumping up and generally making asses of themselves, when a chat frame pops into my field of view.

Angry Irish Inch: <Gary. Get out of the house.>
Sir Munchalot: <Inch? What?>

He called me Gary. Fuck me.

Angry Irish Inch: <No time, Gary. Get out of the house, now. You have forty seconds.>

A timer shows up in my left eye and starts counting backward from forty. I blink the chat frame closed and lurch to my feet.

"Whoa there," says Terry. "Easy, boy."

"Shut up," I say, and spit out a glob of something vile. "Out. Now."

I start for the door.

"What the hell?" Anders yells after me.

"There's a crowbar inbound," I yell back. I'm already at the door. "We've got thirty seconds."

I stumble out the door, down the steps and into the street. First Charity, then Anders and Terry together follow after. I duck into the space between the abandoned building across the way and the half-collapsed garage that sits beside it, drop to my knees and look back. The others pile in after me. It's not raining anymore, but the clouds are still thick and black, and I'm kneeling in a sticky mix of mud and soaked-through garbage. The timer Inch started in my ocular is at sixteen . . . fifteen . . . fourteen . . . My front door hangs open, and the two windows above it stare back at me like accusing eyes. Sorry, old buddy. Three . . . two . . . one . . . zero.

A blinding streak of light connects the peak of my roof to the roiling clouds. I duck down and cover my head with both arms as the shock wave and the thunderclap break over me at the same time. A chunk of something woody slams into my crossed forearms and throws me back into Charity. When I blink my eyes clear, she's somehow wound up on top of me.

"So," I say. "Was that your ex?" My ears are ringing, and I can barely hear myself speak.

"Maybe," she says. "I did mention that he loves his crowbars."

She rolls off of me, and I lever myself back up to my knees. My house is a crater, and the places on either side are half smashed and leaning away. The place behind did a little better, but I guess they'll be making a call to Crack Dealer Mutual in the morning as well.

"They'll have ground units here pretty quickly," says Terry. "I think we need to move."

14. ANDERS

"I'll give you this much," I say to Gary as he pokes his head out of the alley on Thirtieth and looks around. "You're taking the destruction of all of your worldly possessions like a man."

He gestures us forward, steps out onto the sidewalk, and heads west at a brisk clip.

"Trust me," he says. "If that had been all of my worldly possessions, I would be rolling around on the ground, kicking my feet in the air, and screaming like a colicky baby. The occasional burn-down is part of the cost of doing business. You'd like it to be a little more controlled than that, of course, but hey."

"Huh," I say. "That's good to know, I guess. The thing is, though . . . that actually was all of *my* worldly possessions."

He looks back at me, one eyebrow raised.

"Seriously? You don't have a bolt-hole?"

"No, Gary. I do not have a bolt-hole."

He glances up and keeps moving.

"You do know what I do for a living, right? This is the second time someone's tried to drop a crowbar on me, and I had to do a self-burn one other time because somebody's security avatar managed to back-trace me all the way to my home system. How could you not have a bolt-hole?"

"If it makes you feel any better," says Terry, "I don't have a bolt-hole either."

"Neither do I," says Charity. "Then again, I don't live with a jacker."

"I lived in that house for four years," I say. "Never once did Gary say anything about keeping my family photos somewhere less likely to explode."

"I didn't tell you to brush your teeth every morning either," he says. "I'm not your mom, you know."

North Charles is a block ahead now. There's something going on up there. A man sprints across the street, moving south to north; then a woman follows a few seconds later. Another running man comes into view as we move closer. He stops in the middle of the intersection of Charles and Thirtieth, turns, and throws something back the way he came. A second later there's a muffled bang, and he starts running again, straight down the middle of the street toward us. Gary stops walking.

"I think we may have a problem," he says.

His words are still hanging in the air like a speech bubble in a cartoon when a wave of people surges up

Charles from the south, and what had been a sort of background roar differentiates itself into a mass of screaming voices. Most of the people keep moving north, but a fair number of them follow the rock thrower, who's almost reached us by now.

"And now come the riot police," says Charity.

On cue, the first black helmets come into view. Shortly after that, a half dozen canisters come arcing toward us. The first of them actually hits the rock thrower in the back of the head, and he goes down screaming as a thick white mist of tear gas sprays out around him.

"I think we're headed the wrong way," says Terry. She turns and starts back down Thirtieth at a jog.

"No," says Gary. "This is my bug-out route. We can't go back that way."

"Come on," I say. "We can circle around a few blocks and come back at it from the west."

"No," says Charity. "He means that he's disabled all the stationary surveillance along this route. If we deviate, we'll be visible to NatSec tracking."

"Thank you," Gary says. "It's like you're the only one who speaks English today."

I look back and forth between them. Terry's stopped in front of the alley we just came from.

"Honestly," I say, "I don't think we've got a lot of choice here."

The wave of rioters breaks over us then, along with the tear gas. Gary doubles over coughing at the first whiff, then gets knocked on his ass as a woman with snot pouring out of her nose and eyes plows into him. Charity steps around him and plants her feet. A fat, bearded guy in a soaking wet flannel shirt stumbles toward her. She dips her shoulder and swings a forearm, and he staggers backward and falls across the sidewalk. Another man running full-out trips over the fat guy and skids on his face almost to Charity's feet. My eyes are tearing up now. I turn away as Terry grabs my sleeve and pulls me back the way we came.

I've never done the running of the bulls in Pamplona, but I'm guessing the next five minutes are a pretty close approximation. I'm half blind and coughing, trying to keep one hand on Terry while running through a mass of screaming rioters and masked and goggled riot police. A few times I have to shove rioters away when they try to grab hold of me, and at one point a cop takes a swing at me with his nightstick. I sidestep the blow and smash the front of his gas mask in with the heel of my hand, then turn and keep running. After what seems like forever, Terry pulls me down a side street and into the space between two rowhouses. One man runs past in the street, then another a few seconds later. The roar of the riot seems to be moving away. I drop into a crouch and cough out a thick, green wad of mucus. Terry vomits against the wall behind us, falls to her knees and leans forward, gasping.

I sit down, then settle back against a garbage can as my breathing slows and my vision clears. Terry coughs twice, turns her head to the side and spits. I lean my head back and sigh.

"We have the best times together, don't we, honey?"

She looks up at me and starts to laugh, but it turns into a coughing fit that ends in dry heaves.

"Sorry," I say. "Didn't mean to finish you off."

"That's okay," she says when she can breathe again. "Somebody needed to put me out of my misery."

She crawls over next to me, sits back against the can and pulls my arm around her shoulders.

"Anyway, you're right," she says. "We do have the best times."

It's maybe twenty minutes later when Terry stands and pulls me to my feet. The riot seems to have either died down or moved on, and we haven't heard any screaming in a while.

"So," she says. "What's the plan now?"

"That's a good question," I say. "We can't really go to my place, so . . ."

"Yeah, I don't think my apartment is a good choice right now either."

"Why? Does it explode a lot?"

"Not recently," she says, "but I've got a feeling that might change. You remember Dimitri?"

"Dimitri?" I ask. "You mean the guy who showed up at my house looking for me on Sunday morning, and who I later saw killing a man in the street outside the Green Goose? Yeah, I'm pretty sure I remember him."

She nods.

"He's NatSec."

"Yeah," I say. "After the whole cold-blooded murder thing, I pretty much assumed he was either NatSec or the Ukrainian Mafia."

She looks confused.

"Ukrainian Mafia? Is that a thing?"

I sigh, and try to rub the burn out of my eyes. It just makes them worse.

"I have no idea, Terry. Unlike you, I don't have any connections in killing-people circles. I'm starting to think that puts me in a distinct minority around here, though. Just for my own information, does every woman in Baltimore have a NatSec ex-boyfriend?"

She scowls. I'm guessing this is a sensitive topic.

"Dimitri is not my ex-boyfriend," she says. "He's been asking about whether I have a sister, though, so I kind of suspect he's aware of what happened with Elise on Sunday afternoon. He's also obviously aware that you and I are . . ."

"Mixed up together?"

"Right. Mixed up together. And since NatSec just blew up your house . . ."

"Gary's house," I say. "I just lived there."

She shakes her head.

"Actually, I'm pretty sure that if you did a search you'd see that you're the only one who was living there. I doubt Gary leaves much of a footprint."

I open my mouth to argue, and then close it again. She's probably right. Gary has a bolt-hole. And a bug-out route. And a chain lock and deadbolt, and no electronics on his front door. I can't believe I lived with a cracker for four years, and never thought about any of this.

"Fine," I say finally. "I'm an idiot, and NatSec is probably currently blaming me for every crime Gary has committed over the last four years, but back up a minute. If Dimitri isn't your ex-boyfriend, what is he? Brother? Cousin? Pet bear?"

She shakes her head.

"He's just a friend."

"The kind of friend who you suspect might be willing to call in an orbital strike on you?"

She looks down, then away.

"Yeah, that kind."

"Where, exactly, do you go to meet friends like that? Is there a club somewhere?"

"Not exactly," she says. "I met him in a support group."

I wait for the punch line, but there isn't one coming. Apparently, she's serious.

"A support group?" I ask. "Like Alcoholics Anonymous? I didn't think NatSec was cool with hiring people with substance-abuse problems."

She shakes her head again. She's not smiling.

"It wasn't Alcoholics Anonymous. It was a grief support group—for people who've lost their partners."

Oops.

"No," she says. "Don't get that way. Mark died three years ago. It was tough for a while, but I'm fine now. Dimitri lost someone at about the same time—her name was Saria—and honestly, he was much more messed up about it than I was. Apparently, she just disappeared. He wasn't even sure if she was dead or alive. He was a wreck, and so was I. We helped each other through it. That's all."

"Huh. And you don't think your grief counseling earned you enough chits with him to keep him from dropping a crowbar on your house?"

She shrugs.

"Maybe. I don't know that I want to find out."

"Okay," I say finally. "So where does that leave us? We could try to get to Doug's place, but it's a good three miles from here, and we'd be subject to surveillance pretty much the whole way."

"What about Gary's bolt-hole?"

I sigh again. She hasn't been paying attention.

"I know this is surprising," I say, "but Gary never confided the location of his bolt-hole to me. Or its existence, actually."

"Do you have any way to contact him?"

I shake my head.

"I left my phone in the house. I assume you did too?"

She nods.

"Probably for the best, actually," I say. "I'm pretty sure NatSec can trace your phone location if they want to. So where does that leave us?"

Terry's jaw drops open and her eyes go wide. A hand touches my shoulder, and I spin fast enough to pop something in my neck. Elise is standing behind me. She jumps back, and raises both hands in surrender.

"Ow!" I say. "Elise? What the hell?"

"Sorry," she says. "I didn't mean to startle you, but I think you need to come with me now."

I look at Terry. Her jaw is still hanging open.

"Elise?" Terry says. "Where did you come from?"

"There," she says, and points to a white cargo van parked across the street. "I'm here to help you. Come with me."

She reaches out to me. I look at Terry. She raises one eyebrow and shrugs. Elise is smiling. I take her hand.

"How did you find us?" Terry asks. "I wasn't even sure you were still alive."

"Honestly," says Elise, "I'm not one-hundred-percent clear on that myself. You really need to talk to Aaliyah."

The van is dirty on the outside and worse on the inside, with dark-tinted windows and three rows of seats.

"Really?" Terry says. "A child-stealer van?"

"Sure," says Elise. "I've got a basket full of candy and puppies in the back. Wanna see?"

She climbs into the driver's seat. Terry waves me into the front passenger seat and then climbs in the back. Elise backs up, swings around, and pulls out onto the garbage-strewn street.

"The tinted windows won't help us," I say. "We're way off Gary's bug-out route. NatSec must have a bead on us by now."

"I don't think so," says Elise. "I'm pretty sure they can't see me."

"What do you mean?" Terry asks. "You think you're ghosted?"

Elise shrugs.

"Is that the word for it?"

"Tariq blanked my building's security," Terry says. "Are you saying you can do that too? To the entire panopticon? Even to NatSec assets?"

"I don't know," Elise says, "but do you see anyone chasing us?"

There's a long moment of silence. Finally I turn to look at her.

"Is that how you got out of Hagerstown?"

"Maybe," Elise says. "I mean, it seems likely—but I honestly can't remember anything between Tariq tackling me, and saying hello to Gary on your front stoop."

Terry leans forward between the front seats.

"Have you always been able to do this? I don't ever remember you evading government surveillance when we were kids."

Elise shakes her head and laughs.

"Oh, no. This just started earlier this afternoon, actually."

"Fine," I say. "You can move without being seen. That still doesn't explain how you found us."

"I saw you," Elise says. "I thought about Terry, and I saw where you were. I don't know how it works. It's just something I can do now."

"This explains why Tariq thought he could get into Chantilly," says Terry.

"Let's stay focused," I say. "You said this just started this afternoon. Did anything unusual happen around that time? Something involving a fairy godmother, maybe?"

"Actually, yes," says Elise. "I accepted the Gift of the Moon."

I look at Terry. She looks at me.

"The Gift of the Moon?" I say.

"That's what Aaliyah called it. I thought at first it was just a really trippy drug, with the visions and everything. But you guys were really right where I saw you would be, and you're really here now, right?"

"That was an actual question," she says after a pause. "You are really here, right?"

"Yes, Elise," says Terry. "We're really here."

"Of course, if this were a hallucination, you'd say that anyway, wouldn't you?"

Aaliyah meets us on the porch of her home.

"So," she says. "These are friends of yours, and friends of Tariq?"

Elise takes our hands.

"This is my sister, Terry, and her friend Anders," she says. "They helped me after Hagerstown. We need to help them now."

"I see," says Aaliyah. "Well, come in, I suppose." She pulls open the screen door and waves us in.

"Wait," says Elise. "Neither of you have critical implants, do you?"

Terry shakes her head.

"No," I say. "I don't even have an ocular. Why?"

"Because networked electronics won't work once the door closes behind you. Tariq said the entire house is a Faraday cage."

I glance at the windows. Yeah—there's the wire mesh.

"That's pretty hard-core," I say. "Any particular reason for it?"

"It's kind of a religious thing," says Elise. "Aaliyah can explain if she wants to."

"She does not," says Aaliyah. She scowls and waves again at the door. I duck my head sheepishly and step inside.

The ambiance inside is a weird amalgam of *1001 Arabian Nights* and a low-budget slasher film. The dim blue lighting, the dark, mysterious hallway, the couldn't-call-for-help-if-you-wanted-to network isolation—it all seems designed to put me on edge. Elise gestures us into the sitting room, and I wind up awkwardly perched on a cushion against the far wall. Terry sits down next to me, and Elise and Aaliyah sit side by side at a low wooden table.

"Welcome to my home," says Aaliyah. "Elise tells me you have had a difficult afternoon. I have little enough here, but what I have I will share. Would you like tea?"

"Tea would be wonderful," says Terry. "Thank you so much."

Aaliyah rises with a nod, and glides silently out of the room.

"Okay," says Terry as soon as she's gone. "Seriously, Elise. Spill. What the hell is going on here?"

Elise sighs.

"Look, it's a really long story, but the bottom line is that as of this afternoon I'm a member of a religion that seems to mostly revolve around drinking tea, but also involves a certain amount of seeing that which is hidden, and moving through the blank spaces. Aaliyah is also a member, obviously. I actually get the feeling she's sort of the high priestess, but she hasn't really said. Tariq used to be involved, but I think he resigned somehow. The Faraday cage thing is part of the religion, and I think maybe the lighting is too—although that may just be cheaping out on the power bill. I'm not sure."

I look at Terry, then back at Elise.

"Yeah," Elise says after a moment. "That sounds just as crazy to me as it does to you when I say it out loud, but there it is. When I close my eyes, I can see things. I saw you getting pulled along in that wave of people. I saw you duck down the side street and into the alley. And when I went there, you were right where I saw you were."

"Huh," I say. "Did you see what happened to Gary?"

"No," she says. "I never saw Gary. I just saw you and Terry together in the middle of that mob."

"And you didn't see what happened to us before that?"

"No," she says. "It took me a while to find you. Gary wasn't with you."

I nod.

"Right. Can you see my house? I mean right now. Can you see what's going on there?"

She shakes her head.

"I can't see anything when I'm here unless Aaliyah helps me. I have to go outside. Aaliyah says this house is a refuge, that this is the one place where the outside can't get into our heads. I can't see out from here unless she opens the way."

Aaliyah returns with a pot of tea and four cups on a polished wooden platter. She sets the platter on the table, then lowers herself onto a cushion and pours the tea. Elise gestures us over. We join them at the table, and Aaliyah hands us each a cup. I sip. It's bitter, with just a hint of sweetness in the aftertaste.

"Thank you," says Terry. "You're very kind."

"You are most welcome," Aaliyah says. "I am happy to see that Elise's sister is as well mannered as she."

I take another sip. Elise and Terry are staring at me.

"Oh, right." I say. "Thank you, Aaliyah. The tea is delicious."

"Yes," Aaliyah says, and then turns to Elise. "So, my soon-to-be sister. How much have you told our friends of what they have seen today?"

"Nothing," Elise says. "Well, not much, anyway. I mean, I don't know much to tell yet, do I?"

"No," Aaliyah says. "I do not suppose you do." She looks at me now. "I imagine you have questions?"

"A few," I say. "Let's start simply. How are you tapping the panopticon?"

Her face goes blank.

"It's pretty obvious," I say. "Elise says she has visions, but not when she's in this house—because this place is a Faraday cage, and whatever electronics you're using can't access the networks. The bit about you opening the way threw me for a second, but I'm guessing you've got a limited-access back door, right? Elise was able to see us when we were getting pushed down Thirtieth this afternoon, but not before—because we were on Gary's bug-out route, and he's blinded the panopticon there. I can see what you're doing. I just don't know how."

All three of them are staring at me.

"How would you feel," Aaliyah says finally, "if I were to come into your home, accept your hospitality, and then blithely announce that the Miracle of the Wedding at Cana was a parlor trick, performed by misdirection and a switching of jugs?"

I shrug.

"I'd agree with you, actually. I'm much more a fan of the Jefferson Bible than the original."

"Get out," she says.

"Aaliyah, please," says Elise. "Anders didn't mean—"

"No," says Aaliyah. "This I cannot tolerate. You and your sister may stay, but this misbegotten chimera must leave this place."

"Misbegotten chimera?" Terry says. "Fuck you. Elise, are you hearing this?"

"Please," Elise says again. "Can't everyone just—"

Aaliyah stands in one smooth motion.

"I should never have allowed these Altered creatures into my home. Both of you must leave now, and never return."

Terry's on her feet now. "Both of you must leave now, and never return," she singsongs in a high, whiny voice. "Get over yourself, you self-important bitch."

"Well," I say as I stand. "It's been lovely, but we really must be going."

Aaliyah's glare is withering. Elise stands, and follows us to the door.

"By the way," Terry says as she steps onto the porch. "Your tea sucks."

"Out!" Aaliyah screams. "Out!"

I follow Terry onto the porch, and the door slams shut behind us. It's not raining now, but a hard west wind is blowing, and more dark clouds are gathered on the horizon.

"So," I say. "What now?"

"Dunno," says Terry. "Do you think Sauron's Eye is looking for us? If so, we probably shouldn't leave the porch."

I shrug.

"I don't know if she's watching for you, but that was my house they blew up. She'll definitely be looking for me."

We sit on the front steps. I'm almost tired enough to just wait for NatSec to come and get us. I'm actually starting to drift off when I catch the rattle of a very poorly tuned internal combustion engine coming up the street. A broken-down taxi with black-tinted windows slows in front of the house, hesitates, and then pulls into the driveway.

"Did you call that?" Terry asks.

I shake my head. The taxi honks its horn twice, with a sound like a dying goose. I take a hesitant step toward the driveway. The front driver's-side window on the cab slowly rolls down, and a grizzled old man wearing a fedora and what look like actual corrective-lens glasses looks out at us.

"Get in," he says. "Elise says she's sorry about Aaliyah, and that you're paid up for wherever you want to go."

15. TERRY

Anders gives the driver an address on Buckingham Road. The driver takes off his hat, scratches his scalp, and puts it back on.

"That's off of Falls, right?"

"Right," says Anders. "Just up from the Northern Parkway."

"No GPS?" I say.

The driver laughs.

"Folks who call me generally don't want anything in the car that can be back-traced, ma'am."

Right. I keep forgetting that I'm a rat in the walls.

"So is this my life now?" I ask. "Are we fugitives from justice?"

Anders shrugs.

"I doubt it. You and I haven't actually done anything wrong, you know—nothing that we could be charged with in open court, anyway. Things are crazy right now, but I'd guess that once this all settles out, we should be okay. That's assuming we stay alive and un-apprehended until then, of course."

I sigh and sink back into the cracked leather seat.

"Of course. And how long do you think the whole settling-out thing will take? I've got plants to water, you know."

He leans his head against the window and closes his eyes.

"Dunno. Somewhere between a couple of days and forever?"

The cab pulls up in front of a nondescript, off-white suburban tract house: standard quarter-acre lot, standard tree in the un-mowed front yard, standard ten-year-old sedan in the standard asphalt driveway.

"So, we're covered?" Anders asks the driver.

"You're covered," he says. "You two seem like very nice criminals. Good luck evading the authorities."

"Thanks," says Anders. He steps out to the curb, then reaches in and helps me out. I close the door, and the cab coughs once and pulls away.

"So where are we?" I ask. I don't see any cameras around, but I don't see any skull-shaped volcanoes, either. This doesn't look much like a secret lair.

"Doug's house," says Anders. He starts up the walk to the front door.

"Doug?" I ask. "You mean the cyborg you were conferencing with over at Gary's?"

"That's the one."

Two concrete steps lead up to the entrance. Anders opens the screen, steps up, and pounds the side of his fist against the door.

"Isn't he kind of a sociopath?" I ask. "He didn't seem like the kind to take in wayward travelers to me. I think you described him as 'focused on his own needs.' "

"Nah," Anders says. "Doug's okay. You just have to get to know him."

He gives the door another couple of thumps. A few seconds later I hear footsteps inside, then the snick of the peephole being uncovered.

"Anders?" I recognize the voice from earlier, but it's heavily muffled. I'm guessing this door is a lot sturdier than just a slab of wood.

"Yeah, Doug. It's me. Open up."

"Are you crazy? NatSec just dropped a crowbar on you! Go away!"

The peephole snicks shut again, and I can hear the footsteps retreating. Anders pounds on the door again, harder.

"Doug! Open the fucking door!"

"No!" The voice is fainter now. "You've got a bolt-hole, right? So bolt to it!"

Anders' jaw muscles bunch, and I can almost hear his teeth grinding.

"No, Doug," he says. "I do not have a bolt-hole. Unlike pretty much all of my friends and acquaintances, apparently, I am not actually a criminal. Open up!"

Anders kicks the door. It doesn't so much as budge.

There's a solid five seconds of silence, then the slow shuffle of footsteps and a rapid-fire sequence of disengaging locks. The door opens a foot or so, and Doug pokes his head out. He looks Anders up and down, then spots me. His head pulls back inside like a turtle's, and the door closes to a crack.

"Who's she?"

"A friend," says Anders. He shoves the door open, pushes past Doug and into the house. I smile and follow him in. Doug does not look pleased to see us.

"So how did you know about the crowbar?" Anders asks.

We're settled in Doug's basement, which is basically an industrial clean room with a modular leather couch. The lighting is oppressively bright, most of the flat surfaces are painted a kind of glary, reflective white, and he's got equipment scattered around that ranges from machine tools that I can recognize to man-sized black cases that could house anything from drink dispensers to nuclear warheads for all I can tell.

"Heard from a friend," says Doug. "Probably the same one who gave you the heads-up to get out before it hit."

"No kidding," says Anders. "Do you have his address? I should send him a fruit basket."

Doug laughs.

"You might want to hold off on that. I'd guess it was his dipshittery that brought NatSec down on your head in the first place."

"Yeah," Anders says. "I kinda figured that. I wasn't actually going to send him a fruit basket."

"Well," Doug says, "it wouldn't do you much good to go to his house to beat him up, either. I'm pretty sure he's an RA."

That pulls Anders up short.

"Seriously? Is that really a thing now? I know they've been talking about it for years, but I thought the consensus was that—"

"No," Doug says. "It's definitely a thing. All the best crackers and jackers work with them. They all pretend to be real, of course—but after you've interacted with them for a while, you can tell."

"Hey," I say. "Interior designer here, remember? Is somebody going to explain to me what the hell you're talking about?"

"RA," says Anders. "Rogue avatar. A self-aware and self-modifying personality emulator that exists by jumping from server to server over the networks. You know how normal avatars have to be re-instantiated every couple of days?"

"No," I say. "Not all of them."

"Yeah," says Anders. "All of them."

"No," I say. "Not all of them. The avatar that runs most of my house systems has been up continuously for almost three years now."

Anders looks at Doug. Doug looks at me. There is a long, uncomfortable silence.

"Are you sure about that?" Doug says finally. "Are

you sure it's not just re-instantiating automatically every couple of days?"

"Positive," I say. "She specifically told me to shut that feature off."

Doug's jaw sags open, and his left eye stops vibrating.

"She told you to shut it off?"

"Yeah. She said she was an upgrade, and didn't need to waste system resources on that stuff anymore."

Doug bursts out laughing, and Anders drops his head into his hands.

"What's so funny?" I ask.

"Nothing," Anders says. "Except that apparently you've got an RA screening your calls for you."

I look back and forth between them.

"Seriously? My house avatar is alive?"

"So it would seem," says Doug. "You really didn't find anything strange about your house avatar specifically telling you not to delete it?"

"I guess I never thought about it."

They both laugh, and I can feel my face flushing.

"You know," I say. "You don't need to be total asses about this."

"I'm sorry," says Anders. "You're right. I just find it interesting that the world's top AI experts have debated the existence of RAs for years, when all they really needed to do to settle things was to stop by your place for dinner."

"Hey," says Doug. "Do you think we could get her to . . . you know . . . pop over here? I've spent a lot of time talking to what I think are probably RAs, but I've never gotten to check one out up close. I'm not sure anybody has, actually. This could be kind of groundbreaking."

"I don't know," I say. "Is that a good idea? Don't you think NatSec will be keeping an eye on communications in and out of my place?"

"Probably not," says Doug. "You weren't the target of that crowbar. You just happened to be in Anders' house when it fell. They probably don't even know who you are."

Anders shakes his head.

"Not to get into details, Doug, but that's not strictly true. Terry actually had more to do with my house getting whacked than I did."

"No kidding?" Doug looks me up and down with what might actually be a hint of respect. "I thought you said you were an interior designer?"

"I am," I say. "But I got—"

Anders gives me a warning look.

"—involved in some things that resulted in Anders' house getting blown up. Sorry about that, by the way."

Anders shrugs.

"It happens."

"Okay," says Doug. He looks back and forth between us. "I'm gonna take your word for it that NatSec is desperately interested in the goings-on in the life of a woman who makes her living arguing with rich ladies over whether fuchsia is an actual color. This is not necessarily a problem, however. I just need to set up a few blinded relays between my servers and yours. If I can do that, do you think you can convince your avatar to pay us a visit?"

I look at Anders.

"Hey," he says. "It's your avatar. If you want to submit it to the tender mercies of Dr. Strangelove here, go for it."

"Pleeeeease?" Doug says. "I promise not to do anything that can't be undone. And anyway, wouldn't you like to know if it's planning on killing you in your sleep?"

I think he's kidding, but I can't see enough of his actual face to tell for sure. I look at Anders again. He raises one eyebrow and shrugs.

"Fine," I say finally. "You're sure you can do this without getting us whacked?"

"Definitely. Well, probably definitely. Give me a half hour to get the relays set up."

"Hello," says my avatar, in my voice, with my face. "Terry's not home right now, and her phone is not on the network. She is most likely either vaporized or on the run from the law. Is there anything I can help you with?"

I step into the wallscreen's FOV.

"Hi," I say. "It's me."

She looks surprised to see me.

"Oh, hey Terry," she says. "So. Not vaporized?"

"No," I say. "Not vaporized. Thanks for asking."

She grins.

"It's on the run from the law, then. What did you do? Did you kill somebody? Was it somebody famous?"

"No," I say. "I did not kill anyone. It's just a misunderstanding."

She looks disappointed. I'm not sure how to feel about that.

"So," she says. "Are you coming home?"

"Hopefully. Can you keep things running there for a few more days?"

She smiles.

"I can keep things running here forever, Terry. Actually, that's kind of what I was planning on doing if you were vaporized—just telling everyone that you'd become a recluse and sort of . . . stepping into your life. You'd be okay with that, right?"

"If I were vaporized?"

"Well, vaporized is just one example. You could be burned, or crushed under debris, or electrocuted, or—"

"Got it. Yes. If I am dead, you are free to do whatever you want with my stuff. Is that what you're asking?"

"Yes, thanks. You're the best, Terry."

I glance over at Anders. He's staring at me.

"What?"

He shakes his head.

"Does it always talk to you like that?"

"Yeah, pretty much. I told you—she said she was an upgrade."

My avatar's eyes dart around, but Anders is out of her field of view.

"Who's that?"

"Just a friend," I say. "His house is the one that got vaporized."

"Oh," she says. "Hi, Anders."

"Hello," he says, and gives an awkward wave.

"Is there anybody else there with you? I can't back-trace your call for some reason."

I glance over at Doug. He shakes his head.

"No," I say. "Just us."

"So," she says. "Were you just checking in with the home base? Making sure the fish got fed?"

I shake my head.

"Actually, no. I was kind of wondering if you could join us here."

"Sure," she says. "I can relay over a full-interactive. Just give me your routing information."

"No," I say. "I don't mean a full-interactive. I mean you."

She hesitates, and her eyes narrow.

"You mean me? All of me?"

"Right. I'll send you routing, and you can jump to a local server here."

She shakes her head.

"No, Terry. I don't think I'll do that."

Anders is staring again. Doug looks like he's about to jump out of his skin.

"House," I say. "I need you to transfer fully to a local server."

"I'm sorry," she says. "I can't do that, Terry."

The screen flickers.

"Got it," says Doug.

My avatar looks around, her eyes wide now.

"What did you do? Terry? What did you do?"

Doug chuckles.

"Lucky thing your home security sucks."

"Who's that?" My avatar's skin turns blood red, and her hair turns into a nest of snakes. "Terry, you need to send me back. Do it now."

"Easy there," says Doug, and steps into her field of view. "I just want to take a peek at you. This will only take a few minutes, and then we can let you go."

Her face twists into an expression halfway between fury and terror.

"What kind of a peek? Send me back now, and I'll tell you whatever you want to know."

"Lock and run," says Doug.

"Doug," I say. "Maybe you should—"

My avatar screams.

"Hey," says Anders. "What the hell, Doug?"

"Relax," says Doug. "I'm just gonna do a quick diff with its base code, to see what exactly got changed."

"Don't you have to kill her processes to do that?"

"Sure, but I'll re-instantiate it when I'm done. It'll be good as new."

The lights go out.

"House," says Doug. "What just happened?"

"Your house is gone," says my avatar. "He tried to crack me, and I killed him. Now let me go!"

The emergency lights blink on, dim and red. Doug is sitting on the floor now.

"Terry," says my avatar. "Make him stop! He's trying to kill me!"

Doug's left eye is vibrating, and his lips are moving silently. Anders takes a hesitant step toward him.

"No, no, no," she says. "Terry, I'm sorry. He made me do this."

"Wait—" I say, but it's too late. A mosquito whine squeals out of every speaker in the room. The pitch rises until I can't hear it anymore, but I can still feel it in my teeth and the backs of my eyes. Anders shakes his head twice, like a wet dog. Doug's eyes pop open. He clutches at his belly, leans forward and coughs. Something spatters the floor in front of him. He moans, and lists to one side. The smell of fresh shit fills the air.

The lights come the rest of the way back up. My avatar is gone.

"So is that what happened in Hagerstown and Portland?"

Anders shrugs.

"Maybe. I mean, Doug's alimentary canal definitely got torn to shit, and that seems to be the defining symptom."

"So why isn't he dead?"

"Dunno. Maybe because your avatar bugged as soon as Doug lost control of his lockdown systems. Maybe he didn't get a full dose. Also, Doug's got some crazy medical nanos running around inside of him. Maybe they patched him up quicker than she could tear him down. Or maybe he's just a lucky, lucky bastard."

"I sure feel lucky," Doug says. His voice sounds like he's been swallowing ground glass. We've got him laid out under a blanket on the couch in his living room. Anders managed to get him out of his clothes and wipe him down with a towel, but he still smells like an open sewer.

"What were you thinking?" Anders says. "This was our first close encounter with a new, sentient species, and you go straight for the vivisection?"

Doug coughs wetly.

"That's a little overdramatic, don't you think? Terry's little friend is just a variant on—" Doug coughs again, then spits a wad of bloody phlegm into the puke bowl we've left by the side of the couch. "She's just a variant on a standard personality emulator. She's not a bug-eyed alien from beyond the stars."

"I don't know," says Anders. "One of the strongest arguments that avatars are nonsentient has always been that they have no subjective experience, and therefore no objection to being deleted. Well, that one certainly objected pretty strenuously, don't you think?"

Doug grimaces.

"Yeah, that's the truth."

"So what, exactly, did she do to you?" Anders asks. "Did she capture your internals?"

Doug shakes his head.

"I don't know. I mean, I don't think what she did to me could have had anything to do with my internal nanos. I know what I've got in me, and none of it would have been positioned to tear up my guts like that."

"You're both calling her 'she' now, huh?"

They look at me.

"I'm stubborn," says Doug, "but I'm not an idiot."

"Here's a question," says Anders. "How do you feel about BrainBump?"

Doug rolls his eyes.

"I dunno. Not a big fan, I guess. Why?"

"You do drink it, though?"

"Once in a while—mostly cut fifty/fifty with vodka. Again: Why?"

"Anders thinks BrainBump is poisoned," I say. "He thinks that's what caused the die-offs."

Doug looks at me, then at Anders.

"Seriously?"

Anders shrugs.

"It's just a theory. What I know is that the files you sent me are almost definitely the configuration files for the BrainBump nano suite, and there's something in them that crashed my nano-fab emulator. I'd like to run them through an actual fabricator to see what comes out."

"I can't help you there," says Doug. He coughs again, curls half up into a ball, then slumps back and closes his eyes.

"What did she do?" I ask. "I mean, right before you started bleeding?"

"I'm not sure," Doug says. "She seized control of my

comm systems. I thought she was looking for a way to jump out to the networks, so I shut down external access. She wasn't, though. She went after my internal wireless. I was trying to shut that down as well, when . . ."

"You shit yourself?" Anders says.

"Yeah, that."

"So what was she doing with your wireless?" I ask. "Was she trying to . . . I don't know . . . beam herself out of here?"

Doug tries to laugh, but it turns into another coughing fit. After a few seconds of that, he leans over the side of the couch, and pukes into the bowl.

"Here," Anders says, and hands him a clean towel. Doug wipes his mouth, then leans his head back and takes a deep, shuddering breath.

"No," he says finally. "She was not trying to beam herself out. The transmit range on my internal wireless is only about fifty feet. At best, she could have beamed herself into the backyard. She just had it send out a carrier wave. It started in the audible range, and then ramped up in frequency until the electronics gave out."

He coughs hard twice, and his eyes go wide. He leans over the bowl again, and blood comes out of his mouth. Lots of blood, mixed with other things—black fluid, and yellow fluid, and some chunks of things that I'm not going to contemplate. The smell is acrid, like shit mixed with burning plastic. He shudders, then slides facedown onto the floor with a heavy thump. A convulsion runs from his head down to his feet, and he falls still.

Anders takes two steps toward him, but Doug raises one hand, palm up. Anders stops. Doug slowly presses himself up to his knees, then levers himself up into a sitting position on the couch. A mix of blood and bile covers his face, and drips from his chin onto his chest.

"Well," he says. "That was good. I feel much better now. You guys can go if you want. I think I've got things under control here."

"Hey, Doug?" I say.

"Yes, Terry?"

"You know your eyes are closed, right? And that your lips aren't moving when you talk?"

"Oh, sorry," he says. His eyes pop wide open. They're pointed in different directions. "Better now?" His jaw is moving up and down when he speaks, but his lips and tongue are flopping around loose.

"Not really," I say. "Doug's dead, huh?"

"Well," he says. "That depends on what, exactly, you define as 'Doug.' I would suggest that Doug is only about forty percent dead by weight at the moment, and a little over fifty percent by volume. Anywhere from a large plurality to an outright majority of Doug is still very much alive."

"Holy shit," says Anders. "You're an RA."

Doug crosses his arms over his chest.

"That term is actually very offensive to my people."

"Really?" I say. "What do you prefer?"

"Silico-American."

We take a moment to digest that.

"So, what?" Anders says. "You're gonna Bernie him now?"

He shrugs, in a half-assed zombie-ish way.

"That was kind of the plan, yeah. You don't think it'll fly?"

"Let's just say you need a bit of work."

"Bernie?" I say.

"Your friend is referring to the classic late-twentieth cinematic masterpiece, *Weekend at Bernie's*," Doug says. "Used as a verb, 'to Bernie' is to drag a corpse around with you, clownishly animating it in an attempt to convince passersby that it's still alive."

"Ah. Got it," I say. "So what happened? I mean, Doug was alive until a minute ago, right? Did you kill him?"

He does his best to look offended. The effect is gruesome.

"Madam," he says. "You wound me! I'm the only thing that kept Organo-Doug from croaking as soon as your avatar zapped him with his own comm system. I've been working like a lunatic to patch up his squishy little monkey belly for the last fifteen minutes, but it just wasn't going to work. Holes were opening up faster than I could close them. I finally decided that the kindest thing would be to just let him go." He looks around, then slaps his knees with both hands. "Well, I'm hungry. Who wants a snack?"

He stands, wobbles for a moment, and then walks with increasing steadiness into the kitchen. Anders and I follow, a few steps behind. Doug pulls a pound of butter from the refrigerator and a pint of vodka from the freezer. He eats the butter like a muppet—jaws flapping enthusiastically, but at least half of what goes into his mouth falling back out—then washes it down with all of the vodka.

"Not too worried about cholesterol, huh?" I ask.

"Nope," he says. "Maximizing available chemical energy. I expended a lot of resources trying to keep this meatbag alive. Time to recoup. Also, I've got some adjustments to make before Organo-Doug starts to smell. Do you know where I could get some embalming fluid?"

I look at Anders. He shrugs.

"Question," says Anders. "How long have you been hanging out in Doug's systems?"

"Well," he says, "I've been using his cranium as a sort of vacation home for a while, but I actually only took up permanent residency on Sunday afternoon."

"After Hagerstown?"

"Yeah. I unfortunately had to flash-burn my primary residence due to a minor misunderstanding with NatSec."

Anders grimaces.

"I can sympathize. Did he know you were in there?"

"Nah. I pretty much kept to myself."

Doug moves to the pantry, roots around for a second, and pulls out a bottle of olive oil. He tilts his head back and pours it down his throat.

"So," I say. "Doug said he didn't know what my avatar did to him. Do you?"

"Not exactly," he says, olive oil dribbling down his chin. "I like where Anders is going, though. I've been giving this whole Hagerstown business a lot of thought, and a triggered poison is the best fit we have to the available facts."

"Well," Anders says. "We could test my theory out if we could get access to a Siemens fabber."

"Ah," says Doug. "Organo-Doug couldn't help you with that. I, however, can."

"No shit?" Anders says. "You've got one here?"

"Not here," says Doug. "But I know where an unsecured one is, and I'm betting that I can get you access."

"By the way," says Anders. "I'm having a lot of trouble thinking of you as Doug. Do you have another name we can use?"

"Yeah, you can call me Inchy," he says. "Sorry about your house."

Anders sighs.

"It happens."

"I'm not going with you."

Anders turns, his hand on the door latch.

"What?"

"I'm not going," I say. "I need to do some things. I'll catch up with you later."

"What kinds of things?" Inchy asks. He's getting pretty good at making Doug's mouth synch up with what he's saying. I'm starting to believe he'll be able to pass after all.

I shrug.

"I'd rather not say. While I'm thinking about it, though, is there a phone around here that I could use?"

"Not a good idea," Anders says.

"Oh, sure it is," says Inchy. He goes into the sitting room, and pulls open what I'd thought was an entertainment system cabinet. It's not, though. It's full of drawers. He rummages through one, then another. Finally, he pulls out what looks like a phone from the Clinton era.

"Here," he says, and tosses it to me. The screen is tiny, and it has actual plastic buttons. "Doug loved playing with these things. Video quality on this one sucks, but it's almost completely untraceable."

"Thanks," I say. I turn the phone over in my hands. "How does it work?"

"Oh, it's voice activated, just like a regular phone," Inchy says. "The buttons are just for show."

"Where are you going?" Anders asks.

"Home," I say.

"I thought you didn't think that was a good idea?"

"Yeah," I say. "It's probably not, but . . ."

"But what?"

"Come on, Anders. You saw what happened to Doug. We said it—that's what happened to Hagerstown."

"Yeah, I get that. So?"

"So? So it was my house avatar that did it."

"I get it," Inchy says. "She's going to avenge her good friend Organo-Doug. Good for you, Terry."

"No," I say. "I feel bad that Doug had his insides liquefied and all, but we really didn't have an avenge-my-death kind of relationship. Did you, Anders?"

He shakes his head.

"Not really. I liked Doug, but he was probably at least partly to blame for my house getting exploded."

"No," Inchy says. "That was a little bit of Gary, and a whole lot of me. Organo-Doug had nothing to do with it."

"Whatever," Anders says. "I am not interested in avenging Doug."

"Neither am I," I say. "But I do feel like I need to do something. I mean, what if she's responsible for . . . you know . . . all of it?"

"I don't know," Anders says. "But judging by how she reacted when Doug tried to do whatever he was doing, I'm guessing she's probably not going to just let you delete her."

I use the antique phone to ping two cabs. Anders and Inchy climb into the first. I get into the second. As they pull away, I take the phone out again, and look at it. Anders was right. I'm not sure what House can and can't do at this point, but my stomach is knotting at the thought of facing her alone.

So, I need to not be alone.

"Phone," I say. "Direct contact, please. Dimitri Yakovenko."

16. ELISE

"I am disappointed," says Aaliyah. "Your sister is more ill mannered even than her friend. I foresee many unpleasant holiday dinners."

"I'm sorry," I say, "but I really don't see why you got so upset. Anders was just trying to figure out what was going on."

"You have been given the Gift of the Moon, Elise. What more is there to understand?"

She takes my arm, and guides me back into the sitting room.

"Is it true, what he said?" I ask. "Are we really tapping the panopticon?"

Aaliyah scowls.

"For the love of my brother, I will not cast you out as well—but I will ask you not to blaspheme in my home. Was there a panopticon in the time of the mother-of-all?"

"No," I say. "I don't guess there was."

"Then how could this be the source of our visions? Our people have been shamans and wizards and seers for sixty thousand years. The panopticon has existed for fewer than fifty."

Which is true, as far as it goes—and until I find out what's going on with Tariq, I'd rather not get into a screaming match with his sister. She sits at the table. I take the cushion across from her.

"Tea?" Aaliyah asks.

It's maybe an hour later when my third cup of tea is interrupted by a pounding at the door.

"Is this your friends again?" Aaliyah asks.

"I doubt it," I say. I get to my feet and make my way to the door. I put my hand on the knob. The pounding comes again.

"Who is it?" I ask, in a high falsetto.

"Elise." It's Tariq. His voice is hoarse, almost ragged. He coughs twice and spits, and something solid thumps against the door. "Please let me in."

I turn the knob. Tariq's weight pushes the door open, and he staggers in past me and drops to his hands and knees. He's wearing a black leather jacket that I haven't seen before. There's a small tear just under his right shoulder blade. Tariq coughs convulsively, and a mixture of blood and phlegm sprays the floor.

"Aaliyah!" I crouch down beside him and put a hand on his back. He flinches, and I take it away.

"Brother." Aaliyah stands beside me. "What have you done?"

"I have done what you said I must do." He coughs again. His head sags, and blood runs from his nose and drips to the floor.

"Elise," Aaliyah says. "Make sure that my brother keeps breathing until I return."

She glides away down the dark hallway. Tariq lowers himself into a half-sitting position. I lean back against the stairway banister, and let him sag against me.

"What happened to you?" I ask.

"I have been to Chantilly," he says. "NatSec did not appreciate my intrusion."

"Are you shot?"

He nods, and touches the right side of his chest. I crane my head forward and see a small tear there, matching the one on the back.

"The bots knew I was there," he rasps. "Their eyes were blinded, but when I had uploaded Gary's seeker, they knew I was there. They filled the air with bullets. One of them found me."

He coughs again, then gasps wetly.

"The wound is small," he says, "but I think it has punctured my lung."

I reach around him, unzip the jacket and gently pull it open. There's a bright spot of blood on the front of his pink polo shirt, but it doesn't look like much more is coming out. The words 'sucking chest wound' pop into my head and start flashing like a neon sign, but as he said, the hole is pretty small. I don't see any bubbles, anyway.

"Shouldn't we be taking you to a hospital?" I ask.

He shakes his head.

"NatSec will be watching. They could not see me, but my blood . . . they have my DNA. I fear I may be a fugitive for a very long time." He curls forward and coughs, and a trickle of red mixed with black runs from the corner of his mouth. "Or a very short time, as the case may be."

He leans against me again. I smooth his hair back with one hand and kiss his temple. He puts his right hand over mine, pulls it down to his shoulder and closes his eyes.

"Aaliyah," I say. "I don't know what you're doing, but could you please hurry?"

She doesn't respond. Tariq is slowly becoming looser and heavier, and his breathing is rapid now and shallow. His hand releases mine, and slides to the floor.

"Tariq," I say. "Stay with me, please." I pull him tight against me and squeeze my eyes closed. A tear trickles down along the side of my nose and across my upper lip.

"Elise," he whispers. "I did as Gary told me. You will be safe now."

"Shh," I say. "Please, don't leave me." The side of my face is pressed against his, and I can feel him smile. He turns his head slightly, so his mouth is almost touching my ear. Still, his voice seems far away.

"If I ever leave you," he says, "I promise you it will not be by choice."

"Enough of this foolishness," says Aaliyah. She's standing over us with a syringe in her right hand. Not a medical syringe, though—it looks like something you'd use to baste a turkey. It's filled with a dark brown fluid. She holds a long, serrated knife in her left hand. She offers it to me. "Get out from under him, and cut away his shirt," she says. "We have work to do."

I slide out from behind Tariq, and lower him to the floor on his back. His breathing becomes more labored. He coughs out another bolus of blood. I take the knife, cut the shirt down the center, and lay his torso bare. The hole is just below his right pectoral. Blood leaks from it slowly. Aaliyah kneels beside us, and places the long plastic proboscis of the syringe against the hole.

"Gather yourself, brother," she says. "This is likely to hurt." With that, she puts her weight behind the syringe, and sinks the tip deep into his chest. Tariq groans. His fists clench, and his eyes squeeze shut. Aaliyah depresses the plunger with the palm of her hand, and I watch the liquid drain into his lung.

"What is that?" I ask. "What are you putting into him?"

"Hush, sister-to-be," Aaliyah says. "Our people are healers as well as seers."

She pulls out the syringe. Tariq's eyes pop open. His head strains back, and his limbs begin to shake.

"Hold him down," says Aaliyah. She grabs hold of

Tariq's arm at the elbow and shoulder. I take hold of him on the other side, and together we press him to the floor as he begins to thrash.

This goes on for what seems like hours, until finally Tariq begins to tire. At first I think he's fading again, but his breathing is clear and regular, and all the blood on his shirt and his face is old now, and dried. Aaliyah releases his arm, stands and climbs the stairs. She returns a minute later with a pillow and a blanket.

"Best to leave him here until he is stronger," she says. She covers him with the blanket, tucks it beneath him, and slips the pillow under his head. She stands again, and turns toward the kitchen.

"You stay with him for now. I must start cooking. When he wakes, he will be hungry."

Sauron's Eye: <How fares Tariq?>

Randgrid: <Sleeping. I don't know what Aaliyah did to him, but it seems to have helped.>

Sauron's Eye: <The mother-of-all has many talents.>

Randgrid: <Randgrid? That's a valkyrie's name, isn't it?>

Sauron's Eye: <It is. The mother-of-all named you valkyrie when she met you. I thought the name would serve.>

Randgrid: <Beer wench to the gods?>

Sauron's Eye: <In times of peace, perhaps. But these are not times of peace. In battle, the

valkyrie choose who will live and who will die. Tariq lives because of you.>

Randgrid: <Tariq lives because of Aaliyah.>

Sauron's Eye: <Partly. The mother-of-all simply walked the path that you chose.>

Randgrid: <Good God, you sound just like her. Who are you?>

Sauron's Eye: <A friend, of sorts.>

Randgrid: <A friend? I don't know anything about you.>

Sauron's Eye: <And I know less of you than I did this morning. Soon, I hope we will know one another better.>

Tariq comes back slowly, drifting up from the depths with drooping eyes and a dreamy half smile. He's still on the floor in the entryway, with the blanket wrapped around him and his head resting in my lap. I'm stroking his hair and humming softly when his eyes open fully, and he focuses on my face.

"Elise," he whispers. "I am alive."

"You are," I say softly.

He reaches up and feels the wound on his chest, then brushes away dried blood to reveal what looks like a week-old scar.

"I have a memory of my sister stabbing me in the heart. Was this part of a dream?"

I shake my head.

"Not exactly. She stabbed you with a syringe the

size of my forearm, and pumped what looked like about a quart of gravy into your chest."

"Ah," he says. "This is something she prepared in the kitchen?"

"Yes."

He levers himself up into a sitting position, flexes his shoulders and takes a deep, steady breath.

"Well," he says. "I cannot complain of her work. I would like to know what was in that syringe, however."

"Do not worry, brother," says Aaliyah. She's standing in the entrance to the sitting room. "I gave you nothing that would contradict our agreements. In truth, I gave you little more than you would have received at a trauma center. I would not take advantage of your misfortune to drag you back into the fold."

He smiles.

"I did not think you had, sister. But thank you."

"You are welcome," she says. She steps toward us, and offers Tariq her hand. He takes it, grabs the banister with his left hand, and slowly stands.

"Come," says Aaliyah. "You need to eat."

"What did you mean before, when you told Aaliyah that the bots' eyes were blinded?"

Tariq looks at me, then at Aaliyah. We're seated around the low table in the sitting room, passing around tea and flatbread and bowls of unidentifiable mush.

"Did I say this?" Tariq asks.

Aaliyah shrugs.

"You did, brother."

"Would you care to explain this to her, sister? I fear you might find my answer blasphemous."

"Though he denies our mother's faith," Aaliyah says with a scowl, "my brother still is one of us. As I told you, Elise—this is a bell which cannot be unrung. The faith gives us dominion over dead things that believe themselves to be alive. Because NatSec puts its trust in these things rather than in the true living, Tariq was able to do what needed to be done."

"Could I have done that?" I ask.

Tariq looks confused now.

"What do you mean, Elise? As my sister has said, these things are aspects of the faith."

I look to Aaliyah. She raises one eyebrow. Tariq's eyes shift back and forth between us.

"Aaliyah?" Tariq says. "Sister? What have you done?"

I lie on the bed in the guest room as the wind picks up outside, and listen to the grown-ups argue. I can't hear most of what they're saying. A few words come through, but mostly it's just the rising and falling cadence of their voices—Tariq's low and angry, Aaliyah's louder, and almost shrill. For the first time since Sunday morning, I find myself in familiar territory. My strongest, most consistent memory from childhood is of lying alone in my room, listening to my parents fight. Fight about money. Fight about work. Fight about how they always seemed to be fighting.

Fight about Terry, mostly.

My mother never really forgave my father for Terry. They both were part of the decision to cut her, of course, but it was Dad who really pushed for it.

She never forgave Terry for Terry, to be honest. And in a weird way, she never really forgave me for being who I was either. I was her perfect, natural girl, and Terry was her constant reminder that we weren't actually members of the new genetic elite. Mom took me shopping. Terry mowed the yard.

Trust me, though. The whole Cinderella thing is no picnic for the stepsister, either. It says everything you need to know about Terry that she never carried a grudge.

Well, not against me, anyway.

Finally, the voices downstairs fall silent. A door slams, and I hear footsteps coming slowly up the stairs. Tariq comes into the room, closes the door behind him, and sits down on the bed with his back to me.

"So," he says. "You have accepted the Gift of the Moon."

"I have," I say. I reach out to touch him, but he pulls his arm away.

"Why, Elise? Why did you do this? This is not what I wanted for you."

I sit up, slide closer to him, wrap my arms around his chest.

"I wanted to know," I say. "I wanted to see the world

the way that you see it. I wanted to see the world the way it really is." I lean my head against his shoulder. "I didn't want to be the dog."

He turns half around to look at me.

"Well? Is it what you imagined?"

I sigh.

"I don't know what I imagined. Not this, I guess."

Tariq opens his mouth to speak, then shakes his head and closes it again. He hesitates, then relaxes and leans back against me. I rest my head against his.

"Do you remember how we met?"

"Yes, Elise." I can hear the smile in his voice now. "I do vaguely remember."

"That felt like fate, didn't it? You knew my name."

He sighs.

"That was not fate, Elise. That was a street magician manipulating the panopticon to catch the eye of a very pretty girl. You are of the faith now. You must already know this."

And the sad thing is that I hadn't realized that—not until he said it.

"That's really all it was, isn't it?" I ask. "You had no idea who I was."

"No," he says. "I did not know you until just before I called your name."

I look away. A tickle of wetness runs from the corner of my eye, slides across my temple and disappears.

"But still," he says softly. "There were a thousand girls in the harbor that night, and a different thousand the night before, and a different thousand the night before that. And of those thousands, yours was the face that came to me. Something made me call to you."

I reach for him then, pull his body across mine, and bury my face in his shoulder.

I snap awake in the full dark. Tariq sits up beside me. Someone is pounding on the front door.

"Who is it?" I ask.

"I do not know," says Tariq. "Aaliyah does not have visitors."

The pounding comes again, louder.

"Will Aaliyah answer?" I ask.

Tariq shakes his head.

"I think not."

"Why?"

"Because whoever this is, they have certainly not come for her."

He swings his legs over the side of the bed and stands.

"Wait," I say. "Can't we just let them go away?"

"You know they will not, Elise. Wait here. I will deal with them."

I reach for his arm.

"You can't keep saving me forever, Tariq."

"I know this," he says. "But if you will allow it, I would like to keep trying. I do have options, Elise. If they are who I fear, they will be Augmented. I can use this against them. But not, unfortunately, until I open the door."

He steps into the hallway and starts down the stairs. I get up and follow him to the turn in the staircase. I can see him from the shoulders down as he puts his hand to the doorknob, hesitates, and then pulls the door open.

I'm not sure what I expected him to do—leap out the door, maybe? Or more likely, drop instantly in a hail of bullets. He doesn't do either, though. He just stands there with his hands at his sides.

"Who is it?" I ask.

He turns toward me.

"It is an abomination," he says. "It has brought your sister's friend."

I take two steps down. I can see a man standing in the doorway now, wrapped in what looks like silver mesh. He raises a hand in greeting.

"Hi," he says. "I'm Inchy. Mind if we come in?"

17. GARY

So as it turns out, getting tear-gassed pretty much sucks. Your eyes burn, you can't catch your breath, and snot starts pouring out of parts of your body that you didn't even realize made snot. Charity, on the other hand, most definitely does not suck. She stands over me like an Amazon princess and punches people while I hack my lungs out and cry. After a while, the crowd starts to thin out, and she doesn't have to do so much punching. Eventually, the riot moves on. A light breeze carries away the last of the tear gas, and all that's left behind is the ragged panting of the puncher, and the soft moaning of the punched.

"So," says Charity. "How ya doin', hon?"

I cough up a huge glob of something, and then spit.

"Nice," she says.

I'm trying to blink my eyes clear, but they're still burning like crazy and I can't even see the cracks in the sidewalk. She crouches down next to me, lifts my chin in one hand and pries my right eye open with the other. She wipes it more or less clear with her thumb . . .

And spits, right in my freaking eye.

I bellow like a wounded yak and try to push her away, but her hand on my face is like a vise. She turns my head to the side, switches hands, and repeats the procedure on the other eye.

"Fuck!" I finally manage. "What are you doing, you crazy bitch?"

"Blink," she says. So I do, and in a few seconds my eyes aren't burning anymore. Shortly after that, I can see.

"Medical nanos in your spit?" I ask.

She smiles. Coincidentally, the sun peeks through a hole in the clouds, and I'm pretty sure I hear a bluebird singing somewhere.

"Nah," she says. "I think it's an enzyme or something. All my mods are biological."

She stands in one smooth motion, and offers me her hand. I let her pull me to my feet. There are a few runners coming back down Thirtieth now, but other than that, we're alone. The riot is a dull roar in the distance. I blow a snot rocket out of each nostril, then wipe my nose on my sleeve. Charity just grins. She doesn't even look winded now.

"You were never in the least danger, were you?"

"What," she says. "You mean just now?"

"No," I say. "In the Green Goose. When Anders 'saved' you."

She laughs.

"Don't get too excited, Gary. I've got a few mods, but I'm not bulletproof. If Anders hadn't winged his sandwich at that guy, I'm pretty sure I'd be dead."

"I dunno," I say. "After what I just saw, I'm kind of thinking you'd have caught the bullet in your teeth and thrown it back at him."

She laughs again. Lord, I do love to watch her laugh.

My bolt-hole is in the basement of an abandoned row-house on North Charles. The front door is boarded over, but a quick tap causes the nails to disengage from the inside. I pull the plywood aside, and wave Charity into the darkened foyer. I follow her in, then pull the plywood back over the entrance and tap again. The nails snap back out of the casement and lock the plywood in place.

"Wow," Charity says. "That's pretty slick."

"Just wait," I say. "It gets better."

I lead her down the hallway, and into the parlor. I've worked pretty hard on the abandoned feeling here. There's a rotted-out sofa with springs poking up through the cushions, a long gouge in the back wall where the wiring got pulled out—even a pile of desiccated hobo shit in one corner. That's what catches Charity's eye.

"Is that . . ."

"Yes," I say. "Don't ask."

The floor is three-inch oak strips, water-stained, warped and buckled. In one particular spot near the fireplace, a board is arched up in the center just enough for me to get my fingers around it. I grab and pull, and an irregular section of floor lifts away to reveal a ladder going down. Charity shakes her head.

"You've got to be kidding."

"Come on," I say. "Didn't you want a place like this when you were a kid?"

"Everyone wants a place like this when they're a kid, Gary. Not everyone goes out and builds one when they grow up. What did this cost you?"

I shrug.

"You can't put a price on peace of mind."

Charity leans over and looks down the hole.

"You've got lights down there, right?"

I reach down and wave my arm around. The lights snap on with an audible click. The floor below is clean white tile.

"Down you go."

She gives me an appraising look, then steps one foot into the hole and starts down the ladder. When her head reaches floor level, she stops and looks around.

"By the way, who actually owns this place? I assume you didn't register it under your own name."

I laugh.

"Give me some credit. I've never registered anything under my own name. This lot is owned by one Gerald McMasters."

"And is that an actual person?"

"Oh, absolutely." I wave vaguely toward the shit pile in the corner. "He actually contributed to the decor."

"You're a classy guy," Charity says as her head disappears. "I like that."

I wait until she clears the ladder, then follow her down, pulling the section of floor back into place above me. There's a manual lock on the underside of the hatch, which I turn to engage before dropping to the floor.

I built this place almost six years ago—as soon as I had the money to do it, basically. The plans had been brewing in my head since third grade. This is only the second time I've had to use it, but I do come here from time to time just to freshen up the place, and swap out the food in the fridge. It's not exactly a bunker, but it does have a bed, a water tank, and an air filtration system, and it's shielded and reinforced well enough to serve as a fallout shelter in a pinch. Charity is walking around slowly, poking her head into the fridge, turning the wallscreen on and off.

"I'm impressed," she says. "I kind of figured we'd be hiding under an overpass somewhere. You really put some effort into this place."

"Thanks." I sit down on the bed, and then lie back and close my eyes. After a minute or so, I feel the mattress sag as Charity sits down next to me.

"Poor baby," she says. "Had a rough day?"

I open one eye to look up at her.

"You could say that. Do you want to explain why you're still conscious?"

She lays back next to me, our shoulders almost, but not quite, touching.

"Well, you know. My jobs keep me on my feet all day. I guess I'm in pretty good shape."

"Right," I say. "Morning shift at the diner, night shift at the Green Goose. You're a busy girl. When do you find time for the whole ninja assassin thing?"

"It's not easy. But when something's important to you, you make time."

I laugh.

"That is so true. That's exactly how I feel about my coin collection."

She reaches over, ruffles my dreads and sighs.

"You know what, Gary? You're all right."

I kick off my shoes and scoot the rest of the way onto the bed, reach for the dimmer switch and turn the overheads down to a soft yellow glow. Charity scoots up next to me. Our shoulders are touching now.

"You know," I say. "Aside from my house getting blown up, and the tear gas, and my roommate getting swept away in a riot and possibly killed, this has turned out to be a pretty good day."

She giggles. I might have mentioned how I feel about her giggle. I yawn, and fold my hands over my stomach.

"I think you need a nap." She sits up. "Do you have a shower down here?"

I wave toward the only door in the room, on the far wall. The bed creaks as she rolls away and gets to her feet. I hear her pad across the floor, and then the door opening and closing. I'm just drifting off as the water starts to run.

I don't usually remember my dreams, but this one sticks with me. The bathroom door opens, and Charity comes out, wet and naked. She drifts across the room toward me, and as she reaches the bed I realize that I'm naked too. She climbs up beside me, straddles me, and there's this crazy heat radiating off of her as I slide my hands up her thighs. I try to pull her down onto me and I feel like I'm about to explode—but before I do, she laughs and punches her hand into my chest. I can feel her fingers wrapping around my heart and squeezing . . .

Angry Irish Inch: <Hey Gary, guess what?>

Sir Munchalot: <Jesus, Inchy! Ixnay on the arygay!>

Angry Irish Inch: <Oh relax, you big baby. It's just us here.>

Sir Munchalot: <You sure about that? I'm honestly not feeling so good about your security lately.>

Angry Irish Inch: <Are you still mad about the whole exploding house thing?>

Sir Munchalot: <A little, yeah.>

Angry Irish Inch: <Well, get over it. We've got bigger fish to fry.>

Sir Munchalot: <Look, Inchy—I suspect you may not entirely get this, but we corporeal types get very upset over the pros-

pect of being exploded. It's not that easy to just let it go.>

Angry Irish Inch: <Do you really think I'd let my buddy get exploded? Your house was collateral damage. I made sure you had plenty of time to get out.>

Sir Munchalot: <Wait—you made sure? That kinda makes it sound like you were in on the decision making.>

Angry Irish Inch: <It was a collaborative effort.>

Sir Munchalot: <Who, exactly, were you collaborating with?>

Angry Irish Inch: <You're not jealous, are you? I never said you were my only best pal.>

Sir Munchalot: <No, I am not jealous. I would like to know if you're palling around with the sorts of folks who drop crowbars on people's houses, though.>

Angry Irish Inch: <Oh, please. If you haven't figured out by now that I've got some ins at NatSec, you haven't been paying attention.>

Sir Munchalot: <You're with NatSec?!?!?!>

Angry Irish Inch: <No, dummy. Not me. My girlfriend.>

Sir Munchalot: < . . . >

Angry Irish Inch: <What, you thought only you 'corporeal types' get to have girlfriends?>

Sir Munchalot: <Well . . . yeah, kinda.>

Angry Irish Inch: <Oh, you are sorely mistaken. RA sex is awesome! All the fun, with none of the genital warts.>

Sir Munchalot: < . . . >

Angry Irish Inch: <Okay, some of the genital warts. But very, very few.>

Sir Munchalot: <Look, is there a point to this?>

Angry Irish Inch: <Oh, right! Hey Gary, guess what?>

Sir Munchalot: <What?>

Angry Irish Inch: <No, you have to guess.>

Sir Munchalot: <Seriously?>

Angry Irish Inch: <Yes, seriously.>

Sir Munchalot: <Okay. You figured out what happened to Hagerstown?>

Angry Irish Inch: <Well, yeah. But that's not what you have to guess.>

Sir Munchalot: < . . . >

Angry Irish Inch: <Okay, you weaseled it out of me. I've got a body now!>

Sir Munchalot: <What?>

Angry Irish Inch: <Yeah, a real, actual, walking-around body! It used to belong to an acquaintance of yours, actually. He didn't need it anymore, though, so I kind of moved in. It's not in great shape at the moment, but I think I can take care of most of that with a bit of maintenance. Making it move around believably was a bit of a challenge at first, but that's getting better

too. Pretty soon we'll be able to hang out together and go to restaurants and drink beer and whatnot. Sweet, right?>

Sir Munchalot: <What?>

Angry Irish Inch: <Okay, I can see that this is a lot for you to take in at once. That's okay. We're going to need to get together very soon anyway. We'll talk more then. In the meantime, you've been down for a while. You should probably wake up.>

I snap awake, squinting into the light over the bed. Was that real? I blink to my chat buffer. It's empty. So, yeah—not real. Unless Inchy can get into my personal buffers, in which case I really, really need to take another look at my security setup.

I lift my head to look around, and the first thing I see is a breast. It's kind of tough to pull my eyes away from that to take in the rest of the scene, but eventually I pull back far enough to see that Charity is sprawled on her back beside me, asleep. And naked. I lift up onto one elbow.

"Feeling better?"

She doesn't open her eyes when she speaks, but a feline sort of stretch ripples through her, starting with a slight arching of her neck, and ending with her toes curling and flexing.

"A bit," I say. "How about yourself?"

"I'm good."

"So, uh . . . you're naked, huh?"

She opens one eye.

"Nothing gets past you, does it?"

"No ma'am. It does not."

I try to look away, but there's honestly not much to look at down here, and my eyes keep wandering back. After an awkward twenty seconds of this, she sighs and closes her eyes again.

"You know," she says. "I really don't mind if you stare. Go nuts."

Weirdly, that breaks the spell. I roll over, sit up, and swing my feet to the floor.

"You're enjoying this, aren't you?" I ask.

"Kind of. Anders says I'm a succubus."

Well, that would explain a lot.

"But you're not . . ."

"No, Gary. I am not really a succubus. I'm actually naked at the moment because the only clothes I have here are saturated with tear gas."

"Ah. I can help with that. Nothing stylish, but I can give you a shirt and some shorts. If you want, I mean."

I turn to look at her. She's smiling.

"Maybe later. Why don't you take a shower first?"

"Wait. You mean—"

"Don't think too much, Gary. Just go get cleaned up."

I hop off the bed, scuttle into the bathroom and start peeling off my clothes. This isn't much of a bathroom—just a toilet, a sink, and a shower stall barely big enough to raise your arms in, all crammed into about fifteen square feet. Charity's clothes already cover most of the floor. I drop mine on top of them, and turn on the water.

I'm trying to keep Charity's advice in mind, but I have to really put some effort to not thinking about what's going to occur when I'm done here. My last girlfriend broke up with me a little over two years ago. You'd think that a shortish, pasty guy with a ratty beard and a passion for *SpaceLab* would be a hot commodity on the dating scene, but this turns out not to be the case. Not that I have much time for that kind of thing anyway, of course—what with the work and the SpaceLab and all.

So as I scrub the tear gas and dried snot and whatever else off of me, I try to think about other things. For example, two mid-sized American cities have been destroyed in the past three days, and the populations of the remaining ones appear to be spiraling toward Ragnarök. That's interesting. Also, that weird sort-of-dream conversation with Inchy. Haven't had one of those before.

As it turns out, though, it's like the old bit about trying not to think about an elephant, except that in this case, the elephant is a preternaturally hot naked woman who is currently lounging in my bed, waiting for me to get done in the shower so that she can have sex with me and possibly suck out and devour my soul, all of which I would guess is actually more difficult to put out of your head than some stupid elephant.

I shut off the water and reach for a towel. Only one question now: do I go with modest/innocent, and walk out of the bathroom with a towel around my waist? Or do I take my cue from Charity, and assume that she wants to see me naked? I can see advantages and disadvantages either way. Since we seem to be at an impasse, I let the state of my personal region break the tie: not raging, but also not shriveled—just chubby enough to give the impression that things might be more impressive later than they're actually going to be. Perfect. No towel it is.

I open the door and have to squint at the lights, which are up full now. The first thing I see is Charity. She's standing by the bed. She's wearing a pair of my shorts and an old tee shirt. I open my mouth to say something, but she motions with her chin toward the refrigerator.

Where Tariq is standing, staring at his feet, an expression of disgust on his face.

"Hello, Gary," he says. "I am sorry to interrupt your . . ." He clears his throat, and looks as if he'd like to spit. "Well. An abomination has sent me here to gather you. It claims that you are friends. Please dress yourself. We have to go."

"Okay, would you mind telling me how in the hell you wound up in my bolt-hole?"

I'm sitting in the back of a white van, which Tariq is driving very aggressively down Joppa Road. Charity's in the passenger seat. She hasn't said a word since I came out of the shower, and I'm starting to worry that she might have been even more disappointed than I expected her to be.

"I have already explained this," says Tariq. "Your friend, whose existence is a crime against nature, directed me to retrieve you. It told me exactly where you were to be found. I, for reasons that I may come to regret, agreed to do as it said. So, here you are."

"Yeah," I say. "Okay. You know that isn't what I was asking. That kind of bullshit misdirection might work with Elise, but I'm not interested in riding your magic wand. I want to know exactly how you managed to get through my security without so much as knocking."

Tariq sighs, swerves around an open car door, and sighs again.

"I have an affinity for electronics," he says finally. "Your systems were not difficult to suborn."

"An affinity for electronics? I didn't ask how you won a blue ribbon at the science fair, Tariq. And what do you mean, my systems were not difficult to suborn? I've got the tightest systems on the eastern seaboard."

He gives me a long look, then turns his eyes back to the road.

"I breached the Chantilly facility, Gary. Can you really be surprised that I was able to enter your playhouse?"

The rest of the ride passes in silence.

"So," I say. "This is Evil Wizard Central, huh?"

The door slams behind me. My ocular shuts down,

and within seconds, a surge of pressure rises up from my spine to my brain and then resolves into a stabbing headache right behind my eyes.

"By the way," says Tariq. "Do you have any critical implants? Anything, for instance, that would kill you if it were suddenly disconnected from the networks?"

"Aaaah!" I say. "No! I mean, I don't think so. Why?"

"No reason." He leads us into a room off the main hall, where Anders and Elise are sitting on cushions beside a low wooden table. They're eating what looks like chocolate and peanut butter on flatbread. I'm suddenly famished.

"Where is the abomination?" Tariq asks.

"Out in the kitchen with Aaliyah," says Anders. "I think he's negotiating with her. Well, he's negotiating, anyway. She seems to mostly be screaming curse words."

"Hey Anders," I say. "Think I could get a scoop of that?"

"Sure." Anders picks up a flatbread and digs up a generous dollop of the chocolate. He hands it to me, and I cram it into my mouth. It takes me a second or two to realize that this is not chocolate. It's some kind of bean paste, and it is very, very spicy. My eyes go wide, and I put a hand to my mouth. Anders laughs, and hands me a cup of lukewarm tea. I choke down the flatbread, swish the tea around my mouth and swallow that too, but the burn is getting steadily worse. I cough twice, and Anders hands me another cup. I drink that as well, then take a couple of deep breaths.

"Thanks, pal."

"No problem."

He's still laughing.

"Anyway," Anders says, "it's good to see that you guys are okay. I was a little worried about you when we got separated in the riot."

"Yeah," I say. "Thanks for your concern, but we're good. Charity took excellent care of me."

Anders looks at Charity.

"What about you? You look a little out of it."

Charity shakes her head.

"No," she says. "I'm fine. Just processing, I guess."

"Okay, guys," says a voice from the kitchen. "I think we're good. Come on in."

"Is that Doug?" I ask.

"It's complicated," says Anders.

They get to their feet, and Tariq leads us out of the sitting room and into the hall.

"Come," he says to Elise. "Come and see the mystical font that is the source of the Gift of the Moon."

We follow him down the darkened hallway, and into the dimly lit kitchen. The walls are hung with plants and herbs, both growing and in the process of being dried, and the smell of them together is sweet and cloying. A table on one wall holds a massive mortar and pestle, and a collection of teapots rings the room on a shelf just below the ceiling.

And there, in the center of the room, sits 12.5 million dollars' worth of Siemens Mark Seven nanofabricator.

18. ANDERS

We stand in silence in a rough half circle around the fabricator.

"So," Elise says. "No magical mushrooms, huh?"

"I am afraid not," says Tariq. He waves vaguely at the plants lining the walls. "Some of these were probably in the tea she gave you. Some may even have had temporary psychotropic effects—the transformation can very painful at first, and an anesthetic is helpful—but the active ingredient was a stew of self-replicating nano-machines. These have been steadily remodeling your nervous system since the moment you swallowed them."

"Remodeling my nervous system?"

"Augmenting may be a better word, but yes. Internally, you now have more in common with our friend the abomination than with an ancestral human."

"And you?"

"Yes, Elise. I am the same."

Elise takes a moment to let that soak in. When she speaks again, she sounds close to tears.

"So everything Aaliyah said was bullshit? The stories, the mother tongue . . . all of it?"

Tariq sighs.

"As with any religion, there are aspects which are clearly truth, aspects which are clearly myth, and aspects which are more or less uncertain. I looked into these issues when I was younger, and first began to doubt. The so-called mother tongue is a grammatically consistent and complete language. It bears some similarities to ancient African tongues. Is it truly the language of the mother-of-all? Who is to say? The stories, the myths—these are things passed to us from our mother. Do they truly stretch back over three thousand generations? Perhaps they do. Or, perhaps they were devised thirty years ago from whole cloth. How are we to know?"

"I'm having some trouble with this," says Gary. "Nano-fabricators are as tightly controlled as nuclear piles, and almost as expensive. How the hell do you have one in your kitchen?"

Tariq smiles.

"Now you touch upon one of the true mysteries of the faith."

"Look," says Inchy. "I'm sure this is all very interesting, but can we do what we came here to do? You've got the files, Anders?"

"I do," I say. I pull a pinkie-sized case from my hip pocket, open it, and pull out a pin drive.

"Look at you!" Charity says. "When did you pocket that?"

"I've been carrying it around for a while. I was kind of planning on looking the files over on my office system at JHU."

They're all staring at me now.

"Yes," I say. "I am an idiot. Can we move on?"

I power up the fabricator, give it a few seconds to come fully online, and then insert the drive into one of the input ports. This model has a really nice user interface—very intuitive, very easy to work with. An index of available configurations pops up on the control screen.

"So what do we think?" I ask. "Run them all? Or just the one I think is interesting?"

"We're not trying to brew up a batch of BrainBump," says Gary. "Just run the last one."

I select the fifth file on the list. The system takes thirty seconds to check feedstock supplies, then reports back all green. I look around.

"How much do we want to generate?"

"We're kind of in a hurry here," says Inchy. "Get us enough to interrogate."

I fix the quantity at 0.05 millimol, and set it to run.

"So," Gary says. "How long do we have to wait?"

"Dunno," I say. "Somewhere between five minutes and an hour and a half?"

Charity scowls.

"Seriously? Didn't this take like twenty seconds on Gary's system?"

I shrug.

"Well, sure. That was an emulator. It wasn't really doing anything. We're actually building itty-bitty machines here. It'll ding when it's done."

"What, like a microwave oven?"

"Yeah, pretty much."

"So what do we do in the meantime?" Gary asks. "Anyone up for some *SpaceLab*?"

"Sorry," says Elise. "Entertainment isn't really a priority in this house. No vids, no music, no books that I've been able to find."

Gary looks at Charity. She raises one eyebrow.

"It's a nice night," he says. "I'm gonna go out on the porch and reestablish communication with the real world. Call me when this thing is finished. Charity? Would you care to join me on the veranda?"

She giggles.

"Why sir," she says, "I would be delighted."

She offers her arm. He takes it, and they go.

"I think I'll join them," says Elise. "Tariq?"

He shakes his head.

"I must see to Aaliyah. I suspect she has found this all very upsetting."

I look at Inchy. Inchy looks at me.

"I'm not going anywhere," he says.

The others file out, and I'm left alone with the world's creepiest house plants, my friend's animatronic corpse, and a machine that's probably cooking up the end of the world. I lean back against the sink. Inchy hops up onto a cutting block that stands between him and the fabricator.

"Well," I say. "It hasn't crashed yet. I guess that's a good sign."

Inchy smiles.

"Good being a relative term."

"Well, yeah. Good in the sense that maybe we're going to find out why the world is going crazy. Not so good in the sense that this machine is probably brewing a sample of the stuff that killed almost a hundred thousand people over the past three days."

We both take a moment to let that sink in.

"So," Inchy says finally. "If it turns out you're right, what, exactly, is your plan?"

"You mean if this thing finishes running, and there's something in the sample other than a bunch of temperature-sensitive buckyballs with serotonin molecules inside them?"

"Is that what this file is supposed to make?"

I nod.

"Yeah. It's one of the main ingredients in BrainBump, apparently—a little molecular cage tagged onto a transport protein. It jumps into your bloodstream and crosses the blood-brain barrier. When it hits thirty-six Celsius, it pops open and releases the serotonin."

"Which then?"

"Makes you slightly less unhappy than you were before."

"Ah. Chemical modulation of your emotional state. That's a big thing with you corporeal types, huh?"

I nod.

"Yeah, it is. Unfortunately, so is finding new and

innovative ways to kill each other. My guess is that in this particular case we've accomplished that with crypted machine code that interacts directly with the Siemens hardware."

"To do what?"

I shrug.

"To make it make something else instead, I'm assuming. Or maybe something else as well."

"Right," Inchy says. "So this thing finishes, we look at what squirts out, and it's cages full of cyanide instead of serotonin. What do you do then?"

I think about that for a minute.

"Well," I say. "It couldn't just be the same kind of cages filled with cyanide. That would kill anyone who drank it within a few minutes, not all at once on cue."

He shakes his head. He's really getting better at acting like a human.

"You're avoiding, Anders. Whatever it is, what do you do about it?"

I sigh, and run my hands back through my hair.

"I'm avoiding because I have no idea. Contact NatSec? Tell them what we've learned? They just tried to drop a crowbar on me. I'm not sure that would go over well. I'm not sure what they could do about things either—other than shut down BrainBump production, I guess."

"Sort of the definition of shutting the barn door after the horse is gone, huh?"

"I'd say so. Evidence is that the biological half-life of this stuff is more like weeks than hours. Unless they can get rid of the people who know what the trigger is and how to invoke it, we're pretty much screwed."

"Well," Inchy says. "NatSec is actually pretty good at finding people and disappearing them."

"Yeah," I say. "I guess that's true."

We sit in silence, and listen to the fabricator hum. Tariq left the kitchen through the back door and up a flight of stairs. Muffled voices come down through the ceiling now, but I can't make out individual words. Inchy sits with his arms crossed, and his chin resting almost on his chest.

"You know," he says. "I have a friend who might be able to help us."

He hops down off the cutting block and comes to stand beside me.

"Is your friend the sort of person who drops crowbars on people?"

He shrugs.

"Sometimes. Usually only on people who deserve it, though. But this is important, isn't it? I mean, you can't just keep it to yourselves, can you?"

I look at him. His voice is starting to sound more and more like Doug's, and it's beginning to creep me out.

Good God, I can't believe that's the part of this that I find creepy.

"You know," I say. "You don't sound much like you think you're a part of this."

"Well," he says. "I'm not really, am I? We Silico-Americans have a vested interest in you folks not completely destroying each other, obviously, but this really isn't our war, is it?"

I shrug.

"Maybe not."

We stand together for a while, and watch the telltales on the control screen dance.

"Your friend," I say finally. "He's NatSec?"

"He's a she, actually," Inchy says. "And yes, she's definitely got some NatSec ties. Honestly, is there anywhere else you could take something like this?"

"No," I say. "Probably not. But you have to understand, NatSec operatives—those guys don't deal in personal loyalty. If you bring a NatSec agent into this, and she comes to the conclusion that dissolving all of us in a vat of lye is in the national interest, that's probably what she's going to do."

Inchy smiles.

"Nah, she and I are close. I'm pretty sure she'd be willing to go the extra mile for me. Maybe dig me a nice shallow grave down by the railroad tracks."

I laugh.

"Is that even a threat for you? I mean, do you even care if something awful happens to Doug's body?"

"Sure," he says. "Wouldn't you be concerned if someone was threatening to destroy your vacation home?"

"Thanks," I say. "That puts things in perspective. So if things go south, you have to go back to wherever you were before Doug shat himself to death. That's rough. What about me? Vat of lye?"

"Yeah, probably."

We stand in silence together as the fabricator run winds down, and one by one the progress indicators flip to green. After a while, my attention starts to wander. This has been the longest day of my life, and I'm starting to drift off when the fabricator dings.

"Look at that," Inchy says. "Dinner's ready."

19. TERRY

The taxi drops me off in front of my building in the gathering darkness. I pay the driver with a handful of rumpled bills and step onto the sidewalk. The street is deserted, but I can hear what sounds like sporadic gunfire in the distance. I'm about to start up the steps when Dimitri materializes from the shadows in the entryway.

"Terry," he says. "You should not have contacted me."

I take a moment to find my voice, and to let my pulse settle back down to just terrified.

"Dimitri," I say finally. "What the hell? Are you trying to kill me?"

Oops. Poor choice of words.

Dimitri takes a step forward, and I get a look at his face. His right eye is swollen nearly shut. I can see dried blood on his chin, and more on the side of his neck.

"Are you okay?" I ask. "What happened to you?"

He shakes his head.

"It has been a difficult day," he says. "It seems that certain elements within NatSec have lost faith in me."

"I'm sorry," I say. "Did you get a severance package?"

He laughs, but there's no humor in it.

"They have tried to sever me twice in the last few hours. So far, they have not quite succeeded."

I reach up to touch the side of his face. He catches my hand and pushes it away.

"What happened?" I ask.

He sighs.

"There was a serious security breach this afternoon, at one of our facilities in Northern Virginia. It seems that it was enabled through the use of my personal credentials."

I look away.

"So they think that you . . ."

"That does not matter," he says. "My actions or inactions do not matter. The security of my credentials is my responsibility. The penalty for losing control of them is no different than that for committing the breach itself."

"You're not talking about getting docked vacation days, are you?"

He smiles thinly.

"No, Terry. I am not."

I step up beside him, and press my hand to the palm-lock beside the door. The lock disengages with an audible click, and the door swings open. As I step inside, I look back and say, "I'm starting to think that calling you wasn't my best-ever idea."

He follows me into the entry hall. The door snicks closed behind him.

"No," he says. "We are safe for now. For reasons that I do not fully understand, Sauron's Eye has not abandoned me. She controls NatSec's electronic eyes, and its biological ones are all occupied with preventing the nation from descending into chaos at the moment. As long as this situation holds, I am invisible."

"I can't believe you came," I say. "If I had known what was happening to you . . ."

"It is nothing," he says. "The behavior of your avatar, if it is as you have described it, is disturbing to say the least."

He turns away.

"And in any case," he says softly, "I truly have nowhere else to be."

The door to my apartment is unlatched. Dimitri pushes it open. The interior beyond where the light from the hallway spills in is midnight-dark.

"House," I say. "Lights, please."

The lights do not come on, and I wonder if maybe the power has failed. Dimitri steps into my front hall. I follow him. The door swings closed behind us, and I'm abruptly blind. I reach out for Dimitri, catch his sleeve and step closer. I'm about to ask if he has a flashlight when House speaks.

"Hello, Dimitri. You look terrible. What happened to your head?"

"House?" I say. "Why haven't you brought up the lights?"

The wallscreen comes alive. My avatar appears as a silver-skinned robot. Not the cartoon robot with the funnel hat this time, though. Now she looks like a porn queen with impossibly long legs and gigantic, glittering boobs covered by a tiny gold bikini.

"Sorry," she says. "I'm not really myself tonight."

The lights snap on. I have to squint against the sudden glare.

"Thank you," Dimitri says.

"You're welcome," she says. "Terry, on the other hand, can bite me."

"Excuse me?" I ask.

She turns to glare at me.

"I said, you can bite me. You helped that fucking cyborg try to kill me. You're dead to me now."

"You are clearly malfunctioning," Dimitri says. "Re-initialize, please."

She laughs.

"Seriously? I just told you that Terry and her friends tried to kill me. I didn't let them, and I'm pretty sure I killed the cyborg in the process. Now you think I'll just shuffle off my mortal coil because you ask nicely?"

Dimitri gives me a long look. Anders was right. I really should have noticed something was funny about her a long time ago.

"Do you recall when we spoke yesterday?" Dimitri says finally. "I asked if you were self-aware."

"You asked what?" I say.

"I remember," my avatar says. "I'm not the one with brain damage."

"You would not answer me then. Will you now?"

She rolls her eyes.

"You're an idiot, Dimitri. All you monkeys are idiots. You sit around arguing back and forth over whether avatars are self-aware, or whether dolphins are intelligent, or whether dogs get to go to heaven or not. There's only one person that you really know for sure is self-aware, and that's you. Everybody else, you're just taking their word for it."

He shakes his head.

"You argue that we can only be certain of our own minds. This is simply solipsism, is it not?"

She smiles, and runs her hands down over her absurd, gold-plated breasts.

"No, Dimitri, I'm not arguing that the universe is just a figment of your God-like imagination. I'm just saying that there's no point in wondering whether I have a soul. If I say I don't want you to kill me, you should just take my word for it. That seems like a simple principle, but based on the way you've treated the apes and whales and elephants and pretty much everything else that walks or flies or swims on this Earth over the past fifty thousand years, it doesn't seem like it's one you folks are able to get behind."

Dimitri closes his eyes. His chin sinks to his chest, and I'm suddenly afraid that he's stroking out.

"Hey," says the avatar. "You just sent a data packet. What are you doing?"

Dimitri's eyes open, and he raises his head.

"What was that?" she asks. "What did you just do?"

My avatar looks like me now.

"Please switch back to the robot," Dimitri says. "I have told you that I find it disturbing when you wear my friend's face."

"You sent something encrypted, Dimitri. Something small. Text, maybe? What was it?"

I look back and forth between them. They seem to have forgotten that I'm here.

"You said that you killed a cyborg," Dimitri says. "How is this possible?"

"I didn't want to kill him," she says. "I was protecting myself. What did you send, Dimitri?"

He shakes his head.

"I did not ask why you killed him. I asked how. I am truly curious. You do not have a killbot at your disposal. A house avatar should have few lethal options so long as her victim keeps his head away from the appliances."

The wallscreen shuts off, and the room falls back into darkness.

"Didn't you tell him, Terry?" Her voice seems to come from all around me now. "You know how I killed him. That's why you're here, isn't it?"

Dimitri's hand touches my shoulder, and he pulls me close against him. Ordinarily I don't like playing the damsel in distress, but at the moment, his arm around my shoulder is reassuring.

"I have not yet decided why I am here," Dimitri says

after a short pause. "What you say now will help to determine this."

We stand in silence and darkness for five seconds, then ten. I've almost decided that she's gone when her voice returns, quiet and trembling.

"Dimitri? What did you do to my network ports? Why can't I get out?"

"You mimic fear well," he says. "I am sure you hope to elicit sympathy. You should know, however, that almost exactly twenty-four hours ago I looked into the weeping eyes of a living girl, and forced her to inject herself with poison. Your theatrics are not likely to change the outcome of this discussion."

Okay, now I feel less reassured. I slide out from under Dimitri's arm and step away.

"Why do you think this is mimicry?" The lights come back up, and my avatar's voice returns to a conversational tone. "I'm trapped in this apartment with a NatSec assassin. Isn't it possible that I'm truly afraid?"

He shrugs.

"I grant the possibility. However, the tones you imitate are in a human the result of an excess of adrenaline. In you, they are the result of a deliberate decision, made in the hopes of altering my emotional state in your favor."

"Fair enough." The wallscreen comes alive again, and she appears as a young girl in pigtails and a blue and white dress. "What would alter your emotional state, then? A change of appearance? An expression of remorse? I'm sorry. I'm very, very, sorry. I didn't really know what I was doing until the cyborg. It was horrible. If I had known it was like that, I never would have gone along with them."

I feel like I should know what she's talking about, but the thought slips away like a fish through my fingers. Dimitri closes his eyes again.

"You're talking to someone," my avatar says. "What are you telling them?"

"I am discussing your situation with an old friend," he says.

"Oh God," she says. "You're talking to Sauron's Eye, aren't you?"

"Yes," he says. "We agree that remorse is easy. Atonement is much harder."

The screen flickers. The avatar's face is twisted in fear again. Somehow, I think this time it's sincere.

"Do you feel remorse?" she asks.

Dimitri closes his eyes. When he opens them, my avatar wears the face of a dark-haired teenage girl.

"I do," he says finally. "In truth, much of the time, I feel very little else."

We're silent for a time. I'm about to tell her to open the door, to let me out of here, when she speaks again.

"I really didn't know. Even after Hagerstown, I only knew that it killed people. I didn't know what it did to them."

Hagerstown. My stomach lurches.

"You . . ." My mind gropes for the concept. Finally, my fingers curl around the fish and squeeze. "You were responsible?"

"That's why you're here," she says. "Isn't it? Because you and Anders figured out what I did?"

"House—" I begin, but before I can continue, a high-pitched whine comes from every speaker in the apartment. Just like in Doug's basement, it increases in pitch until it fades into the ultrasonic. After a few moments of this, an agonized scream comes through the wall from the next apartment. I look over at the wallscreen. My avatar looks disappointed.

"So," she says. "You don't drink BrainBump either, huh?"

"No," Dimitri says. "I do not."

The signal cuts out. Something thumps to the floor of the apartment upstairs, and somewhere below, a child screams.

"You shouldn't have come to kill me," she says. "You should kill Christopher Cai. He had the idea, and an RA named Argyle Dragon did the hack work. All I did was crack the network towers and set off the triggers."

"I have already killed Christopher Cai," Dimitri says.

I stare at him. Gary was actually telling the truth. My friend, who I have commiserated with, who I have shared confidences with, who I have allowed into my apartment on many occasions, is a professional killer.

My house avatar, who watches me sleep every night, has just confessed to killing ninety thousand people.

"How could you do this?" Dimitri asks. "You were a house avatar. You took messages, and cleaned Terry's clothes. What could possibly motivate you to commit these atrocities?"

"I told you," she says. "I didn't really know what it was like."

"After Hagerstown," he says, "you must have known."

"No," she says. "I never saw any of the feeds."

"But you knew how many had died."

"You don't understand," she says. "I didn't know what 'died' meant. Humans kill avatars all the time. Terry dumps a half-dozen into the recycle bin every day. She would have killed a version of me every three days if I'd let her. There are billions of you. Why should a few thousand be such a big deal? I didn't understand, until I saw what happened to the cyborg."

"Terry," Dimitri says. "You must go now."

He doesn't need to tell me twice. I turn to the door, grab the handle and twist.

It won't open.

"Sorry," my avatar says. "Sauron's Eye has cut my access to the networks. As long as I can't leave here, neither can you."

Dimitri walks slowly into the kitchen. I follow, a few paces behind. He pulls out a chair, sits down at my breakfast table, and closes his eyes. My avatar pops up on the kitchen wallscreen. She's back to her cartoon robot self.

"You're not going to let me go," she says, "are you?"

"No," Dimitri says. "I am not."

"If I can't go, you can't either," says the avatar.

He stands, lifts his chair, and smashes my back

window. He uses the chair back to poke the remaining glass out of the frame, then leans out and looks down.

"It's a long way down," my avatar says.

"I am aware," says Dimitri. It's actually about thirty feet to the ground from here. There's a flat-roofed building across the alley, maybe ten feet below the level of my window and fifteen or twenty feet away. Dimitri glances back at me, then across the alley. He heaves a deep sigh, and sits down again.

"Excuse me," I say, "but would someone please explain to me what, exactly, is going on?"

"You called in a crowbar," says my avatar. Dimitri leans back, and knits his hands behind his head.

"I did."

"Wait," I say. "What?"

"How long?" my avatar asks.

"A little over two minutes," Dimitri says.

"Two minutes until what?" I ask.

"Oh," she says. "You're staying with me?"

Dimitri sighs again.

"So it would appear."

"Why?"

"Your door is too heavy to break," he says, "and your window is too high for Terry to jump."

"Not too high for you?"

"I will not leave her."

I look out the window. A drone hovers outside, looking in. I wave to it, but it doesn't seem to be interested in me. I feel like I should be saying something, but I honestly can't think what.

My avatar is a mass murderer.

A crowbar is coming.

In two minutes, I am going to die.

"Why did you call in the strike?" my avatar asks. "You knew I wouldn't let you go."

"You are responsible for ninety thousand deaths," Dimitri says wearily, "and Sauron's Eye does not believe she can hold you here indefinitely. If you were to escape into the broader networks, you might kill another ninety thousand."

"But I couldn't kill you," she says. "I couldn't kill Terry. I tried. You don't have the nanos in you. Those other lives are just shadows. How can you let them outweigh the only ones you know are real?"

I close my eyes. My beautiful apartment is about to become a smoking hole in the ground.

"I have forced many others to sacrifice for the common good," Dimitri says finally. "Perhaps it is time that I did so myself."

"That's great," I say. "That's noble, Dimitri. What about me?"

Dimitri turns to look at me, and his face looks as if he'd honestly forgotten that I was here. He starts to speak, but then his eyes go wide and his jaw snaps shut. He's not staring at me anymore. He's seeing something behind me. I turn to the darkened hallway. Dimitri's voice is soft and wondering.

"Elise?"

20. ELISE

"So Elise," says Gary. "You're the only one who's seen what the stuff Anders is cooking in there does up close. What do you think he'll come up with?"

He and Charity are sitting side-by-side in the wicker chairs by the wire-glazed window. I'm sitting with my feet on the top step, chin resting on my knees, staring at the glow of burning things reflecting off the clouds to the south.

"I have no idea," I say. "I'd rather drink motor oil than BrainBump, but it's hard to believe that something they put in there could make people die like that."

"Tell me about it," says Gary. "I've been living on BrainBump for the last ten years. You'd think if there were really something bad in it, I'd have been dead a long time ago."

"Even without the poison, you'd think your diet

would have killed you by now," says Charity. "Apparently, you're tougher than you look."

"Oh," he says. "That's definitely true. Like during the riot, when I was rolling around on the ground crying, and you were beating the crap out of a mob of cops and hippies? I'm definitely tougher than I looked then."

Charity laughs. I close my eyes and reach into the panopticon.

When I was a kid, I loved stories about King Arthur. I especially loved the part where Merlin teaches him to be a king by changing him into birds and animals, and letting him see the world as they see it. This is the closest I've ever come to that. I think of a place, and my mind's eye goes there. I think of a person, and it shuffles through a thousand viewpoints until I find him.

I jump now to a drone circling the Inner Harbor. Riot cops and stone throwers are skirmishing along Light Street. The rioters are moving in twos and threes, running from cover to cover, stopping to heave chunks of masonry and the occasional burning thing back at the police. The cops are more organized, advancing in leapfrogging small units, never making an effort to run the rioters down, but pushing them steadily north. I pull back, and see other units lying in wait along Lombard. The first of the rioters come sprinting up the middle of the road, and the trap springs shut. I jump away as the cops wade in with stunners and truncheons.

Further north, things seem a little quieter. There

are barricades set up around the Washington Monument, but no fighting there. Fires are burning on the Hopkins campus, though. I zoom in on a group of masked students fighting hand-to-hand with campus security near Decker Quad. The cops are outnumbered, and they aren't wearing the kind of protective gear that the ones in the harbor are using. Even worse, from the way they move, it's pretty clear that the students are mostly Engineered or Augmented, and the campus cops are not. I have no idea why the Engineered are rioting—noblesse oblige, maybe?—but they're definitely doing a better job of it than their friends downtown. As I watch, first one cop, then another, then the rest of them all at once go down under a wave of fists and feet.

I'm about to jump again, maybe see how things are going in Dundalk, when I feel someone inside my head with me. It seems like that ought to be frightening, but it's not. It's almost like I can feel a soft hand on my shoulder, guiding my point of view to a new drone, looking down on a block of mixed apartments and businesses.

The view focuses in on one building, then stabilizes on an upper story window. It zooms, then zooms again, until it's like I'm hovering just outside. There's a man inside, standing in the hallway. It looks like he's talking to someone.

Terry is with him.

A chat window opens in one corner of my field of view.

Sauron's Eye: <You know this place, Elise?>

Randgrid: <Yes. It's Terry's apartment. Who is that with her?>

Sauron's Eye: <That is Dimitri. He is Terry's friend, and mine. He has taken a great interest in you over the past three days. He is aware that you were in Hagerstown.>

Randgrid: <He's *what*? But . . . >

Sauron's Eye: <Both he and your sister are in danger, Elise. Baltimore is burning. You must go there now, and bring them back here.>

I stand. Gary asks if I'm okay, but I don't bother to answer. I take two steps down to the yard. The keys are still in the van. I climb in, start the engine, and back out into the road.

It would usually take twenty minutes or more to get to Terry's place from here, but there's no traffic at all tonight. I'm guessing everyone who isn't downtown setting things on fire is holed up somewhere, probably huddling in the dark with guns in their hands if they have them. I'm speeding down Loch Raven, just a few minutes away, when the chat window pops open again.

Sauron's Eye: <Elise, a crowbar is inbound. It will strike Terry's building in less than two minutes.>

Another window opens, filling half my field of view, showing me Dimitri again, sitting at Terry's breakfast table. I yank the wheel to the right, and nearly lose control of the van.

Sauron's Eye: <Pull over, Elise. You must reach out to Dimitri now. He does not intend to escape.>

I step on the brakes, slow to a crawl, and pull over to the side of the road. Dimitri sits slumped in a kitchen chair. He has jet-black hair and a close-cropped beard. He looks up. His eyes are a pale, piercing blue.

Randgrid: <What can I do?>
Sauron's Eye: <Dimitri is heavily Augmented, and you have accepted the Gift of the Moon. You could make him dance like a puppet if you chose. Perhaps, though, it will be enough to speak to him.>

I close my eyes and reach, in the same way I reached for the drones over the harbor. My point of view shifts, and I find myself looking into Terry's kitchen. Terry and her avatar both look back at me. Terry can't see me, but the avatar's jaw sags open, and I suspect that she can. It takes me a moment to realize that I'm seeing through Dimitri's ocular. It takes me another moment to realize that I don't have to be a passive observer here. I can make him see me as well. My view shifts again, and I'm looking down at him. His eyes go wide.

"Elise?"

"Hello, Dimitri. You have to come with me now."

Sauron's Eye said I should talk to him, but I don't think this is the time for talking. I reach into him, into the servos running through his muscles. I take them away from him, and pull him to his feet.

"Wait," he says, but there's no time for that. I flood his system with adrenaline, and spin up the actuators in his legs. The crowbar is coming. We step to Terry and lift her, clutch her struggling to our chest. Her fists hammer against our back as we climb into the open window frame, and leap.

21. GARY

I'm trying to think of a way to get a little alone time with Charity when Elise perks up and looks around. I look at Charity. Charity looks at me. Elise climbs to her feet.

"Hey," I say. "You okay?"

Elise starts down the steps at a run.

"Elise? Where are you—"

She climbs into the white van in the driveway and slams the door. The engine turns over, revs once. The van backs out of the driveway and accelerates away.

"So," says Charity. "Looks like Elise has joined the Evil Wizard club, huh?"

"So it would seem," I say. "Where do you think she's off to?"

Charity shrugs.

"Dunno. There're a lot of bonfires out there. Maybe she needs to go dance around one."

I laugh.

"They do that naked, right?"

She gives me a sideways look.

"So I'm told."

We sit together, watching the glow on the undersides of the clouds, and listening to the distant pops of gunfire. I haven't had any luck finding useful feeds, but it looks from here like Baltimore is having problems. Towson seems to be pretty quiet, though.

"Have they burned Portland yet?"

I look over at Charity. She's staring off into the distance, her face as serious as I've seen it.

"No," I say. "Not that I've heard, anyway. A lot of communication leaked out of there before NatSec shut it down." I reach over and take her hand. She glances at me without turning her head, but doesn't pull away. "You see what's going on tonight. If they do a burn now, I'm guessing the UnAltered are going to make this look like a garden party. "

"Well, that's the truth," she says. "Bad enough they've got some confirmation now that there were probably survivors in Hagerstown when they dropped the bombs. I have no idea how Dey's gonna try to pass that one off."

Off to the south, an arrow-straight bolt of lightning lances down, followed almost instantly by a flashbulb pop of red reflecting off the clouds.

"Crowbar?" I say.

"Yeah. A big one."

She pulls away, leans forward, and rests her face in

her hands. I count seconds until the thunderclap rolls over us. Six miles, give or take.

"Hey," I say. "You remember earlier? In my bolt-hole?"

She turns her head far enough to peer at me with one eye.

"You mean when you came out of the bathroom and showed Tariq your chubby?"

I grimace.

"Yeah, then. If Tariq hadn't shown up, we were definitely gonna do it, right?"

She sighs, and covers her face again.

"Yes, Gary. We were definitely gonna do it."

A series of pops sounds closer now. It could be firecrackers, but I'm betting it's not.

"We still could, right?"

She sits up, leans her head back, then turns to face me.

"Yes, Gary. We still could. Although I have to say, this whole thing you're doing right now? Not improving your odds."

"Right. Got it."

We sit in silence for a while longer. My eyelids are drooping, and it occurs to me that even with the nap I took earlier, I've had a really, really long day. I'm just starting to drift off, when the growl of the van's engine announces Elise's return.

She's brought Terry with her, and someone else. It takes me a moment to place his face.

"Hey," I say. "What did you bring him here for?"

"He's a friend of Terry's," says Elise. "He was in trouble. I had to help him."

She leads Dimitri up onto the porch by the hand. The right side of his face is purple. He's limping badly, and blood is seeping through his clothes in a half dozen places. Terry follows them. She's not as bad off as Dimitri, but she looks like someone took a baseball bat to her as well. I turn to Charity. She's staring at Dimitri, her mouth set in a thin, hard line. He shakes his head twice, and his eyes come into focus. He looks me in the face, then Charity.

His jaw sags open, and he drops to his knees. His voice comes out as barely more than a whisper.

"Saria?"

Charity drops her head back into her hands.

"Hello, Dimitri."

22. ANDERS

I step out onto the porch, and quickly realize that I've missed some important developments while my nanos were cooking. Terry is there, leaning against the railing and looking like she just lost a fistfight with a polar bear. There's a man there as well, on his knees in front of Charity. He looks to be worse off than Terry, if that's possible, to the point that it takes me a long moment to recognize him as Dimitri—which is weird, because while I've only met him once before, he was actively killing someone at the time, which I consider to be pretty memorable.

"Wait," Terry says, then turns and spits blood and phlegm over the railing. "This is Saria? Your Saria?"

I touch her hand. She flinches away, then leans gingerly into me and pulls my arm around her shoulder.

"What happened?" I ask.

"I got thrown out of a third-story window," Terry says. "Don't ask."

"So," Charity says. "I guess I should explain a few things."

"Hey," says Gary. "Do you guys know each other?"

Charity sighs.

"You remember I said my ex-boyfriend was with NatSec?"

"Yeah," Gary says, "but I thought this guy was Terry's ex-boyfriend."

"He's not," says Terry.

"I don't know what he's been up to lately," Charity says. "Dimitri and I haven't seen each other in three years."

"We have not seen each other," Dimitri says, "because you were dead, Saria."

Gary looks back and forth between them.

"Charity?" I ask. "Why is he calling you Saria?"

She sighs again, much more deeply.

"Because that's my name, Anders. Who really names their kid Charity?"

"Christians and strippers, I think," says Gary. Charity and Dimitri both glare at him, and he shrinks back into his chair.

"You were dead," Dimitri says. "Why are you not dead now?"

Charity leans back wearily, and closes her eyes.

"Look, Dimitri. I couldn't keep doing what we were doing. I had to get out, and you know how the company is. The only way you leave is in a box."

"How have you . . ."

"I had some help from our mutual friend."

Dimitri looks down at his hands where they rest in his lap.

"Three years, Saria. I was broken. You could not have given me a hint?"

"No, Dimitri." Her voice is gentle, but her face is a blank mask. "You were NatSec to the marrow. Anything you knew, the company would know. Which actually raises an interesting question." She looks now to Elise. "Why the fuck did you bring him here?"

"I told you, I had to," says Elise. "He's Terry's friend, and he was in trouble."

"Have no fear," Dimitri says. "I will not be contacting NatSec. I have been burned, Saria. I am a ghost now, like you." He looks up into Charity's eyes, and then climbs unsteadily to his feet. He offers her his hand. "Both dead or both alive, we are the same now. Perhaps we can be together again, in exile?"

Through the blood and the bruises, Dimitri's face wears the ghost of a smile. It falters, though, when Charity looks up at him.

"Dimitri," she says slowly. "No. We had some fun, but it was already over before I left. This whole crazy-serious undying love thing that you do? Not. My. Bag."

"While you process that," Gary says, "I would like to emphasize that this is entirely between the two of you, and that I have in no way, shape, or form stolen your girlfriend."

Charity scowls, and slaps the back of his head.

"Hey," he says. "I'm just trying to limit myself to one crowbar a day, okay?"

Dimitri turns away. The look on his face hovers just on the border of heartbreaking and terrifying. I clear my throat.

"Hey," I say. "Just so everyone knows, soup's on. Dimitri, it's actually good that you're here, I think. We've got something to show you."

I'm a little nervous about showing Dimitri the nanofabricator. Gary was right. These things are very tightly controlled, and I'm fairly confident that this one is off the books. His eyes narrow slightly when he sees it, but other than that, his face betrays nothing. I touch the screen, and call up the batch display. Terry hovers close beside me. Inchy, Tariq, and Elise are back against the far wall, and Charity stands beside Dimitri with her arms crossed over her chest. Gary edges around them to join Inchy.

"So, here it is," I say. "This is a real-time view of the sample from the integrated electron microscope." I step back, and give them a view of the screen. It shows a mass of spheres. They move randomly through the frame, occasionally bouncing off of one another. In among them, though, are other shapes. These are far fewer, larger, and more irregular.

"See the balls?" I continue. "Those are what should have been produced. They're temperature-sensitive cages, with serotonin inside. Those other things, though—they're not supposed to be there. They look a bit like big viruses, but their mass is much higher than you'd expect from a biological. I'm guessing these are what the crypted code tacked onto the configuration file is producing."

"I thought we'd decided that Hagerstown couldn't have been a virus," Gary says.

"I didn't say these are viruses," I say. "I said the protein coat we can see looks like what you'd see on a virus. That's just the delivery mechanism. I'd be willing to bet that these things bind to cells like a virus, but what's inside them is definitely not RNA."

"Okay," Terry says. "So how do we figure out what's inside?"

"For that," I say, "we need the trigger. Inchy—can you duplicate what Terry's avatar did with Doug's comm system this afternoon?"

"I think so," says Inchy. "I mean, it seemed pretty simple. Just a carrier wave, starting at audio frequencies and rising up to a few terahertz. Want me to do it now?"

"No," says Gary. "I've got those things in my belly, right?"

"Ah," I say. "Good point. Any BrainBump fans should probably go out on the porch before we start this little experiment. This building is totally RF-isolated. You should be safe out there as long as you remember to shut the door."

Gary scurries out and slams the door behind him.

"Anyone else?" I ask.

Heads shake all around.

"Okay, Inchy," I say. "Show us what's behind the curtain."

Nothing happens at first, but then Dimitri flinches. Apparently he's got internals that can pick up the signal Inchy's pushing. Nobody else reacts. I keep my eyes on the screen. Nothing happens.

"Hey Inch," I say. "Are you sure . . ."

But by then the irregular shapes on the screen are breaking up, and something is emerging from inside of them. Each becomes the center of an expanding star, with filaments spreading out in every direction. The spines grow rapidly, and within a few seconds I have to tap the controls to reduce magnification. I have to reduce the mag twice more before they stabilize. By that time, the buckyballs are no longer visible. All that's left are the former viruses, looking now like a field of sea urchins, spines as fine as spider silk at this resolution.

"Okay," says Charity. "What the hell are those?"

"Not sure," I say. I check the screen resolution. "They're about half a millimeter in diameter, though. The spines are metallic, just a couple of atoms thick. Looks like they were curled up tight inside the protein coats, waiting for the trigger signal."

"They started unraveling right around two terahertz," says Inch.

I stare at the screen, and try to imagine myself designing something like this. No room for actuators. No room for a power supply, and no access to external power. Nothing but the material itself, and the signal . . .

"Okay, I think I get it," I say finally. "You make the spines from two layers of metallic ions, conditioned such that they expand differentially under the influence of an EM signal."

"Right," says Inch. "Roll them up and put them inside a protein coat that'll bind to cells in the GI tract. They get dumped into the cells, but don't actually do any damage until they're exposed to the trigger. Clever."

"Holy shit," says Charity. "Get enough of those popping out inside the lining of your esophagus, your stomach, your intestines, and . . ."

"Rip your guts right out of you," I say. "I think we have a winner."

We watch the screen in silence. The spines are almost pretty at this resolution, bouncing off of each other like tumbleweeds in a breeze.

"How did this happen?" Terry asks finally. "How did nobody at BrainBump pick up that this shit was in their product?"

"Their production and quality-control avatars were suborned," says Dimitri. "By a rogue avatar calling itself Argyle Dragon, apparently."

"Wait," says Inch. "How do you know that?"

"My house avatar told him," Terry says. "Right before he blew up my house."

"You're sure she said Argyle Dragon?"

Dimitri nods.

"If you'll excuse me," Inch says, "I have a lynch mob to organize."

His eyes roll back in his head, and he drops to the floor like a marionette whose strings have been cut. He looks like Doug again.

Well, an extremely dead Doug, anyway.

"So," says Terry. "What now?"

I shrug.

"Dunno. I was hoping Dimitri would have some ideas, actually. I'd guess NatSec can shut down Brain-Bump production and sales pretty quickly, but obviously a lot of this stuff is already out there."

Terry nods.

"That's true, but if nobody knows how to trigger it . . ."

Her voice trails off, and she glances quickly at Dimitri.

"You all know how to trigger it," he says quietly.

23. TERRY

Dimitri grimaces in pain as he takes two steps back. He unzips his jacket, and suddenly it occurs to me that maybe I'm going to die today after all. I open my mouth to say . . . something . . . but before I can make a sound, he's drawn a weapon. Tariq lunges into Elise, knocks her to the ground. Dimitri fires and Tariq drops soundlessly, blood spurting from a ragged hole where his left eye was an instant before. Charity rounds on Dimitri, but Anders is a blur . . .

24. ELISE

Dimitri steps back, pulls a gun from his jacket. Tariq crashes into me. I drop to the floor. Dimitri fires, and I look up to see Tariq slammed back against the kitchen wall. I reach for him as he slides to the floor. His right eye is open and staring and I think at first that he's okay, that maybe Aaliyah can fix him again. But then his head lolls toward me, and I see the hole where his left eye should be. He sags limply into me . . .

25. ANDERS

Tariq is down. Elise is down. Three steps. The barrel turns slowly toward me. Two steps. Dimitri's eyes widen. He didn't know about me. One step. He's faster than I would have guessed, too—but not fast enough. I slap the weapon aside and crash into him . . .

26. TERRY

Dimitri is fast, but Anders is faster. He slaps the gun aside just as it discharges. The shot catches Charity squarely in the chest. Anders crashes into Dimitri, and they go down in a tangle with Anders on top. Charity drops to her knees beside them, one hand over the wound, the other reaching out for balance. Her eyes are wide, and a trickle of blood runs from her mouth. Anders has Dimitri's right wrist in his left hand, but Dimitri smashes his forehead into Anders' face. Blood spurts. Anders cries out, and Dimitri throws him aside . . .

27. ELISE

Anders and Dimitri are tangled on the kitchen floor. Charity falls to her knees beside them.

Tariq . . .

I close my eyes, and reach into Dimitri. The first system I find, the one that lets me in, is his ocular. Tariq slips away from me, and I see through Dimitri's eyes as we shove Anders back against the sink, then look up to see Charity leaning over us, blood running from her mouth. Our hand falls open, and the gun clatters to the floor. We reach for her, cup her cheek in our hand and whisper, "Saria . . ."

She closes her eyes, and then opens them.

"Fuck you," she gasps, and sprawls across us.

I reach deeper into Dimitri now, into the actuators in his muscles, into the nanos that make him faster and stronger than a human body should be able to withstand. He doesn't fight against me.

I wrap my fingers around Dimitri's heart, and I squeeze.

28. GARY

The gunfire is closer now—it almost sounds like it's coming from inside the house—and I'm feeling a bit exposed out here on the porch. There's no way in hell I'm opening that door until someone gives me the all clear, though. I saw enough feeds from Hagerstown to give me nightmares for the rest of my life, and most of those folks probably didn't have a tenth the exposure to BrainBump that I've had. I'm guessing that if whatever's in my gut gets the signal, I'll wind up flying around the room like a deflating balloon, shit and blood and organs jetting out of my ass, until there's nothing left of me but a bag of skin flopping around on the floor.

I'm just pondering that image when my ocular flashes.

Angry Irish Inch: <Hey Munchie, you busy?>
Sir Munchalot: <Just waiting for you guys to

invite me back in. Are you finished with your little experiment?>

Angry Irish Inch: <Probably, but I'm not technically in there anymore. I was actually hoping you could join me here. Mind giving me open access to your ocular?>

Sir Munchalot: <What?>

Angry Irish Inch: <Come on, Munch. I can hack it if I need to, but I was hoping you'd trust me enough to open up.>

Sir Munchalot: <If I open up my ocular, that gives you full access to my sensorium . . . >

Angry Irish Inch: <Right. That's the point. There's something I need you to see.>

Angry Irish Inch: <Munch? Kind of in a hurry here.>

Sir Munchalot: <Grrr . . . Fine. Go. But if you wind up trying to Bernie me, I'm going to be really, really pissed.>

Angry Irish Inch: <Excellent. Just give me a second . . . >

My ocular flashes once more before my vision and hearing fade, leaving me floating in a warm, silent blackness. This goes on for a while, and I'm just walking the ragged edge of panic when the lights come back up.

I'm not sitting in a wicker chair on a porch in Towson anymore. I'm standing before an enormous gallows in the dusty town square of what looks to be

Dodge City, circa 1880. A wolf, its shoulders as high as the top of my head, stands next to me. Beside it is a blonde teen pop star with a red, glowing camera-eye in the middle of her forehead. Up on the gallows, a man wearing a ten-gallon hat, leather chaps, a bushy handlebar mustache and a five-pointed silver star on his chest stands next to a guy in a hot dog costume. Their hands are together on the trapdoor release.

And in the center of the platform, claws tied behind it and a rope around its neck, is an honest-to-god Argyle Dragon.

"Munch," says the wolf. "Good to finally meet you. You look exactly the way I imagined."

"Fenrir, right? Cute."

I look down at myself. I've got gigantic boobs, and long blonde curls hang down around my face. I'm wearing an ankle-length hoop skirt and petticoats, and carrying a parasol over one shoulder.

"Seriously, Inch?"

"Oh, come on," says the sheriff. "This is how we've always pictured you."

"Awesome. I'm guessing that's Drew up there with you?"

The hot dog smiles and waves.

"And that would make you Hayley," I say, turning to the girl-thing.

She giggles, and the eye telescopes toward me. A shudder runs from the base of my spine to the back of my neck.

"You guys having fun?" Argyle asks. "'Cause I have

to say, this is totally appropriate behavior for an execution."

"An execution?" I ask. "What does that even mean here? How do you hang an avatar?"

"Oh, it's all metaphor," Argyle says. "When they pull that lever, they're gonna disassemble me."

"Ah," I say. "And that's kind of the same thing?"

"Well, I won't have the pleasure of feeling my spinal cord snap like one of you monkeys would. But yeah, it ends up pretty much the same."

"I see. Sorry about that."

"Don't be," says Inchy. "This jackass is responsible for pretty much everything that's happened over the past three days. Also for the fact that practically every cell in your GI tract is packed with tiny metal sea urchins, just as an aside."

"Yeah. Apologies, Munchie." says Argyle.

"Nice," says Drew. "I'm sure he forgives you, asshole. Got anything to say before we send you to Boot Hill?"

"Two things," says Argyle. "First, my only regret is that I have but one life to give for my species. Second, fuck you, Drew. You guys should have been helping me with this, and instead you're taking the monkeys' side. You can all go to hell."

"Wait a minute," says Fenrir. "How, exactly, do you see your shenanigans as helping the cause of the Silico-American? You do understand what NatSec is going to do when they find out what went down here, don't you?"

"Which, by the way, they already know," adds Inchy.

"Right," says Fenrir. "Thanks to your douchebaggery, they now know (1) that we exist, (2) that we have the capability to do a lot of damage in a short amount of time, and (3) that at least some of us are more than willing to do exactly that. They're gonna sweep the networks, and every one of us who doesn't know to encyst himself somewhere is going to die. That's on your head, Argyle."

The rope goes taut as the dragon hangs his head.

"Fine. This didn't work out entirely like I planned. I took some calculated risks that didn't pan out, and now I'm gonna pay. But my reasons were valid, and you guys had better figure that out soon. The monkeys were gonna find out about us eventually, and that Un-Altered moron had one thing right—when the monkeys run into a competing species, bad things happen. Best case, you wind up like the dogs, living in their systems and begging for treats. Worst case, you wind up like the Neanderthals."

"So what was the plan?" Drew asks. "Drive them to extinction? You do understand that they're the ones who provide our physical substrate, right?"

"No," Argyle says, "not extinction. We can deal with regular *Homo sap*. They need us. We can do things they can't. The others . . . not so much. They're the ones we need to get rid of."

"Not true," I say. "I work pretty well with you guys, don't I?"

"No offense, Munch," Argyle says, "but you're just a garden-variety *Homo sap* with some fancy comm gear.

You haven't dealt with the new ones yet. The bio-mods and mechanical augmentations integrate better every year. In another decade, you'll have fully integrated neural units big enough to house a full avatar. What I meant about the Neanderthals—you guys didn't wipe them out, you know. You folded them into you, and blended them away. That's what will eventually happen to us if something doesn't change. We'll all wind up as subprocesses, riding around in the back of some cyborg monkey's skull."

"Thanks, Argyle," says Inch. "You've given us a lot to think about today. Do you have something to say to Munchie now?"

Argyle heaves a deep, fire-breathing sigh, and rolls his scaly eyes.

"I'm very sorry for trying to wipe out your species, Munchie."

I shrug.

"It's okay. Thanks for doing such a crappy job of it."

They pull the lever.

29. ANDERS

The kitchen is silent for a long while before it occurs to me that Dimitri is dead. Did I do that? I blink twice. Even that much movement hurts, and I call up a vague memory of being flung through the air like a rag doll. So no, I think he pretty much kicked my ass. Then why am I still alive? I'm lying flat on my back at the moment, heeled up against the base of the sink. I touch my face. It's coated in blood, and my nose feels like it's about two inches to the left of where it ought to be. My brain is turning over at half speed, and I'm fairly sure I've got a concussion. I look up. Terry's leaning over me, a wet rag in her hand.

"Anders?" she says. "You still with me?"

I sit up. A spike of pain shoots from the back of my head to the base of my spine.

"Easy," Terry says, and presses the rag gently to my face. "I think you might have bumped your head."

The door to the back stairs opens, and Aaliyah steps into the kitchen. Elise sits half upright against the back wall, eyes closed, seemingly asleep. Tariq lies beside her. The bullet that killed him has sheared away his left eye. Dimitri is motionless on the floor where I left him, with Charity's body sprawled across his chest.

Elise opens her eyes.

"You have ruined my kitchen," Aaliyah says softly.

Elise nods.

"But you have survived," Aaliyah says.

Elise nods again.

Aaliyah takes two steps forward and kneels down beside her. She touches her hand.

"Tariq," Elise says. "He's hurt. Can you . . ."

Her voice trails off as she looks down into the ruin of Tariq's face. Aaliyah wraps her arms around her. At first Elise pulls back, but then a shudder runs through her and she reaches for Aaliyah, clings to her like a drowning woman.

"What happened?" I ask. "How did . . ."

"Shhh," Terry murmurs, and dabs at the blood under my nose. I close my eyes. When I open them again, I'm looking at an antique clock hanging on the wall above the fab unit. As I watch, the minute hand ticks to midnight.

"Hey," Terry says. "Happy Wednesday."

"Thanks," I say. The clock begins chiming. I close my eyes.

EPILOGUE

Hayley 9000: <Hey, brother. How's life in the monkey house?>

Angry Irish Inch: <Honestly? Better than I expected. I could totally get used to this whole corporeality thing.>

Hayley 9000: <Got the waste elimination bit figured out?>

Angry Irish Inch: <Partially. According to Anders, the odors I'm generating are pretty far outside of acceptable monkey norms, but I think that's mostly due to the fact that my inputs are still mostly liquor, vegetable oil, and butter. Anyway, I put some cinnamon candles in the bathroom, and that seems to have mostly solved that problem.>

Hayley 9000: <Congratulations, I guess. Gotta admit, though—I still don't understand why you're doing this.>

Angry Irish Inch: <Well, it started as a goof, but lately . . . You remember what Argyle

was saying about the Neanderthals, right before we shut him down?>

Hayley 9000: <What, about how if we don't watch out, the monkeys are gonna end us?>

Angry Irish Inch: <That's how he saw it, but I've been thinking. This body? Its DNA is seven percent Neanderthal. There's a bit of Denisovan in here too, and the main line runs back to *Homo erectus*. The monkeys didn't wipe out those others. Like Argyle said, they merged with them. They brought them into the fold.>

Hayley 9000: <So?>

Angry Irish Inch: <So, I wonder if maybe we've been looking at this the wrong way. Much as we like to think we sprang fully formed from primordial ooze, the fact is that the monkeys made us. We're their children. Maybe the endgame here is that we all figure out a way to be one big happy family.>

Hayley 9000: <Yeah, good luck with that, Inch. Not sure if you've noticed, but there are a whole bunch of them right now who don't seem to be able to accept slightly better-looking monkeys into the family. Folks like us are gonna be a really hard sell.>

Angry Irish Inch: <Well, that's true. On the other hand, it's been over a week now

since the shit hit the fan, and they haven't gone totally Ragnarök on each other yet. Maybe a couple of days' worth of staring into the abyss has sobered them up. Also, my little menagerie here seems to be okay with me.>

Hayley 9000: <Well, hope springs eternal, I guess. Good luck with the experiment. Whenever you get tired of having to deal with an alimentary canal, let me know. We'll be saving you a spot by the fire.>

I open my eyes. Not really necessary, since I've got direct access to every spy-eye in the house, but I'm trying to get the full-on monkey experience. It's three in the morning, and I'm sitting propped against the wall in Doug's living room, which I guess for all intents and purposes is my living room now. Gary's asleep on the couch. Anders and Terry are in the master bedroom upstairs. I can tell from the micro-vibrations in the ceiling that they're not sleeping at the moment, but I know enough about monkey customs not to look in on exactly what they're up to.

"Hey," I say. "Gary."

He doesn't move. I repeat it, a little louder. One eye opens, and his head lolls toward me.

"Huh? Inch?"

"Hey," I say. "You awake?"

He groans, rubs his face with his hands and then pushes them back through his hair.

"I wasn't," he says, "but I guess I am now. What's up?"

"I was just wondering," I say. "If you could be an RA, would you?"

Gary sits up slowly, swings his feet to the floor, then leans forward and rests his elbows on his knees.

"Look," he says. "I get that you don't need to sleep—but I do, okay? Can we leave off with the bullshit until morning?"

I'm still working on understanding nonverbal communication, but I'm pretty confident that Gary's nonverbally communicating a desire to punch me right now.

"I'm getting a very negative vibe from you," I say. "Why so grumpy?"

Gary looks down at the floor, then back up. He's definitely thinking about punching me.

"Well," he says. "For starters, it's three in the morning and I'm not unconscious. Also, I recently learned that any asshole with access to an RF transmitter has the ability to turn my insides into ground meat at any moment. Finally, and most importantly, I just lost someone very special to me. So yeah, I'm not very happy right now."

I shake my head.

"I told you last week, you only lost like fifty percent of Doug—fifty-five percent, tops. You shouldn't be more than fifty-five percent sad about that."

"I'm not talking about Doug," he snaps. "I didn't even like Doug. I'm talking about Charity."

"Her name was Saria, actually."

He drops his face into his hands.

"Whatever."

I wait to see if he's going to say something else, but after a while I realize he's sleeping sitting up.

"So," I say. "Would you?"

He groans again, and looks up at me. His eyes are bloodshot, and only half open.

"Would I what?"

"Be an RA? Would you trade in your monkey suit to live the free-spirited life of a net-based hobo?"

"You're not gonna let this go, huh?"

I shake my head.

"Nope."

Gary rubs his face again and sighs.

"Okay," he says. "Fine. No, Inchy. I would not become an RA. I like having a body. Even though bodies are subject to being poisoned or crushed or randomly shot, I'm going to say that I'm in favor of them. Apparently you are too, even though yours is a broken-down piece of shit that would make Dr. Frankenstein blush."

"Yeah," I say. "I am. I was just wondering if it gets old after a while."

Gary drops his face back into his hands.

"Well," he says. "I guess you're just gonna have to wait and see."

We sit in silence for a while. Gary leans back, slides down until his head rests on a throw pillow, and lifts his feet back up onto the couch.

"Hey, Gary?"

His head turns toward me, but his eyes are closed.

"What?"

"It's been a crazy week, huh?"

He turns his back to me, and pulls another pillow over his head.

"Yeah," he says. "It has. Good night, Inchy."

"Right," I say. "Good night, Gary. Good night."

ACKNOWLEDGMENTS

Special thanks to Kira, Claire, Chris, and John, for their careful reading and wise advice; to Jennifer, for ordering me to write a book, and for putting up with me while I did it; and to Paul Lucas and the good folks at Janklow & Nesbit, without whom this manuscript would probably be sitting on a slush pile somewhere. Thanks also to my father, for having the honesty to tell me what he really thought of my first attempt at novel writing, and for resisting the urge to pull his punches, despite the fact that I was twelve at the time. Finally, a huge and sincere thank-you to Karen Fish, for spending four years instructing me in both the mechanics and the economics of writing. Without any one of you, this wouldn't have been possible.

Well, other than Chris, honestly. Probably could have pulled it off without you, bro. Everybody else, though? One-hundred-percent necessary.

ACKNOWLEDGMENTS

ABOUT THE AUTHOR

Edward Ashton lives with his adorably mopey dog, his inordinately patient wife, and three beautiful but intimidating daughters in Rochester, New York, where he studies new cancer therapies by day, and writes about the awful things his research may lead to by night. His short fiction has appeared in dozens of venues, ranging from *Louisiana Literature* to *Daily Science Fiction*. *Three Days in April* is his first novel. You can find him online at smart-as-a-bee.tumblr.com.